KILL FOR LOVE

a novel

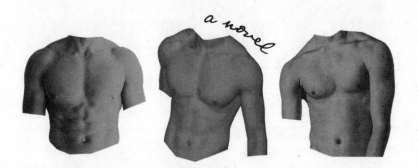

LAURA PICKLESIMER

The Unnamed Press
Los Angeles, CA

KILL FOR LOVE

1

EVERY NIGHT I DREAMED OF FIRE. I WATCHED AS SANTA MONICA descended into flames: blocks of designer merchandise torched to the ground, windows shattered, and mannequins melted onto their steel pedestals. It was one spectacular disaster each night.

The flames always swept east, immolating strolling shoppers and Lululemon moms, toppling over palm trees. Clouds of smoke sent wheezing men in suits to the ground. Closer to the flaming epicenter, hair extensions ignited like wicks of dynamite up women's backs, and silicone implants exploded out of their mesh sports bras with wet pops.

The fire gained momentum once it reached Brentwood, moving on to destroy the rest of the storefronts and organic cafés in its way. I could feel the heat lick at me, but I was always safe from the fire's reach. After its fury was spent, the flames would eventually calm, and bodies would litter the street like charred anorexics, still smoking.

Then I'd wake up alone in my four-poster bed, my skin burning.

It was the September heat wave that hit every fall across Los Angeles. While the basic bitches in other parts of the country sucked up pumpkin spice lattes, L.A. got one more lethal hit of summer. Temperatures climbed, and the central air conditioning in the Delta Gamma sorority house ran nonstop. But it was never enough to keep the heat from pressing in.

I'd wake each morning in a chilled sweat that would quickly sour. After a cold shower, I'd head downstairs for a breakfast of ice cubes. I'd dash salt on them to feel a pucker of flavor before braving a hair dryer on my scalp.

Earlier in the summer, I'd been able to follow the entirety of my morning routine alone, in peace. But now the sorority was back for the new school year. Classes had started last week, which meant twenty girls were crammed into an eight-room Victorian mansion. In teen comedies, sorority living was a wet dream of pillow fights and towel-clad bimbos.

The reality was that girls were disgusting. Living in the DG house involved stray hairs of every length, texture, and color filling the sinks and showers. Blooming red tampons spilled out of Target trash cans, and watered-down Starbucks drinks sweat across every spare surface.

The last week of September, I woke up to two DMs: an RSVP reminder for a refugee cupcake drive in the quad and a photo of the deep V-cut of some boy's abs, his boxers hung so low I could see the wiry growth peeking from underneath. I deleted both messages.

Camilla, DG president and bane of my existence, stopped by my room with a white poster board before I even had a chance to get dressed.

"What am I supposed to do with this?" I asked.

"It's a vision board for the new school year. Fill it out with visual representations of your goals and other aspirations."

I had seen hers; I wasn't sure what kind of life goals a bunch of fluffy accent rugs and wellness smoothies signified.

"This sort of bullshit is for the pledges," I said. "I'm a fifth-year."

"I wouldn't be proud of that distinction," Camilla said, and finally buzzed off.

Fall rush had just ended, the time when sororities hosted a slaughter of social mixers recruiting for the upcoming school year. It had once been the highlight of the season. I used to revel in the chance to disassemble every potential new member, relentlessly break down each girl's deficiencies in the group chats.

This year, I had skipped recruitment and gone to Cabo with a group of girls who were also graduating soon and didn't give a flying fuck about protocol anymore. After five years at the sorority, I couldn't stomach another afternoon sorting through girls in knockoff Louis Vuittons and cheap skater dresses or smiling at the eager faces of pledges.

At least most of the house would be gone today now that classes had begun. I entered the shared bathroom, and the air was still heavy with fruity body wash. Mandy and Amy, fellow fifth-years, were shaving their legs over the sink.

"Dan says you can't get herpes from giving head," Mandy said.

"Dan's a fucking liar. That's why I stick with chicks," Amy said. "Most of the time."

We had spent the last four years living under the same roof, and yet Mandy and Amy weren't my friends. I didn't even like them. I'd graduate, unfollow the two on social media, and never think about them again.

"Want to go to the rec center later, Tiffany?" Mandy asked me as I dried my hands and snatched somebody's bottle of Gucci Guilty from the bathroom counter.

"I have some pretty important errands to run today," I said.

I structured my weekdays around four important categories: fitness, self-care, shopping, and socials. It was harder than it looked. I often found myself in my Mercedes, winding down random streets. It was so easy to get lost; one extra turn off the main thoroughfare, and I'd dead-end at a deserted park or ugly stucco apartment complex facing yellowed lawns.

Today I took the Mercedes west toward the mansions above San Vicente Boulevard, passing clipped grass and gardener trucks. A street I had never heard of before dumped me out near the ocean, over the cliffs of the Pacific Palisades. I parked near the Third Street Promenade and walked past misters and fountains, moms and their little brats. The stores were too low-end, and I found nothing. Those were the worst days. I settled for a manicure even though I had just had one three days before.

"Strip them," I instructed the nail technician.

"What color?"

I looked over the samples, the several dozen key chains of replicated, matching oval nails, and thought of a Technicolor corpse. I settled on the color I was already wearing: pink but a shade darker, a slight neon over the cotton candy of the old coat. I had her file my nails at an even sharper angle.

I needed an escape from the heat, so I checked the movie times. It was a novelty, but I wanted a distraction. Romantic comedies were my preferred film genre. There was such a clear ride of emotions: I could let my mind wander and still clearly register each character's emotional trajectory, even if I couldn't feel those things in myself most of the time.

I settled on *Will You Be Mine*, featuring Ben Affleck as a mining tycoon working somewhere in South America during the 1950s. Jennifer Lopez played his sassy secretary, who was thinking of a new career as a cabaret singer. She was just about to quit when the evil head of a rival mining company plotted to leave the two for dead in the wilderness. When they were first ditched in the rain forest together, they hated each other. But after an unrelated mining disaster allowed Ben to rescue Jen from a random band of rabid tree monkeys, they fell in love and got married at a conga lounge.

The movie contained all the expected beats, but as I was walking back to my car, the dry heat of another 95-degree day bearing down on me, I could only think about how fucking old Ben Affleck was starting to look. It ate at me on the drive home.

I had forgotten it was rush hour. I crawled along Wilshire, inching slowly behind the backlog of cars waiting to enter the 405 Freeway.

I heard screaming. Two guys about my age, with the bloated body types of croissants, were waving from the sidewalk, trying to flag me down. I met their gaze, and one of them barked, "Show me your tits!"

When I didn't react, they began miming, pointing. I thought briefly of what it would feel like to swerve to the right and plow into them. I thought about how far their bodies might fly, if their barreled guts might explode.

The fantasy was shattered by a loud, low honk from the Prius behind me. The light had turned green. I rolled up the five feet that traffic had moved and saluted my middle finger to the driver.

When I finally returned to the sorority house, I found my roommate, Emily, home from her classes and plowing through a bag of Milano cookies.

"Hey, Tiffany," she said, and tried to wipe away the crumbs she had dropped on her bed.

Emily was a second-year and nowhere near Delta Gamma material. She wore her hair in frizzy curls and refused to pluck her eyebrows. Her style was bold in a bad way: uncoordinated, baggy, in overly optimistic colors. She looked like the type who hunted for bargains at thrift stores. We had brought her in last spring to raise the collective GPA of our house. It wasn't so bad rooming with her, though—Emily's grandmother lived in a shitty neighborhood south of Pico Boulevard, so she left every weekend.

I threw myself on the bed. "I need a shower."

Emily offered a cookie, and I shook my head.

"You know I don't eat processed food," I said. I sat up and stared at the mirror, angling myself for a selfie. "You don't look like this on a diet of simple carbs."

My empty stomach made a gurgle in agreement.

"Skipping meals can cause you to overeat in the long run," Emily said.

"How do you know that?" I asked.

"I read it."

"What, like in a newspaper? Get your facts the normal way," I said.

I scrolled through my phone, looking for that rare fitness influencer who had sharper ab cracks than me, trying to block out both Emily and my hunger pains.

By nightfall, the entire chapter had crammed into the living room to watch *The Real Housewives: Retribution*, a long-anticipated special that pitted the OG of every major *Housewives* franchise against one another in a dating competition. If you wanted to see desperation and fury, watch middle-aged women fight it out for the same soft fifty-something real estate developer.

The competition began with a recap of the long-standing feuds across all cities. I had hoped the on-screen drama would substitute for my disappointing shopping run, but I couldn't get enough of a rise from the shouting matches, the occasional shattered glass. I wanted spilled blood, not wine—something more violent from the divorcées, but it never came.

The climax of the episode arrived when a loudmouth from New Jersey ripped out a Dallas housewife's hair extensions. The Texan shoved the woman's head into a giant punch bowl of Sunset Sangria, the sponsored drink for the night. The catfight ended as quickly as it had begun, when a New York housewife revealed her ex-husband was being sent to prison for tax evasion: suddenly, there were tears and slurred apologies, and then a shampoo commercial came on.

I had one of the couches to myself and was applying La Mer self-tanning moisturizer to my forearms.

"You're so tan," Mandy remarked.

I looked down at my arms, the smooth inward curve my biceps made as it met my elbow. I grabbed my phone and snapped a shot of my body, making sure the product label could be seen in the background. I'd post later, when the number of likes would be higher.

"So who's going to the black-and-white party next week? Show of hands," Amy asked.

Camilla said, "I've said it before: I seriously think we need to rebrand. It just doesn't feel very sensitive."

Camilla was the type of goody-goody who even the teachers wanted to punch in high school. When she wasn't taking semesters off to try to save leukemic babies, she was usually sticking her nose in my business, informing me that I was late for meetings or short on volunteer hours, as if I was expected to follow the same rules as the other girls.

"The black-and-white party refers to the most iconic duet of colors in a style wardrobe," I explained. "It's a classic party theme, and it's not going anywhere."

"I'm just thinking about optics," Camilla said as the show spotlighted an Orange County housewife who had gotten her upper lip sewn to her nose in a freak plastic surgery accident.

"Tiffany, what season was your mom on the OC show?" a recruit named Julie interrupted. Most Delta Gams knew to avoid mention of Pam and her brief stint on the show.

"She was a friend of, not a cast member. And that was over four years ago."

Pam had never even told me about it. I had found out freshman year, when I suddenly caught sight of the marble staircase and backyard of our estate, and realized that the feng shui wine cooler party was taking place at my house. Pam had come in hot, immediately accusing one of the show headliners of taking a bite of her Pomeranian's custom birthday cake, but she was always too self-aware, too insecure. There were shots of her checking mirrors, primping her hair, looking into the cameras out of the corner of her eye. And she was incapable of committing the appropriate level of backstabbing.

My phone vibrated, and I looked down to see a text from Tristan, my date to the black-and-white party. He was shirtless, flexing his biceps in a bathroom mirror, ratty towels visible behind him. His text read, *Sneak peak.*

I slipped into the downstairs bathroom and pulled out the small bottle of Gucci I had nabbed earlier. I sprayed the air and took a long breath. I fixed my eyes on the curves of the perfume bottle and anchored myself back through the momentary high of mandarin and patchouli. Tomorrow, I'd go shopping and buy something extra expensive.

Still, my body itched with a strange dissatisfaction. It reminded me of the low, grating hum the electrical wires made when the Santa Anas came in, the static white noise that filled the air right before they exploded onto unsuspecting streets.

2

MY NIGHTMARES CONTINUED. THE FIRE SPREAD TO WEHO. I would wake up in the middle of the night to a gnawing sensation in my gut and wonder if I'd somehow forgotten a hair conditioning appointment or a wellness session with my life coach.

On Tuesday, I missed a morning fitness class at Elite Elegance, a Beverly Hills workout studio that combined belly dancing, yoga, and trapeze work performed with an aerial hammock. Instead, I had to settle for a standard spinlates session all the way over on Fairfax Avenue, the type of simplified, modifications-heavy class that attracted still-tubby new moms and the over forty set. Out shopping, the new outfit I wanted for the black-and-white party on Thursday failed to materialize, and I returned to my Mercedes with just a pair of Louboutin heels and a Prada clutch. I felt dejected driving back into Westwood with only a couple of accessories.

"I need you to record me," I told Emily when I returned to my room. Maybe playing back my figure, watching the likes stack up, would brighten my difficult day.

"Make it look spontaneous," I instructed her as I pivoted and blew a kiss.

Emily's appreciative gaze would help soothe my nerves. The assurances mothers gave their daughters, that those blondes in the magazines had been photoshopped into impossible sizes or that Barbies couldn't anatomically exist because women couldn't support that hip-to-waist ratio—those were lies. I could prove it.

I paired the Louboutins with a white strapless cocktail dress embellished in black. It was a month old, but I hadn't worn it in public yet. I hoped that Emily's hungry gaze over my curves would be enough to boost my spirits, get me excited for another weekend of the typical drinking and slutting.

"You look amazing," Emily said, handing back my iPhone. I'd post the video across three platforms and get at least a few thousand views in the next half hour.

I grabbed the white clutch and held it against my outfit. "I'm going to wear this combination to the party. What do you think?"

"That'll be perfect. Who are you going with?" Emily asked.

"Tristan."

"Tiffany and Tristan. That's cute."

"Sure," I said. Other than being about 95 percent certain I had slept with him once during freshman orientation, I didn't know much about the dude.

I didn't bother asking Emily about her date; she wouldn't be going. The prude didn't even drink.

I had picked up a bakery item on the way home, a doughnut-type pastry with an explosion of confetti and pastel frosting. I carefully untied the twine around the box and slid it open, careful not to disrupt the decorative collage inside. After I had taken it to the spot in the hall with the best natural light, I shot a dozen photos from different angles and then smashed the thing in the trash.

I went to the kitchen and grilled up some soy blocks, cutting them into tiny fourths and counting to ten between each bite. I looked at my watch. It was only 4:00 P.M.

In the common room, Mandy and Amy were sorting through a pile of fashion and style magazines. The sorority had a mail subscription to all the major publications that had never been canceled over the decades. I usually joined them at the beginning of each month: we liked to pore through the magazines and rip out advertisements for must-have products or fashion items, stopping occasionally if an intriguing title like "25 Naughty Uses for a Q-tip" caught our eye. We'd wait until we accumulated a fair number of ads and then order everything on our iPhones, sending a customized tally of our transactions to one another.

Amy looked up from her *Cosmo*. "Did you know that fifty-seven percent of five thousand men polled would rather undergo brain surgery than submit to anal penetration during foreplay?"

"Not Dan," said Mandy. "He loves it."

I grabbed an issue of *Allure* and flipped through it.

I had at least ten products from every major designer listed in the thing. I felt a sudden weightlessness, like when you're slipping off to sleep, only to be jolted awake by the certainty that you're free-falling, that nothing around you is real.

I realized that I'd be sitting on this couch again next month, when the winter issues were mailed, and I'd have every single item in those magazines, too. And I'd still have time left over because a two-hour workout and a four-store shopping spree weren't enough to fill up an entire day. My hunger was back, and I wouldn't eat again for hours.

My phone vibrated: a text from an unknown number, this time a 323 area code. I opened it, and a curved cock filled the frame of my screen.

I threw my phone down and felt for my throat, finding the pearl-drop necklace I'd worn every day since I was seventeen. My life coach called it my "force center" and encouraged me to touch it and count backward with slow, steady breaths any time I felt alone or anxious. I usually didn't need to be calmed. I liked being alone, and I was rarely anxious. I felt numb most days, unsurprised, bored. Today, though, was different. I resisted the urge to put the necklace in my mouth and feel the smooth pearl against my tongue.

When I returned to my room, Emily was eating from a tray of celery and carrots. She smiled and held it out, proud of herself.

"Nice try," I told her. "But that ranch dressing contains more saturated fat than a cheeseburger."

I grabbed a pile of celery sticks and fell back on my bed. I began snapping them in two.

"Have you ever had an existential crisis?" I asked her.

"Would all of middle school count?"

"No, being awkward and unpopular isn't what I'm talking about. I'm referring to real problems. Do you ever feel like you're not acting like your true self?"

"No."

The vision board Camilla had dropped off was still a blank white, propped against my bedroom wall.

"I mean, is there more that you wish you were doing than just living in the sorority house?" I asked.

"Of course. I've always wanted to visit Cambodia. And I dream all the time about finishing med school, maybe starting my own clinic."

What would happen when I was forced to finally graduate? I'd live alone, that was for sure, no more roommates. As relieved as I would be to no longer sync my menstrual cycles with a dozen other girls, I wondered what I'd do with my time every day. People got jobs, I supposed, but wage earning wasn't exactly my vibe.

"Seriously, that's it?" I said.

"Well, what do *you* want?" Emily asked.

I didn't have an answer. The soy blocks had failed to fill me, and I was already feeling the familiar pangs of hunger again. I scrolled through my phone, past the hearts and likes and confirmation emails from the day's purchases. I looked through my photo library of sunsets and tiki drinks, uneaten buffet feasts, hollowed stomachs, that perfect triangle of emptiness between my inner thighs and the sky. I stroked the soft leather of the Prada purse I had bought that day and thought about the carcass it had been peeled from.

"I want everything."

3

ON THURSDAY, I WRAPPED UP MY DAILY ACTIVITIES EARLY, giving myself two hours for makeup contouring and hair. Tristan was picking me up at ten. Thursday was the night of the week that the frats hosted their biggest parties and everyone got the most wrecked. We'd spend the remaining weekend in recovery mode.

As I got ready, I thought briefly about canceling. I'd barely slept the night before. Tristan wasn't worth all this primping and plucking. I wondered if any guy I had slept with was. The alternative, though, was sitting in bed for the night, trying not to sabotage my diet on Emily's arsenal of junk food.

Tristan arrived in a Corvette, which was pretty annoying, since it practically skimmed the ground. My legs sprawled out under me, and I could tell my dress was starting to wrinkle on the drive to the party.

I caught a glimpse of Tristan's outfit. He had chosen the exact same color distribution that I had: a solid white base with accents of black. We looked way too matchy-matchy, especially since our hair was pretty much the same shade of blond. I entered the party with him praying that no one would think we had coordinated.

The party was typical, held at a rented space about a mile from Greek row. A cheap wooden stand served as the open bar, stacked with midrange liquors, and the dance floor was already inundated with a bunch of Sigma Nus. About a half hour into the party, a dozen Delta Gammas stumbled in. My house had pre-partied heavily. I usually laid off the alcohol because it made no sense to spend the day limiting my intake to 800 calories and then go ruin it with a bunch of cheap frozen margaritas.

An hour into the party, I had downed only a vodka and Diet Coke. Tristan was pretty drunk. I pulled him away from his frat brothers, and he took it as a come-on.

He slid his hand from the small of my back over my ass and kept his hand huddled there like a moron. Then I had a sudden vision of Tristan screaming. The image was brief: a guttural yell equal parts pain and satisfaction. I felt a burning urgency, like a shot of Bacardi 151 fanning out through my system. I suddenly knew that tonight, *something* worthwhile was going to happen. And I would be in control every step of the way.

"Do you want to ditch the party and go back to the frat house?" I asked.

"We just got here," Tristan said. He grabbed my wrist and leaned closer. "There's a back room that we could use."

He pointed off the dance floor to a small lounge area. A girl was puking into a trash barrel nearby.

"I want to go back to your place," I said, twisting away from his grasp.

"Let's stay here," he said.

I went ahead and revealed the plan half solidified in my head: "I'm interested in exploring more deviant forms of sexual expression tonight. I think a private room would be best."

He looked at me for a second. "I'll get the car."

"You don't need to tell anyone else we're leaving," I said, and pulled him toward the exit. "You good to drive?"

"It's only a few miles away," he said.

On the car ride, my stomach tightened, intestines knotted. I had eaten only a veggie cauliflower rice bowl and some kale chips that afternoon, which put me at about 600 calories for the day. I clutched my abdomen as hunger pains sliced through me. Reaching for my phone out of habit, I counted the views from the videos I had taken at the party. Then I turned it off. I stared at the dark of my eyes reflected in its blank screen.

"Do you have any gum?" I asked Tristan.

"Look in the passenger-side door. I'll take one."

I pulled out a pack of peppermint Trident and popped three pieces in my mouth, then gave one to Tristan. I chewed for the entire car ride over, but the gum only further roused my appetite. I swallowed it when we got inside. The smell of the frat house was welcome after a long summer at the sorority, the stifling scents of competing perfumes, all too fruity and candied. Here there were notes of piss and beer, a trace of vomit, and the overriding ripeness of fresh boy.

Tristan's room was on the top floor of the empty frat house, away from the main hall. The space was bigger than I remembered. Next to his bed were a small wet bar, a table, and chairs. I sat down at the table and motioned for him to do the same. He was reluctant.

"Why don't we relax on the bed?" he asked. "These chairs are pretty uncomfortable."

"Sit here first," I insisted.

Tristan approached the bar and poured a shot of Jack Daniel's. "You want something? I've got Malibu," he said.

I liked to set up a bottle of Malibu behind me when posing for selfies—it always lent a carefree, Californian mood to the occasion, but I never actually drank the stuff. I let him pour me a glass and didn't touch it.

"Why are you attracted to me?" I asked, after he had taken a seat next to me.

He sighed and took a drink. "Because you're hot. And seem interesting. And popular."

I didn't know exactly what answer I was expecting from a fuckboy like Tristan.

"Popular?" I asked.

"You know, well liked."

"I'm popular, but I don't know about liked."

He shrugged. "Well, being beautiful is more than enough."

I smiled. It was true, I was beautiful. *I'm also smart*, I wanted to add. But that had never gotten me likes. Or laid.

Tristan's hand reached for mine—only for a second, though—then slid down my thigh and under my dress. I could foresee the usual course of events. If he could even get hard at this point, there was probably no way he'd be able to finish in a reasonable length of time.

"Let's go to the bed," he said again.

I looked at his bed—it wasn't even made—and back at Tristan. Behind him, I caught a glimpse of a knife, serrated and about six inches long, resting on a cutting board next to a chopped lime. Such a simple tableau, and yet I suddenly saw the possibilities, the promise. The knife could do so much more than service drinks for frat boys.

"I want to play a game first," I said.

I took his hand and placed it palm-down on the table.

"Keep it there," I said.

I went over to the bar and grabbed the knife. The weight of it felt good in my hand, appropriate.

"What are you doing?" he asked.

"Put your hand back on the table. I want to play that game where I try to get it in between your fingers."

"No," he said, pulling his hand away.

"I'm not going over to that bed until you play."

"Fine. But you don't even know how to fucking play. I place my hand on the board," he explained, putting his palm down, "and *I* get the knife." He reached to take it from me.

In one fluid motion, I swung it down as hard as I could over his hand. He pulled back with lightning speed, and the knife stuck into the wood of the table.

"Dude!" he said, jumping up to his feet. "You almost got my hand!"

"You have amazing reflexes," I said, feeling my first flash of attraction toward him. I stood up.

"That was not cool."

"Calm down," I said, touching his shoulder. "I was playing around. It's just a game."

But I was anywhere from calm. In that moment, I recognized the developing desire that had been circulating unnamed in my head for the past few weeks, that had been slowly crystallizing inside me over the course of the night. My heart beat against my chest, and I felt a rush of anticipation, a new energy. I was a predator. And Tristan was prey. I wanted to see blood, to feel the same fire that fanned across the streets in my dreams.

"Calm down," I said again. I stroked the pearl on my necklace, my hands trailing lower down my body. I pulled my phone out from the hollow between my breasts, where I had stored it earlier for safekeeping, and I threw it on Tristan's bed. I grabbed the hem of my dress and pulled it up my thighs and over my hips, revealing the La Perla lingerie set that I had bought over the summer. By the time the dress rounded over my chest, Tristan was beside me, helping lift it over my head.

I pushed him back into his seat and straddled him. As we began making out, I eyed the six inches of knife, still stuck in the wood. I'd need to keep him distracted for another few minutes, long enough for him to miss that one of my hands was reaching away from him. Tristan tried to pull down my panties, but I widened my legs and made him take off his shirt instead.

He was a blank canvas. The perfect masculine equivalent of me physically, only I noted that he didn't regularly tan, so there was a discrepancy between the skin tone of his face and chest. I ran my hands over his pecs. He shaved his chest—I had never decided exactly what my opinion on this matter was, since aesthetically, it helped display muscle tone, but practically, it scratched like hell and could produce unsightly rashes. This wouldn't be an issue, though. We were never making it to Tristan's bed.

I gave myself one last appreciative glance of his upper body, my hand reaching between his legs. With my other hand, I pulled the knife out of the wood, and in one swift motion, I drew the blade back behind me and jammed it as hard as I could under his rib cage.

The skin was much tougher than I had anticipated. I had to let go of Tristan and use both hands before his chest relented and took in the knife. He had frozen, long enough for me to pull the blade back out.

Suddenly, he came to and knocked the knife from my hand so hard it flew against the back wall.

He pushed me off him and stared down.

"You stabbed me," Tristan said. Blood was starting to flow out of him. "You stabbed me! You fucking stabbed me!"

"No shit!" I said. I needed to get around him and find that knife.

"You crazy bitch!" He shoved me, knocking me against the table, where I banged the back of my head before falling to the floor. I climbed to my knees as Tristan ran to the bar. Maybe he was looking for a weapon. There'd be no way I could defend myself against him; I was just starting to recognize my size, how much smaller I stood. Instead Tristan went for a towel to cover the bloody mess across his stomach. He seemed more annoyed than anything else.

"Now I've got to call an ambulance to take me to the fucking hospital, sit around waiting in the ER," he said, and stumbled over to the door.

"Stop!" I yelled, pushing myself to my feet. "Come back!"

He was at the door, but his hands slipped off the knob, coated now in his blood. The pain finally blasted through whatever barricade the night's whiskey had provided, and he let loose one long scream.

He was growing weaker. I didn't have enough time to run across the room and find the knife, so I flew on instinct. I spotted an aluminum bat near his bed by the door. Tristan reached for the knob again and managed to wrench the door open just as I secured the bat and approached him face-on. When he saw the bat, he threw up his hands to block his upper body, so I fell to my knees and swung low, taking out his right kneecap. He was down instantly.

I circled around him, above his head, and aimed the bat. It connected with his skull so hard it made a soft plop, like a shovel pushing into damp earth. He fell down hard, the floor beneath me shaking. I looked at his body, his arms spread.

He was mine.

Tristan was still, but he wasn't dead. His body blocked the door from closing, so I dragged him by the arms toward the center of the room, using every muscle in my body since he had at least eighty pounds on me. My biceps burned by the time I had finished, way more than a class at Elite Elegance or even a private session with my personal trainer, Sergio.

Once I had Tristan moved, I kicked the door closed and found the knife. I brought it back over to his body and straddled him for a second time. I stabbed him in the abdomen again, but I was much more effective. Blood bubbled to the surface and spilled over my forearm. I kept going.

When I finally looked up from his chest, I had stabbed Tristan a good twenty times and assumed that he was dead. But his cobalt-blue eyes were still open, alert. The terror in his eyes captivated me, kept me frozen in place, until his body let out a tiny twitch, and it was over.

I thought about taking a photo of the wild angles of his limbs, the siren splash of red slowly surrounding his body. It would have been a beautifully artful shot. I wouldn't have even needed a filter.

I slid off Tristan, gliding right across his chest. My lingerie was soaked and ruined. My legs were shaky, but I was satisfied. I felt for the first time in years proud of my labors, a day well spent. I wouldn't need to go to aerial lifting class tomorrow. I could sleep in, maybe just go for a walk. Every muscle in my body was exhausted, but I still had one final urge.

I walked across to Tristan's minifridge and pulled out a Pabst and a leftover chicken drumstick wrapped in foil, the skin hanging off the bone. I tore into it, letting the fat and grease fill my mouth, my stomach, my entire being. I washed it down with the beer and turned back for another look at what I had done.

4

I HAD RIPPED THROUGH THE CHICKEN LEG AND STARTED ON A box of Carl's Jr. French toast sticks before the slow-moving tide of Tristan's blood across the linoleum near the refrigerator jolted me from my binge. His blood had hardened over my entire torso and down my thighs, almost reaching my feet. I rotated my arms and could feel my pores screaming, begging for exfoliation. I looked down at the French toast sticks, crusty around the edges, probably at least a week old. I started to realize what I'd done, the mess I'd stumbled into. I needed to fix it, fast.

I stuffed all the food I'd started to eat into a plastic takeout bag, along with the bloodied knife. A panicked voice in my head told me it was just as important to get rid of the food, that evidence of my binge would be as damning as the murder weapon if found. A jerk of movement by the door, and my eyes darted across the room, but it was only Tristan's body stiffening, warning me that it was time to bail.

In the hall I listened for a creak of the hardwood, a door closing below. The house was still empty. I hurried to the communal bathroom on tiptoe, trying to avoid pressing my bare feet into the tile. The shower walls were stained with the accumulated piss of two dozen drunk frat boys who couldn't make it to a urinal. The sight made me nauseated, and I almost slipped on the slick tile. I forced myself under a spray of ice-cold water until the blood rolled off my skin and down the drain. Squeezing the cups of my bra, I attempted to wring out the blood as best I could until the fabric transformed from red to a soft pink.

I put my dress back on without drying off and found my phone on the bed. I grabbed a towel and wiped frantically at the baseball bat, my chair, the fridge, anything I could remember coming into contact with.

Scanning the room, I noticed my untouched tumbler of Malibu sitting across from Tristan's empty whiskey glass. I carried it to the sink. I had never watched *CSI* or *SUV* or whatever they called it. I had no idea if this would do me any good. I briefly considered googling "how to clean up a murder scene," but thought better of it and kept my phone off.

A minute later, the stench reached my nose. I looked at the pulpy mess of limbs at my feet. It wasn't much different from the tail end of a bad hookup, when you're left lying in a small pool of fluid on the wall side of a twin bed, when you feel that small wave of disgust before you can get the hell out and pretend it never happened. Though the smell had never been this bad—this wasn't the usual sour beer and body odor; it was human shit mixed with something even more rancid that I couldn't place.

Then a door rattled and slammed downstairs. My heart hammered into my throat so hard I could barely pick up the noises from below. If I had any chance of pulling this off, I needed to disappear. Now. I couldn't take the front door, but I could leave through one of the back balconies. I snatched up my stuff, along with a ratty sweatshirt from Tristan's bed, and raced down the empty hall into the darkness of a back bedroom. I used the sweatshirt to open the sliding door and threw the fabric over the side of the railing. I hoisted myself over, hanging down far enough to leap onto the wet grass in front of an abandoned building behind the frat house.

Two fraternity members moved above me as I took cover under the pilings. My hands clenched the sweatshirt. I waited for a scream, an *Oh shit!* or a *Dude! Tristan got carved!*

Nothing. I followed the sound of their footsteps and the path of light to the other end of the house. I knew that room. They were settling into the stoner dungeon.

I pulled the sweatshirt over my wet dress and stumbled onto the street in my heels. It was still before midnight, and the local parties would be going for at least another two hours.

I took a longer route home to avoid being seen by other Greek members. I cut up along a row of grad school apartments, filled with med students and Ph.D. nerds. Rushing from street to street, shower water still dripping between my legs, was grosser than any walk of shame from my past, and that included sophomore year, when I had lost my underwear and somehow swapped outfits with a WeHo drag queen dressed in lederhosen.

A campus police cruiser rolled along behind me. Two quick beeps sounded, and its lights came on. Had Tristan's brothers already called 911? I tried to dissolve into the nearby shelter of a tree. I couldn't breathe until the cruiser slowly passed.

A few blocks from my sorority house, almost in the clear, I caught sight of three guys wearing Beta sweatshirts. I tried to turn up the next street to avoid meeting them.

"Hey," one of them said as I crossed to the opposite sidewalk.

"Party's this way!" another shouted.

I pulled the hoodie farther down my forehead.

"Looking for a good time?"

The three guys had stopped. I ignored them and jogged away.

"Well, fuck you!" one of them yelled, their laughs carrying across the street.

The road was empty after that. I tried to pretend it was just another Thursday night, that I'd left the party early and ditched Tristan with a semi-hard-on and a hangover.

Approaching the sorority house from the rear, I spotted lights on upstairs. I decided to travel by window again. I kicked off my heels and scaled the brick wall onto Camilla's private balcony. I'd done this plenty of times before when I was on probation, sometimes having to crawl on hands and knees across the floor if Camilla was already asleep in bed. I slid the door open and entered her bedroom. No one was around upstairs.

I tore off my clothes as soon as I had locked myself back in my room. *You're fine,* I told myself. *You just need a loofah to wash off any remaining traces of blood on your skin and to open up your pores. You can meet with a dermatologist tomorrow, take home an antioxidant-rich moisturizer to apply for the next week or so.*

My stomach contracted, like a finger jabbing from the inside, telling me, *Do you realize what you've just put into your body? The saturated fat? The simple carbs? All the empty* calories?

The wonderful burn I'd felt hauling Tristan's dead body across his room was gone. The last time I had eaten this much was fifth grade, before Pam had enrolled me in Donna Delaney's Preteen Booty Camp.

"Who's there?" someone slurred from the hallway. "I know someone's in the house!"

I heard the sound of footsteps outside my bedroom, and there was a bang on my door. I whipped on an oversized shirt, scanned for any leftover blood across my arms, and opened the door. It was Ashley, still clad in a tight black dress that had ridden all the way up past her cheap thong. She leaned against the wall, barely able to stay on her feet.

"Tiffany? Where did you come from?" she asked.

"You wanna keep it down? I'm trying to sleep."

"You weren't here before?"

I looked into her cloudy eyes and gauged how much of this conversation she'd remember in the morning. Not much, if any.

"I've been home for the past two hours," I said. "I had my date drop me off early."

"I was sent home. Johnny told me I got too drunk again. He wouldn't even have sex with me."

"That's too bad," I said.

"I puked into a keg tub."

"Wonderful."

"Do you have any Cheetos in your room?" Ashley asked.

I bristled at her mention of food. "No."

"What about some Fritos?"

"Do I look like I have chips stashed away like some tubby squirrel? Go check the kitchen."

I could barely contain the urge to shove her away from me. But I needed to be careful. Ashley had to be on my side tomorrow.

"Take an Advil and drink some water," I instructed. "And sleep it off."

Her thickly padded steps on the hardwood shook the hall, and I waited until I could hear her stumble down the stairs before retreating from the door.

I had pulled it off and was in the clear, for now. Tomorrow, I'd face whatever fallout came. I couldn't do anymore tonight.

I saw the spreading red around Tristan's body, the tiny air bubbles popping on the wash of blood across his chest. I pushed him out of my mind. He had asked for it, in a way, luring me into his room, keeping that knife right in my line of vision, a bat conveniently by the door. He had wanted fun, but he hadn't specified what kind—or who would be getting off tonight. He shouldn't have gotten so drunk. Tristan could have taken me if he hadn't drank so much, if he had really wanted to live. I felt a chill thinking about how the night might have gone down if he'd fought back.

I touched my necklace. There was a tiny bit of crusted blood over the pearl. I scratched it away. I had killed somebody. I was afraid, shaking, but I felt no guilt about it. Not even a little bit. I weighed that realization for a few moments, trying it on.

Then I looked down at my full stomach and remembered the chicken skin and fried dough I had eaten, enough greasy food for five meals. I grabbed a nail file, entered the shared bathroom, locked the door, and fell onto my knees in front of the toilet, letting the taste of meat, grain, and acid come up. I stared at the flakes of chicken floating in the water. They swirled and danced, tormenting me. I kicked the toilet lid shut, flushed, and climbed into bed.

That night, I dreamed of chicken legs, ten feet tall, chasing me, holding me down, forcing themselves down my throat. I woke up choking until I realized it was simply a strange new nightmare.

5

RECOVERY FRIDAY WAS SURPRISINGLY ROUTINE, CONSIDERING the murder off campus. Mandy had ordered breakfast sandwiches for the sorority, and I ignored the tempting smell of eggs, cheese, and croissant, sticking to pressed juice. Every member was plastered to her phone, but today, it was for news bulletins, not last night's drunken stories.

"Any updates on Tristan?" Emily asked.

"All of Sig Nu is on lockdown," Amy answered. "It's so fucking weird. One day, Tristan's helping me fundraise for Volleyball against VD, and the next, he's dead. Life is truly so transitory."

"It wasn't an accident," Mandy spoke up. "I heard he got shot by his dealer."

The police had kept the details of Tristan's death a secret throughout the day. A couple of Beta members claimed they had seen an entire campus cleaning crew visit the frat, while others insisted he had just choked on his own vomit, Hendrix style.

"Tiffany, you went to the black-and-white party with him, right?" Emily asked.

I sucked on an ice cube so hard it cracked. "I already told you, I left early."

"What about before Tristan dropped you off at the sorority house?" Amy asked. "Did anything weird happen?"

I felt the back of my head, over the small lump that had developed overnight.

"Nothing seemed off," I answered. "He got wasted at the party and asked me to come back to the frat house with him, but I said no. I could tell he was so gone at that point, he'd just go soft on me and make me watch *Starship Troopers* or listen to Journey with him. One of those nights."

Amy rolled her eyes.

"My guess is that one of the delivery guys from Jose's went off on Tristan," Mandy said. "His frat orders burritos from them all the time, and they *never* tip."

Mandy dug into her egg sandwich before moving on to the next item from last night.

———

The cops questioned me two days later. I had been sent over to the station, along with five other girls from different sororities.

The detectives were all so friendly, asking about our different sorority events and hobbies. I gave a statement, telling them I'd been dropped off directly from the party after refusing Tristan's advances.

"As a young woman, I know the importance of remaining vigilant during these types of alcohol-fueled events. You can't be too careful when there are potential predators lurking out there. This school is woefully unprepared in dealing with issues of consent," I told two middle-aged detectives.

"Your parents taught you well," the heavier one said.

I laughed in spite of myself.

"And where do your parents live?" the other asked.

"Excuse me?" That threw me. I didn't want to talk about Pam. Or my father. "Orange County. My mother lives there."

"And your father?"

"He's dead."

"I'm sorry to hear that. Recently?"

"He died when I was seventeen. Are we almost done?"

"Simple protocol," they described it.

But after I left the station, my mind started cycling through the details, what I'd left out, and wondering if their reassuring glances were only meant to throw me off, lure me into complacency, assure me that the revealing top I had worn during questioning was working. I'd be tallying up my calorie count for the day and paranoia would hit. Did I tell them I was back at the house by 11:00 or 11:30? Had those dudes from Beta recognized me on the street? I had stuffed the random contents of the night—the knife, my lingerie, Tristan's sweatshirt—in the closet safe I had bought to keep my good jewelry away from the other girls. I hadn't touched it since. I didn't know what next steps to take.

I came to an inevitable conclusion: I couldn't do this on my own. I needed to make sure this indiscretion was put away, taken care of by a professional, so I could move on and turn back to more important matters. The yearly sorority bikini calendar would be shot in a few weeks, and I was three pounds over my target weight. I had been asked to judge the upcoming fraternity Strip-A-Thon. These were important upcoming events, calendared items that required my full attention.

I called Pam the next afternoon on the way back to the sorority house. A CBS van was parked along frat row, and a young reporter in a hideous peach pantsuit stood drooling over an SAE member.

"How has the murder made you feel?" she asked him. When she got no articulate response, she continued: "Do you worry for your own life, knowing there is a murderer out there, lurking uncaught?"

He shrugged. "Maybe. I guess."

Another frat brother snuck up behind the oblivious reporter, palms resting against the back of his head, and thrusted his pelvis at her.

The cameraman was about to intervene when Pam picked up.

"Tiffany, your tutor told me you're already failing two of your classes. The term just started."

"Miscommunication. My tutors are imbeciles. Besides, that's privileged information."

"It wasn't privileged when I hired Mr. Pete to fill out your application. Get a tutor who will bring your grades up, okay? It's time for you to oversee some of these things."

"Fine by me. Listen, I need the name of Dad's attorney."

"He had several."

"The one with the spray tan and blondish hair."

Pam didn't seem too concerned. She probably didn't even know that there had been a murder on campus.

"Richard Slade. Why do you need a lawyer?"

"You just said I should be taking care of things myself."

"Please don't tell me you spent your stipend on crypto."

"What? Give me a break," I said.

I had just hung up when the reporter turned to me.

"You!" she shouted. "We need a female perspective."

"Angle that camera a bit higher, and I'll talk," I instructed the cameraman. The reporter thrust the microphone at me.

"How has the murder made you feel?"

"Terrified," I answered.

And I was terrified: terrified that I'd somehow be caught and sent to prison, forced to barter scissoring sessions for tampons and plastic hairbrushes. I'd live my most fuckable years with a horde of hairy convicts. It'd be worse than the sorority. But I also felt something else. Tearing into Tristan had been how YouTube unboxings were supposed to feel, that rush where you surprise yourself and feel completed, whole. Alive.

———

Richard Slade's law office overlooked Beverly Hills, ten stories above the city. He had swathed himself in Ralph Lauren and a heavy spray tan. I had chosen to wear an all-Chanel ensemble in a demure shade of blush. He met me at the door to his office. There was a hint of anxiety cloaked under all the rich fabric and cologne. The last time we had met I had been seventeen. He had visited my father one final time to sort out the estate. I remembered my father's booming voice echoing across the downstairs hall, still strong despite the cancer.

Slade and I assessed each other for a second.

"Tiffany. Look at you. All grown up."

Slade didn't seem surprised when I mentioned my concern about being questioned.

"Sounds like typical protocol. Just trying to put together a timeline of the evening. Unfortunately, you appear to be the one who was with Tristan for most of the night. Who did you speak to at the station?"

"Guy named Jenkins, I think. I can't remember the other one. Look, I'm not worried, I just need to know what to do if I'm called in again. I'd really like to get back to my life, you know, back to studying and volunteering and all that."

"Of course. I typically deal with white-collar issues."

"Can you help me or not?"

"I can consult you, sure. Your father was one of my best clients. I would be happy to help if I can."

A pretty but overweight secretary interrupted us to bring me a sparkling water. Slade waited until she had closed the door. I nodded my head, and he resumed.

"Is there any possibility you could be traced to the scene of the murder?"

"Tristan's room?" I realized my misstep. "That's where the cops told me he was found."

He nodded for me to continue, and I caught the beginnings of a receding hairline, despite the honey-blond highlights.

"Yes," I answered.

"There's a possibility?"

"There are parties," I said. "Every Thursday. Sometimes Tuesdays. Occasionally Wednesdays. Anyway, there was an around-the-world party just last week. I think Tristan's room was Russia. They were serving Moscow mules and Putin shooters. Dozens of people were there."

I piled on the details out of habit. These scattered pieces of truth were usually the trick to pulling off a successful lie. I still didn't know if I could trust Slade.

"What would you have touched in the room during one of these parties?"

"Well, everyone's pretty drunk. Sometimes we stumble into chairs. Tables. Beds."

"Beds. Have you ever slept with Tristan?"

"No. Not that I remember."

He gave me a patronizing look, and I wanted to smack him.

"You can't quite remember?" he asked. "Did you engage in any sexual conduct with him the night of the incident?"

I thought about the shock wave I'd felt between my legs when I'd first broken through Tristan's skin.

"No. Definitely not."

Slade didn't have much else for me other than an instruction to not talk to the police without consulting him first. He also advised me to forgo any upcoming parties and carefully screen my social media content. He was asking a lot from a sorority girl with a reputation to maintain.

"Is that it?" I asked.

"For now. Hopefully, for good."

I opened the door, all thirty pounds of slick metal barricading him from the rest of the city.

"Wait."

Slade's voice stopped me. I turned around, uncertain. He stood in front of his desk. He seemed small, much shorter than I remembered.

"Take care of yourself, Tiffany."

"Sure," I said.

"Find yourself a nice guy, a boyfriend. Your father would have wanted it. He could be a difficult man, but he was fond of you."

A difficult man. What an understatement. That was what good lawyers did, though—took the truth and diminished it until it was a dot, barely seen.

I took the elevator down and walked back into the heat and traffic.

———

Then I waited. The police never called me back. I got a five-figure bill from Slade's office and never heard from the detectives again.

Ashley had sworn I was back at the house around 11:00 P.M., holding her hair over the toilet. Smashley wasn't exactly the definition of an airtight alibi, but I'd take it.

A Metro bus on its way downtown had a stop right in front of the frat house, so over the next week, speculation grew that a transient may have hopped off to steal some shit from the empty unlocked house when Tristan arrived early from the party and fatally foiled his plans. A local headline ran: "Are Homeless People Preying on College Students?" Fox News was there the following week.

Once this theory gained some traction, everyone started to calm down a little. It made sense; order was restored. Soon it became an accepted fact solidified in the *L.A. Times*. The sleeping bags near the billboards of nearby bus stops were gone one day. The shopping carts and makeshift forts disappeared. Residents said the streets looked safer, cleaner. I'd done the city a service, really.

6

AFTER TRISTAN'S MURDER, AFTER THE CANDLELIGHT VIGILS and news reports about his perforated lungs and savaged chest, there was a return to the mundane. Lectures. Football season. An accidental drowning at the rec center. I embarked on a strict raw food diet, eating a maximum of 1,000 calories daily, no cheat meals allowed, with two-hour workouts scheduled six days a week. I tried to avoid thinking about that night at Sig Nu.

The days still burned, sunny and hot, but the nights had finally cooled down. I stopped dreaming of fire, but I woke instead from new nightmares: accidental blood on my blouse, a knife toppling out when I reached to pull my platinum card from my purse.

I tried to distract myself with Delta Gamma's upcoming activities. Strip-A-Thon was the third weekend of October, when ZBT hosted an annual male strip show. After the murder, off-campus parties had been suspended, but those rules were already loosening. The school couldn't expect the ban to last, for students to mourn one dead dude much longer.

The Strip-A-Thon was technically classified as a charity event, since we'd be using our singles to raise money. I had been asked to judge and score the guys on their individual and group routines, alongside representatives from two other sororities.

It felt good to represent what was being billed as the trifecta of hot girls from our campus, but dealing with the different sorority houses could be a real pain in the ass. Tammy, the judge from Pi Phi, had the IQ of a small dog, but she had gotten a new nose over the summer, which spurred a temporary surge in her popularity. Stephanie, the judge from KKG, was another matter. She was a legacy from one of the wealthiest families in the Bay Area and exhibited a raw malevolence that made me think of myself.

I dressed casually, since the emphasis would be on the guys for once. Casual ensembles, however, were the most difficult outfits to nail, since appearing effortless actually required the highest level of preparation. I went with a feminine Dior top, flared jeans, and extra-tall nude heels that would put me at five-foot-ten. Stephanie was taller than me, and I wanted to make sure I matched her.

Selecting an outfit had distracted me from the nervousness I felt returning to another fraternity house after Tristan's death. I sat in front of my bedroom mirror, second-guessing the shade of Urban Decay on my eyelids, about to smear it all off. In five minutes, I'd be late to the event. Emily's voice startled me.

"It hit you hard, didn't it? Tristan's death."

I hadn't realized she was in the room.

"There's a line you can call," Emily continued, "if you want to talk to someone. I've used it."

"Why? What problems do you have?" I instantly regretted asking.

"Sometimes I don't feel good enough, to have gotten into the school, the DG house."

"That must be hard for you," I said. I put my hand on her shoulder and counted to three. Best behavior, I reminded myself.

The truth was I felt plenty good enough. In fact, I felt like the world was only beginning to deliver on everything it owed to me. But I kept my mouth shut. I was officially late.

It always baffled me how some people could put their battered souls out there. Emily thought I was struggling with Tristan's murder, that sadness was what had thrown me off these past weeks. Emily always saw the best in people. Her mistake.

"Thanks for the advice, but I've done the whole therapy thing."

I'd spent $50k in therapy sessions through middle and high school. Some volunteer phone worker wouldn't help me sort out my daddy issues.

"And?" Emily asked.

"I have to run."

———

The scent of weed and cheap beer flooding through ZBT's front door matched the smells I had taken in that Thursday night at Sigma Nu, right before Tristan had led me up to his room.

The second I arrived in ZBT's main room, Stephanie brought her hand up to my face so quickly I thought she was about to slap me, and I prepared to kick her in the gut. But she only wanted to flash a gaudy three-stone ring in my face. She fluttered her fingers around and whipped her hand over to Tammy, who immediately shielded her face.

"Watch my nose!"

"Jeremy gave this to me last weekend when he took me to Napa," Stephanie said.

I'd already seen the ring. Stephanie's socials were full of shots that clearly had been staged for a solid hour by a full-time Instagram boyfriend: splashing under waterfalls, floating on flamingo inflatables, cartwheeling across remote desert landscapes.

"Are you two engaged?" Tammy asked Stephanie.

"Are you kidding me? This isn't the South. It's a six-month anniversary gift."

"It's beautiful," Tammy said.

"Tiffany, did you get a good look at it?" Stephanie said, trying to blind me with it again.

"I saw it. I prefer a teardrop."

"Oh please, that cut is so passé," she said, staring pointedly at the teardrop shape of my necklace.

I changed the subject. "We should probably prepare something to say about illiteracy." Tammy and Stephanie stared at me. "We're here to raise money for illiterate adults, right?" I asked.

"I thought this was a protest against fracking," Tammy said.

Donnie, the ZBT president, emerged from the crowd juggling three Solo cups of beer. He directed us to the front row and handed us silk sashes with our sorority monikers spread across them. Then he pulled out pink tiaras for us. Tammy immediately put hers on, but Stephanie and I caught sight of the tiny crystal-studded dicks lining the front band.

"Classy," Stephanie said.

"You're sorority royalty," Donnie said. "Wear it proudly."

"I'm doing this solely for charity," Stephanie clarified.

Tammy took a seat between Stephanie and me as the other girls began crowding in: they well surpassed the twenty-five-girl limit. A legion of Delta Gammas lined the front right side of the stage where an MC stood. He had us come up and introduce ourselves, and we were given little whiteboards to write our scores on. I zoned out staring at Stephanie's ring—it did sparkle, especially under the fluorescent light.

The house darkened as strobe lights began to pulse across the stage. A pair of guys dressed as firemen came out, holding plastic hatchets. They swung off their jackets to loud cheers and then went for their helmets. One fireman flung his offstage, but the second dancer threw his into the audience, and the helmet clipped a Tri Delta girl across the forehead. The dancing firefighters sensed something was wrong, and their routine disintegrated into a humping charade until they were booed off the stage.

I gave them a –3.

The firefighters were quickly replaced with ten dancers, all dressed in Tarzan jungle gear, beating bongos. They stripped down until I could see every muscle in their bodies strain. Girls surrounded me on all sides, but I was convinced I could catch the smell of sweat and Old Spice coming off their bodies in sheets. My heart pounded to its own feverish rhythm, faster than the beat of the music.

My eyes stayed fixed on the empty stage long after they'd left. I imagined being in a room with just their naked bodies and a fully charged power drill. I shook my head and scribbled down an 8.

"Did you seriously score them that high?" Stephanie turned to me. "That was too appropriative."

For the third set, only one performer walked out. He wore a suit tailored within an inch of his life. The music had been cut, and he stood there in silence, a lone red spotlight on him. He loosened his tie from his collar and removed his jacket, placing it over a folding chair. He meticulously undid one button after another down his shirt as a hush went over the crowd. He pulled it off, and my eyes traveled down his chest, to the perfect V-cut that framed his abs.

He bypassed his pants and began removing his shoes, his tie still on. He was like the Warhol of stripping; the utterly ordinary way he slowly and unceremoniously removed all his clothing defied logic.

"A bit too abstract for my taste," Stephanie mumbled.

Every muscle in my body tensed, and my legs wrapped themselves around my folding chair so hard I became part of the cold metal beneath me. I tried to write on my scoreboard, but my hand was shaking too hard. I could only produce a wandering zigzag. As I lifted my arm, a bead of sweat rolled from my armpit past my triceps to the floor. He was down to just his briefs. Then, without waiting for the applause of an audience, he walked off the stage.

"Your score, Tiffany," Stephanie said.

I looked down at the scribble on my whiteboard.

"Are you okay?" Tammy asked. "Your eye is twitching."

I could see her scan down and catch the sweat clouding under my top. I stood up so fast I overturned my chair.

"It's just too soon, what with Tristan's death," I said, scrounging up a suitable explanation.

"You can't leave!" Stephanie shouted over the music and screaming girls. "The next act is starting!"

But I was already fleeing for the outskirts of the room, pushing past sorority girls to find the exit.

I burst through the large double doors of the house and stumbled down the stone steps. I couldn't stay in there; I couldn't trust the urges that had been stirred in me yet again. Ever since Tristan, it was all I could think about. There was no going back to normal parties. I'd had a taste of real fun.

I took off my heels and rushed down Strathmore Avenue. I might never be able to set foot in a fraternity house again. Those guys were barely 7s. What would happen when I got close to a 10? I was out of control. I was on fire.

I approached the Village. I was a good mile away from sorority row. I kept walking. When I spotted the sign, I knew I had taken this route on purpose. The building had been there all through college—I drove by it almost every day but had never been inside. Tonight, it called out to me, beckoning me with that wonderful yellow arrow.

I walked in and headed straight to the counter, bypassing the line of people.

"Double-double, animal style," I told the cashier, who looked about seventeen and wore a ridiculous paper hat.

He stared at me for a moment and said, "Three fifty-five, please."

I had left my purse back at the judging booth. I dug through the pockets of my jeans and found two bucks. I handed the salvaged wad of cash to him and took the receipt before he could count it out. He sighed and motioned for the next customer.

While I was waiting for the burger, I caught a boy giggling at me. I had no idea what the chubby little fuck was looking at, but I soon realized that other people were staring too, like they knew I shouldn't be here, that I was the type of girl who should be drinking a soy shake and picking at some carrots over at Whole Foods, not ordering stacks of beef at an In-N-Out. It wasn't until I glanced down at my dirty feet that I realized I was still wearing my judging sash. I felt the top of my head: the crown of penises. I ripped the thing off and stuffed it into the round maw of a nearby trash can.

When they finally called my number, I took the order and retreated to the side of the building away from any windows. I squatted down on the other side of the drive-through, free from wandering eyes, and sunk my teeth into the soft skin of the burger bun. I gave in to the wild blur of flavors, the complementary taste of greasy beef and creamy Thousand Island dressing. I couldn't calm myself until I had eaten the entire thing, including some of the paper wrapping it came in.

I could hardly remember walking back up the hill to the sorority house. When I got inside, I found myself in front of the bathroom door again, waiting to let the guilt of my nearly-1,000-calorie meal force me onto my knees in front of the toilet. But I couldn't do it tonight. What was wrong with me?

I wandered down the empty hall to my room. Emily was gone, probably off to visit her grandmother. I unlocked my safe and pulled out the knife that had gone into Tristan, feeling its serrated blade. I returned to the hall and sat on the floor outside the bathroom, running my finger up and down the knife's smooth middle, waiting for some sort of answer or sign.

7

I WANTED TO BE AN EXPLORER WHEN I WAS YOUNG, BEFORE I thought about being an influencer or a personal shopper or a fashion model. Before I later realized I didn't have to *be* anything, that jobs were for people with shitty credit and student loans who aspired to someday buy a condo.

I liked testing things out, pushing boundaries: a finger over the flame of a candle or along the blade of a razor. The catapulting snap of the mouse trap in the pool house. It was even better when I made other people play with me. Like my younger sister, Celeste. Sometimes I messed with the Pomeranians. But usually it was Celeste, since Pam freaked out way more about Tiki and Sergeant Sparkles.

Pam would pile up all my little sins and wait until the weekend, when my father came back from his business in the city. Then she'd snatch me by the hand and pull me up the stairs to his office, which was always dark and cold no matter the season. She had to knock first. We all did. The door remained locked, whether he was inside or not.

"Tell your father what you did yesterday."

My father usually turned his back on us, his gaze toward the window at the ocean below.

I'd admit to some sliver of the truth: "Celeste got stuck in the closet."

"'Stuck'? Interesting choice of word," Pam might say, tapping her Jimmy Choos on the hardwood, already regretting coming upstairs, already wanting to escape. She hated my father's office, its emerald and mahogany.

"Someone locked her in the closet," I might admit.

"*You* did! Celeste was in there for hours! She peed her new Burberry overalls."

"It was an accident," I'd promise. Around this time, my father might finally turn to face me. At some point, he would cut in with follow-up questions for Pam.

"And where were you during all this? Where was the nanny?" My father approached all angles of an argument. He narrowed in on my mother's weaknesses like he was watching her through the scope of a hunting rifle. And he always took my side.

He liked to click the spark of his lighter back and forth. It sounded like the hammer of a gun.

"Why did you do it, Tiffany?"

I usually answered him honestly. "I don't know. It was fun. A joke."

"Don't do it again," he would say, whether the "it" was locking Celeste in a closet, knocking her head against a counter, or dumping her Barbie Jeep into the pool.

I'd nod, and the conversation was over.

Pam always forgave me, though. Over a glass of champagne and an awful home design show, she'd lean over and admire me: "Look at you, that face. You're just like me. You don't even have his eyes. Not a single thing."

She loved commenting on my looks, the green of my eyes, the lines of my cheekbones, the even longer lines of my legs. They were all her features. My mother was perfectly symmetrical through a combination of genes and plastic surgery. Celeste, meanwhile, was gawky, horsey. She never grew into either her nose or her jaw.

Pam and I matched, it was true, like halved hearts to a keepsake necklace. She actually gave me one of those things, a broken half of a heart on a silver chain. You give those to your friends when you're twelve (and it's still lame), not one of your daughters. She'd act like we were members of the Baby-Sitters Club. I'd dangle the necklace over Celeste and taunt, "Where's yours?" until she shrieked. Otherwise, I never wore the stupid thing.

When I started high school, Pam's face grew tighter, more pinched. That was when she started to get desperate. Pam's basic-mom antics really began to embarrass me sophomore year, when she started trying to hang out with my friends. She'd coax us with alcohol like she was the mom from *Mean Girls*.

"A little champagne, just a dash," she'd say when I had girls over.

Once we plotted to TP the sad loser on the cheerleading team, and we caught Pam eavesdropping. She wanted to join in.

"I'll take you girls. I can be stakeout. Drive the getaway car."

I answered for all of us. "Thanks, but no thanks, Pam."

My junior year, she'd try to give me dating advice, plant her ass on my bathroom counter while I was applying my makeup, a glass of the grigio in her hand.

"Smile more!" she'd tell me. "It gets you what you want."

But my father never smiled. And he seemed to have all the power. Besides, I wasn't like Pam, born in some backwoods in Missouri. I didn't spend my late teens "dancing," as she called it, waiting for someone with money to take me away to somewhere better. I came from the OC. I was born this way, with sea salt in my hair and an iPhone in my hand. I had an ocean view from the beginning. Someday, I'd marry someone who was the same way, who could also smell desperation from a mile away.

"A guy will do almost anything to get laid," Pam had said that same day in the bathroom. "At least for the first month. I'm kidding, of course."

She wasn't. And she was right. Guys *would* do anything to get laid. This was only truer the older I got. For example, you could totally tell a dude, *There's a high probability I'll stab you repeatedly with this knife after I go down on you*, and he'd just think, *Wait, so I'm about to get head?*

Maybe he'd think the girl was only kidding. That was on him.

I'd said it before to boys, that I'm dangerous, and they thought I was just showing off (I was) and that I didn't mean it (they were wrong). I'd prove myself later with a brush of flame against their body, a bite on the thigh a little too close or hard for comfort. Nothing serious. Nothing close to what had happened to Tristan. The truth was I didn't know

I had it in me, that the ability not just to maim but to *kill* had been lurking within me the whole time. If I had known, I would have tried a long time ago.

—————

After Tristan's name faded out of the headlines, the question on everyone's lips soon became what would happen to Halloween. The school had banned all major parties in the wake of the murder. The sororities were worried less about being stabbed by a homicidal maniac and more about what Halloween would look like without the traditional night of ghosts, debauchery, and ODs at the frat houses. There were protests along the row, homemade signs championing the right to party strung across balconies and staked into front lawns. I even spotted a few sit-ins at the library on Instagram.

I caught Amy on the local news one day being interviewed in an American flag bikini.

"How are we supposed to get through the appropriate stages of grief without Halloween?" she asked. "We can't move on unless we can celebrate! We have rights, too! It's in the Constitution!"

She had a point. Our parents had been able to indiscriminately party and fuck their way through their college years, so why couldn't we?

The truth was the university wanted the murder gone, wiped clean, as quickly as possible. It got its wish when the news vans found a better story to report on: an overworked engineering student hanged himself at the rival school across town and live streamed the whole thing on YouTube.

Two days before Halloween, the administration lifted the moratorium on parties, and there was a mad rush among the sororities to solidify their plans. Delta Gamma ended up committing to a party at SAE. On the thirty-first, I returned from an evening spin class to find most of the girls already dressed in costumes.

A bunch of them had taken an excursion to Hustler and were dressed as varying versions of a Playboy Bunny. Slutty *Sesame Street* costumes were really popular this year, too.

Amy stood in the common room wearing the remains of a nurse's dress. Mandy was crouched at her feet, cutting the hem of her skirt with a pair of scissors, until the red of her underwear popped out like a bull's-eye. Mandy herself had dressed as a topless zombie with pasties crafted to resemble rotting pieces of flesh.

"Dan is going to jizz himself when he sees you," Amy told her. "Boobs and zombies are his two favorite things."

Mandy stood up to admire her work. "What do you think, Tiffany?"

"The hookers on Hollywood Boulevard are more covered."

"Thanks. Where's your costume?"

"I don't have one."

I hadn't planned on going because I knew I couldn't trust myself. I didn't want to feel that same panic, that chest-constricting lack of control I'd felt when I was at In-N-Out on my knees with a mouthful of meat patty shoved in my face. Just like the murder, it had happened before I could stop myself. I was supposed to listen to Slade, to stay clear of parties and any dangerous circumstances. But I had never been good at following rules.

Halloween night was unusually dry and windy, with a crackle of electricity to the air. As I climbed the stairs, a strong gust from the outside rattled the framed portraits in the hall. I looked out my bedroom window, at the tops of other houses and the palm trees that punctured the sky.

"Aren't you getting ready?" Emily asked. She had come in from the bathroom.

I told her the truth, one of the rare times: "Emily, I've been feeling off lately. I don't think I should go."

"You never called that phone line I gave you, did you?"

"No."

"You should consider getting help. We all need it sometimes."

I was about to answer when I turned and caught her outfit, the pointy hat and ridiculous amount of extra fabric. "*What* is that?" I asked.

"They're dress robes."

"What?"

"I'm a wizard."

She might as well have worn a sign over her chest that read NINE-TEEN-YEAR-OLD VIRGIN.

"You've got some important World of Witchcraft party to go to?" I asked her.

"I'm going to the SAE party like everyone else. I've decided to stay here for the weekend. And you know what? I think you should go, too. I think it would be good for your recovery," she said.

Emily never went to parties. If she was going, that would mean I might be the only DG missing. That would be even more suspicious. And what would happen to my socials if I wasn't tagged in the night's activities? "Get ready with me" videos were already flooding my feeds. Most of the house had left. From my window, I watched girls filtering out, heard the clacking of heels that would be lost or thrown aside by the end of the night.

Emily was right. I had to go. There was no other option, really. And I needed a quick costume.

I decided to dress as a black cat, which was the LBD of Halloween costumes. I slipped on a black lace lingerie set I had picked up at Agent Provocateur and paired it with thigh-high fuck-me boots. I sculpted a perfect cat eye that highlighted the green of my own.

A lot of girls like to sport the lingerie look without thinking about mobility, which is not smart. Whenever I wore my underwear out in public, I always anchored myself in with double-sided tape. I tore off a strip and taped it around the curve of my hip. I turned back to the full-length mirror for one last look, just to make sure my chest arched perfectly. I slipped on full-length black gloves that reached past my elbows to complete the outfit.

Stephanie would be at the party, since Jeremy was SAE's vice president. I needed to look knockout hot. Drop-dead gorgeous. I was still missing something.

"Will you walk over to the party with me? I can wait for you," Emily said.

I looked her over. I hated being seen with such a dork, but then again, arriving with Emily would only make me look better.

"Fine. I still need something for my costume."

I went downstairs and hunted through the discarded costume accessories, the unwrapped candies, and the empty vodka shooters, until I found a cheap headband with glued cat ears. It still had the seven-dollar tag on it. I picked up a pair of sewing shears from the coffee table. My reflection split into two along its thin blade. I sliced the tag off and found myself unable to put the scissors down. They could fit snugly, comfortably, in my boot, resting along my calf.

"You ready?" Emily called out. She was at the door, opening it, when the wind caught hold and swung it hard into the wall.

I slid the scissors into my boot before I could stop myself. *Just as a precaution,* I told myself, already knowing it was a lie. *Protection.*

8

THE MAIN ROOM OF SAE WAS EMPTY WHEN EMILY AND I ARRIVED, and the dance floor held only two losers listening to techno and drinking Bud Light. This was usual protocol, though, since people were slow to arrive and usually went straight upstairs to get wasted first.

I clutched the banister, pausing at the bottom while Emily lumbered up. I prepared myself for the wave of masculine heat that had hit me at the Strip-A-Thon and then climbed up the stairs into a cloud of smoke. Halfway up, I spotted a guy dressed as a keg, naked from the waist up, a beer spout protruding from his groin. I rubbed my gloved hands across my thighs, attempting to distract myself from flesh and ab muscles.

But soon the sight of Alpha Chi and Tri Delta sorority members squeezed into costumes three sizes too small slowed my pulse. I was in better shape than every girl here. My focus on the guys waned, and I began rating each female who passed by, tracking muffin tops and sausage legs. It was like walking through the greasy salad bar at a middle-American Sizzler.

A guy who was already so faded he could barely keep his bloodshot eyes open wandered into me. Even though he was high as hell, he must have realized he didn't have a chance with me, because he approached Emily.

"You're at a bar and you've just died, and God appears and he tells you—"

"Don't answer," I instructed Emily. "Don't even make eye contact with him."

I pushed him back into the hallway traffic, and he was lost in the crowd.

"Tiff! Emily!" Ashley called out to us.

A couple other Delta Gammas had gathered away from the crowd in a bedroom off the hallway and were passing a loose bag of Franzia around the room. Ashley had already spilled red wine all over her Tickle Me Elmo halter top.

"You must be sweating balls in that outfit," she said to Emily.

"I didn't realize how hot it would be in here."

"Is this your first frat party?"

Emily nodded.

This did not reflect well on me; as her big sister, I should have taken her to a party as soon as she pledged last year, but I figured as long as she left every weekend to go hang with her grandma, it didn't matter.

"First-timers have to slapbag!" Ashley screamed, thrusting the bag of wine toward Emily.

"I don't really like wine," she said.

"Dude, don't think; just drink," Ashley said.

Emily looked at me with the eyes of a calf on its way to slaughter.

"You have to chug if it's your first time," I told her, gently pushing her into the circle of DG members that had formed around us. Ashley hoisted the bag up, and I pulled Emily's head back as her body naturally fought against the gush of wine propelled into her mouth. She spit most of it out across the carpet. It was the worst binge attempt I'd seen in a long time, but the girls cheered for her anyway.

"Tiffany, your turn!" Julie screamed.

The girls began chanting, and soon we were attracting male attention. A hot blond who wasn't in costume had walked into the room. I didn't recognize him from any past Greek events.

"Fine," I said. "I can do it myself."

I took the bag, grabbing hold of the warm plastic, and positioned the nozzle over my open mouth. I didn't take much of it in before I had to slap and pass it on. Warm red wine rolled down my throat, and I quickly wiped my neck before it could hit my lingerie. The move brought me back to the night with Tristan, when his blood had soaked right through my bra. I felt light-headed.

"Are you DGs seriously drinking that cheap excuse for wine?" a shrill voice cut in. Stephanie had entered the room with Jeremy. As if they weren't already cheesy enough as a couple, they had chosen to dress as Romeo and Juliet. They had obviously picked up the "explicit" costume versions: Stephanie was in a tiny corset, and Jeremy wore some sort of vest that showed his nipples.

"Tiffany, you're a fifth-year. You should know better," Stephanie said. She stroked Jeremy's biceps. "Have you all met Jeremy?"

"This isn't your room, is it?" Ashley asked Jeremy, picking up a leaking Franzia bag she had just tossed onto a nearby bed.

"No, I'm down the hall," he said.

Jeremy stayed for only a few minutes, but Stephanie parked on the bed.

"Did you all see what Jeremy got me last week?" she asked, holding her hand out.

"Jesus fucking Christ, everyone has seen your ring already, Stephanie," I said.

Her eyes burned. "That's not true. But whatever." She spun the rock around her finger, casting flashes of light across the room. "Tiffany, Jeremy told me that he saw you at In-N-Out, the night of the Strip-A-Thon. You couldn't wait till the end of the event to stuff your face with a cheeseburger?"

The other girls were listening. I clenched my jaw. "I have absolutely no idea what you're talking about."

"Oh, I think you do." She smiled.

"Do we need to take this outside?" I asked.

"Calm down. This isn't East L.A. Besides, I'm coming from a well-meaning place." Stephanie's eyes traveled down my body. "You wouldn't want to outgrow your lingerie."

I sucked in my stomach as though I had just been punched.

"I better find Jeremy. See you around, ladies," Stephanie said, tossing the girls a wave as she strolled out.

To get my mind off taking a baseball bat to Stephanie's skull, I joined the sorority for more drinking games. We had just polished off another five-liter bag of wine when a stampede of frat members rushed the room, squeezing us in to capacity. Sweat from a nearby guy in a hula skirt smeared down my arm.

"Body shots!" he shouted. He hoisted a bottle of Patron above his head. "Who's first?" he asked.

"Emily should do it. It's her first frat party," Amy said.

The blond I'd seen earlier volunteered and took his shirt off, revealing a defined succession of ab muscles. Happiness briefly lit Emily's face for the first time that night. The fool: he was mine. I pushed her out of the way.

"Emily doesn't want to do it," I said, forcing myself past the press of bodies to the center of the room.

I faced the hot, shirtless blond. "You first," we both said at the same time.

He relented and reclined across a desk, knocking down a row of plastic cups. I crouched over him, licking him across the stomach. I sprinkled salt on him, making sure to press into his abs a little. When I went to lick off the salt, I gave him a little bite.

I took the shot, and he immediately swung me off my feet and onto the table. Instead of leaning over me to lick off the salt, he went to the end of the table and came up between my legs. He hooked his arms under my thighs and took a double shot, then crawled up toward my mouth for the lime. We sent the room into hysterics.

I didn't catch Blondie's name, but I found out he was an SAE member from a chapter in San Diego. He had just mentioned going downstairs to the dance floor when I heard the splash of liquid hitting a hard surface, and a sour stench invaded the room. Some chick dressed as slutty Snow White had spewed burgundy chunks across one of the desks.

The smell sent a wave of people fleeing from the puking Disney princess. The force of bodies hit me like a slow-rolling earthquake, shoving me into the wall. The upstairs became complete chaos.

Blondie fled immediately, pushing his way through girls with those magnificently muscled arms, not even a backward glance my way. I tried to fight against the rush of bodies and felt someone grab hold of my arm. It was Emily latching on to me.

"Let go," I said, dragging her along as I attempted to follow Blondie.

When I finally managed to get out of the stifling upstairs room and detach from Emily, Blondie was nowhere in sight. I wandered down to the dance floor. It was now packed with sweating, heaving bodies. I pushed through the crowd and got my ass grabbed twice, but I couldn't spot him anywhere.

At 1:00 A.M., the music was cut, and people began staggering for the exit.

The dance floor was a sticky mess, and the beer kegs were drained dry. Another typical frat night. I wished I could have felt as excited as Emily, but that wouldn't happen unless I scored some serious Molly.

I headed back upstairs. I was sober again, and it seemed to be only getting hotter. I entered an empty room that had been left unlocked and stepped onto the balcony for some air. A catcall sounded to my left.

The tease was one room away, on the next terrace. I walked out to the edge of the balcony. Only six feet of air separated us.

"Do you believe in fate?" he asked, and smiled.

"Depends on how this night turns out," I said. "You left me back there."

"I knew we'd meet again."

"So you're a fortune teller now?"

"Did you come out here for the view?" he asked.

"There's a better one on the roof," I said, instinct taking over, the words out of my mouth before I knew what I was saying, what I was about to do.

"Yeah? You've been up there?"

"I have," I said. "You wanna see it?"

He nodded.

"I'll meet you back inside," I said, and tilted my head toward the door. I stopped at a mirror to adjust my hair. The hallway was empty.

Bedroom doors were beginning to slam as couples came up from the dance floor to hook up. I felt the hard edge of the sewing shears under the leather of my boot.

"This way," I said when Blondie emerged from the other room. I'd been up there a few times with other SAE members.

We had to pull down a ladder at the far side of the upstairs hallway to reach the roof. Blondie let me go first, and I could feel his eyes lock on to my ass while I climbed up one rung at a time. I pulled myself up and walked across the roof to overlook Westwood. There wasn't much to see: a layer of smog distorted the view of Century City skyscrapers in the distance, and I could count only three stars when I glanced up.

"It's gorgeous," Blondie said.

I led him over to a vertical slant against the side of the building that offered an easy way to hook up without having to roll around in the gravel.

I pulled at his shirt, and he raised his arms, letting me yank it over his head. He reached around to unhook my bra, but nothing happened after the clasp was freed.

"What's going on?" he asked.

"I have double-sided tape on."

He gave the bra a pathetic tug.

"Harder," I said.

He ripped the tape off, tearing at the soft skin under my breasts and leaving a curved line of red across my chest. My heart pumped. I pulled Blondie closer to me with my legs, wrapping my left thigh around him tight. He lowered himself over me, his mouth on me.

I whispered in his ear: "Tell me a secret."

He paused for only a second. "I didn't shower today."

Was he fucking serious?

"That's really weak," I said.

"You can top it?"

"I can." I leaned in close. "I killed a boy."

Blondie let out an immediate laugh. "With your man-killing pussy? I believe it."

Both his hands were occupied now with his fly. He was having difficulty getting his dick out because whenever he'd get close, I tightened my legs harder around him.

"Stop," he said, laughing. I did it again. "Seriously."

The restraint I'd promised myself at the beginning of the night was gone, and I didn't care. I understood how guys felt when they promised to pull out, the initial intent behind the words betrayed by the need of the moment. At that second, nothing else mattered. I was going all the way.

I reached into my right boot, feeling for the handle of the scissors, sliding them slowly out. I'd have to stab quickly and with full force, jam them straight into his jugular, then maybe push him back and stab him in the eye or somewhere on the face, just to make sure he was fully incapacitated. What if it didn't work like it had with Tristan? What if he hit back, sent me flying off the roof? I paused, suddenly unsure. *Keep going,* the voice in my head said. *Ignore any doubts.*

I readied myself for the metal to connect with soft flesh, the puncture and then the warm flow of his blood.

"What the hell?" Blondie yelled, almost causing me to drop the shears. He had given up on his pants and was trying to pull off my panties now. "You got a chastity belt on?" he asked.

"The double-sided tape," I hissed. My hand was shaking. "Figure it out."

"Goddamn, they all said this would be easy," he said under his breath.

I rolled my eyes, and then the full weight of his words hit me. I slid the shears into my boot, barely escaping his line of vision. *They said?*

"Who told you that?"

"No one," he muttered. I squeezed Blondie hard with both legs, knocking the wind out of him.

"Did you tell anyone you were coming up here?" I asked, trying to mask the frenzy in my voice.

"No," he said. I glared at him. "I don't know. I guess I mentioned it to a couple of the guys before I left."

"By name?"

"What?" he said.

"Did you mention my name? What's my name?"

"Tiffany, right?"

"How do you know that?" I screamed. I hadn't even told him. It totally figured—the time I needed a completely anonymous sexual encounter with a guy, he knew my fucking name.

"Chill out," he said.

"And you told them you were going to the roof with me?"

"Yeah, what's the big deal? I'll tell them we just made out or something. But seriously, do you know what kind of reputation you have?"

My plans for the night were shattered. I could kill him anyway—he was only from San Diego—but to explain it to the cops, to the school, how he had ended up dead in the very spot I had taken him alone to was pushing it. Slade would have an absolute meltdown.

I shoved him away from me.

"Oh, now you're angry?" he said.

"Do men show any discretion at all these days? Can you do anything without bragging about it to your stupid frat bros?"

"Look, I'm sorry."

He picked up my bra. I went to snatch it from him, and he yanked it away.

"Come on. You can't do this to me. I'm still hard."

I crossed my arms. "You think you're the only dissatisfied participant in tonight's events?"

"Just get me off. You only have to give me a hand job or something," he insisted.

"Go beat yourself off alone, asshole," I said.

"You're a real bitch," he said, and pulled out his phone. "I hate L.A."

I took his phone and heaved it off the building. I could hear a loud crack when it shattered on the pavement.

"You fucking cunt!"

"You're lucky it wasn't you! Give me my bra!"

I wrestled him for it, and although he was angry at first, he must have thought it was some sort of belated come-on, because he started grinding his thigh against me while holding the bra over my head. I bit him on the forearm as hard as I could, the taste of salt and coconuts filling my mouth.

Blondie punched me in the jaw. Hard. By the time I had finished spitting blood out onto the gravel, he was long gone.

I found my bra hanging from one of the satellite antennas, waving like a surrender flag. I let out a bloodcurdling scream across the rooftop into the night.

9

MADE MY WAY OFF THE ROOF FEELING DISGUSTED AND USED.
What did I think would come from some asshole from San Diego?
And did I really think another murder could be so easy?

The remaining tape on my bra had peeled off and was chafing
against my raw skin. I felt my head: my hair had rubbed against the
side of the roof into a tangled mess. I needed a mirror. I tried door after
door in the dark, but they were all locked. It was after 2:00 A.M., and
people had progressed from hooking up to passing out. Socks and a
few condoms hung over the doorknobs.

The only thing to disrupt the silence in the hall was the sound of
Bob Marley's voice drifting up from the stoner quadrant downstairs.

I finally found an open door and let myself into the room. The
moon's reflection bounced off a full-length mirror, and I fixed my hair
under the green glow of my iPhone. Emily had texted, asking me to
wait for her to walk home, but I ignored her. I reapplied the tape on my
bra, checked my swollen lip, and was about to raid the nearby closet for
a sweatshirt when my eyes adjusted to the darkness enough to notice
the couple behind me.

Stephanie and Jeremy rested alone, oblivious to the world in a giant
bed reserved for council members of the fraternity. A bottle of pills
lay on the dresser over their heads. My anger at Blondie disintegrated
when I looked down at their bodies. They were still dressed in their
ridiculous Shakespearian outfits. Even passed out in some sort of Ambien coma, Stephanie managed to show her ring off, draping it loosely
across Jeremy's chest.

The two of them were pathetic. I caught sight of a picture of Jeremy on his wall with the words "MY HERO" on a felt letter board. I had to laugh. This was why I didn't have a boyfriend, why I was smarter than all that college relationship bullshit that had twenty-one-year-olds wearing matching Greek sweaters and self-medicating themselves every night.

I hated everything about these assclowns: The way they snuggled together. The clichéd selfies of them kissing in front of the Eiffel Tower. The Hallmark-card prom portraits. The fact that they had an entire king bed, but bunched together, intertwined like they were one person.

Stephanie leaned in closer to Jeremy, laying claim to his broad chest even in drugged sleep. I wasn't smiling anymore. I wanted to punch holes through the cork board over their bed, strike a match and burn every posed photo of them.

I thought about Blondie, my missed opportunity, and I had to bite my tongue to stifle another scream. Without another thought, I shut the door, locked it, and returned to the bed. I dissected Stephanie feature by feature. I came out ahead on everything: straighter nose, higher cheekbones, bigger chest, more lustrous hair. What did she have? I gave Stephanie's blond hair a little tug, then a harder one, so forceful her head hit the top of her shoulder. She made a small noise but barely flinched. I rolled her away from Jeremy, just enough to leave space to wedge my body between them.

I tried to ignore the heat coming from Stephanie and focus instead on Jeremy. I just wanted to get myself turned on a little, to feel the same energy that had burned me up that night with Tristan. Lying there beside Jeremy, running my hand up his thigh, I imagined I was choking him out with a wide leather belt, a scream struggling to surface from his strangled throat.

But soon, my mind led me to an unexpected place—I suddenly wondered what our names would look like written in curling script across a bulletin board. "Tiffany" and "Jeremy" could be written on top of each other, the "y's" in our name touching. I imagined a lazy

Sunday in bed with him watching a *Bachelor* marathon, eating full-fat Rocky Road ice cream. Jeremy's cologne—it was an all-American scent, Calvin Klein, most likely—was like a slow-moving poison, subverting my thoughts.

Their relationship was so basic, and yet I wanted some of it, just a taste to try the flavor. So I gave in, sliding my hips across his body, so his scent would rub off on the lace of my lingerie as I straddled him.

I closed my eyes and leaned down to kiss him, a simple, chaste kiss. The metallic taste of blood was still in my mouth, and I licked at my lips, so they wouldn't stain his perfect, rose-tinted ones.

I froze. I had to make a choice. Hearts and daisies, or something darker tonight.

I smacked Jeremy's cheek, challenging him to wake up. A different sensation started to come over me, one that felt stronger and more welcome. He was finally starting to stir.

I slid my hands up his arms and across his chest and ripped off that stupid vest, tearing the cheap stitching right down the middle. My pelvis dug against his, the pulse between my legs quickening, until the excitement I had felt on the roof returned. I took one last look at the tousled copper of his hair and his full lower lip, the square of his jaw and his wide, strong neck.

I grabbed one of the throw pillows on the bed and positioned it over Jeremy's face, gently at first, applying increasing pressure. I pulled the shears out, aimed them over his neck, and, without time to think, stabbed them as hard as I could into his waiting throat.

There was a jerk, a muffled sound under the pillow, but I was ready. I shoved the pillow into his face harder and pinned his arms down on the bed with my knees.

Once the shears were buried to their handle into his flesh, I ripped them horizontally across his throat so hard it tore into the fibers of his neck. A jet of blood sprung out of him in a high solid arc, like the swift jet of water from a drinking fountain. The spray of blood showered Stephanie with a thin trail of red. The tightness that had built up in me found its release, and I was able to take a breath.

Jeremy's body barely convulsed, but the blood spilled out in swift gushes. Luckily, his sheets had a superhigh thread count and were doing a remarkable job of absorbing most of the blood. Stephanie, however, had shifted positions and rubbed her face, smearing blood across her cheek. She was going to have one hell of a hangover tomorrow.

I pulled myself off Jeremy, crawling away from the parade of blood marching down his quilted coverlet. I had done it again. The intensity, the fleeting rush of pleasure, subsided to pure lazy satisfaction, and I calmed my breathing by looking at my reflection in the mirror. A substantial amount of blood had soaked my gloves, but it was nothing like the mess I had made with Tristan. I pulled the sticky gloves off and stuffed them into my boots.

It was so much easier to regain calm this time. I was already thinking about what kind of breakfast I'd have tomorrow. I craved bacon, could almost hear the sizzled pop.

I made sure to leave silently. The hall was still quiet, but I ran into a girl passed out across the floor in the hallway, blocking the stairs. I stepped over her and went down each step carefully, leaning forward on the balls of my feet so my heels wouldn't hit the wood. I could hear the last remnants of the party downstairs. Emily had kept texting me, no doubt scared to go back by herself, and I prayed that she had stuck around. I was going to need an alibi.

I found her downstairs, with three guys passing around a bong. The loser I had steered her away from at the beginning of the night had lit it up for her and held it to her mouth.

"Hey, Tiffany," Emily said, coughing out a cloud of smoke.

"Hey," the stoner said. "I know you."

"Shut up," I told him. "Are you ready to go, Emily?"

Another dude had moved seats and motioned for me to sit next to him on a stained brown couch that looked like it had been there since the '70s.

"Not happening," I told him.

"I was waiting for you and Chase to come back," Emily said.

"Chase?"

"Timothy said you went up to the roof with him."

So that was Blondie's name. And word of our hookup had already spread to even the deadbeats.

"Right," I said. "That was who I've been with the whole time. I came right from the roof. And now it's time to go."

"Just have one toke," the third stoner said.

I glanced toward the hall and up the stairs, where I had left Jeremy leaking out quarts of blood.

"It's two A.M. Party's over. We're leaving, Emily."

"I think this is the first time I've ever gotten drunk," Emily said. She zigzagged across the length of the sidewalk as we made our way back to the sorority house.

"I wouldn't advertise things like that," I said.

"I had fun," she said.

I sighed and watched her circle a lamppost three times. I needed to get her drunk ass in gear. We had to reach the sorority house, the sanctuary at the end of a long night.

"I talked to two guys tonight," Emily said.

"I hope you used protection," I said.

"It's a big deal for me," she muttered. "I don't have a guy like you . . ." She stopped. "Who was your last boyfriend?"

I answered with the truth before I could stop myself: "I've never had a boyfriend."

"But you're so beautiful."

"I know, right? It makes you really wonder what's wrong with men."

"Did you hear that?" Emily asked. "From up in the trees?"

"You're paranoid because you smoked," I told her, annoyed with her swerving line of questioning. She was ruining my high with her own.

A car approached, its headlights sending a long beam of yellow light over the road ahead of us. I waited until I could tell it wasn't a cop, then grabbed Emily by the shoulders, pretending to push her into the car's path until she shrieked. Maybe that would wake her up a bit.

"That's not funny!" she screamed. She hit me across the arm, then latched on to me. Is this how girlfriends joked? "Especially after what happened with Tristan. We shouldn't even be walking alone. This is exactly how *Walk in the Woods* started before those girls got hacked into pieces."

"I'll protect you," I said. She leaned into me, and I tried to pull her along.

Emily was limping in her heels, still wearing a smile despite her bleeding ankles. I hadn't realized how wrecked she'd gotten.

"I think I might stick around next weekend," she said.

I remembered back when it was exciting to binge on wine coolers, when frat parties still held their allure. Back when a four-minute fuck with a fraternity president in the front seat of a Mustang meant something. How quickly that stuff wore off.

"I don't think there will be more parties for a while," I said.

"I had fun," she said.

"You already said that," I told her.

We arrived back at the house and headed through the front room, where Emily walked right into a side table. I shook my head.

"You know, Emily, you can only do so many keg stands and go to so many frat parties before you need to move on to something more sophisticated, a little more meaningful. You're only a second-year, so I won't fault you for that. Me, however . . ." I cleared my throat. I wished there were other girls around to witness my declaration, but the bedroom doors were all closed, the lights out. "My days frequenting frat parties are over. I'm ready to move on and find myself someone successful, real boyfriend material."

Emily ignored me and crawled on hands and knees up the stairs.

"Are you listening to me?" I asked.

She rose to her feet and looked at my chest.

"You're bleeding," she said, motioning to a small line of blood smeared under my bra.

"It's nothing," I said quickly, rubbing at it. "I cut myself on the roof hooking up with Chase."

"I don't feel good," Emily said, turning away from me to resume her crawl up the stairs.

She spent the next hour puking up box wine in the bathroom. I could hear her down the hallway while I locked the shears and gloves in my safe. I left a glass of water and some Tylenol by her bed with a signed note, so she'd know it was *me* who had helped her. I was going to need her tomorrow.

Then I sat in bed until the pinkish rays of morning light snuck into the room, taking in the last moments of calm before the news of last night swept through campus. I imagined Stephanie rising out of her hibernation to the same interplay of light across the wall, the slow sinking realization of her circumstance. How long after finding Jeremy's emptied body would she figure out that something else was gone?

I had kept it in my right boot, safe on the walk home. I pulled my trophy out and felt the round metal of Stephanie's ring, the jagged edges of the stones. I slid it over my finger. Perfect fit.

10

THE NEWS CREWS WERE BACK. NOT JUST ON CAMPUS THIS TIME, but throughout the whole city: at Starbucks, boutiques, juice bars, yoga studios. Armed guards replaced doormen at the nicer apartment complexes along Wilshire Boulevard.

The cops were looking in all the wrong places. I would stroll out of Erewhon and spot the police patrol cars, windows down, rolling along, scoping out the alleys, the nearby cemetery, the underpasses. I'd crunch into a carrot stick and smile as they passed by.

When I looked in the mirror, I wore the murders so clearly across my face. I had to remind myself that other people saw a different reflection. The cops were looking for somebody else, someone who didn't wear pale pink sundresses and ballet flats. Girls with clear skin and breathless smiles couldn't kill men, slit their throats and watch them bleed out on a bed. They obviously hadn't experienced rush.

People binged on details about Jeremy's murder like they were at a Vegas buffet: the angle the knife had gone into his throat, that he died gushing blood beside his girlfriend—it all came out in sweeping profiles that took up everyone's feeds. A five-part podcast soon broke the top one hundred.

I didn't think anyone was really scared at that point. They were thrilled by it. The murders brought an electricity to the neighborhood. News vans parked all across West L.A., from Bel Air down to Culver City. Reporters stopped students, residents, faculty, asking us how we were dealing, if we were scared for our changing way of life. I gave a great performance with a group of other DGs.

"They had so much to live for, both of them," I said of Tristan and Jeremy, lying through my teeth. They were the most basic of bros. The sum of their lives amounted to keg stands, porn, and burrito runs.

Posters soon went up at bus stops, replacing the ads for designer brands and boutique workouts, warning instead of the new threat lurking across the streets of Westwood, different words for the same thing: HOMELESS, VAGRANTS, TRANSIENTS, THE HIGHLY MOBILE. I'd be leaving sorority row for a run in the closing gasp of daylight and catch the glares of other Tri Delts crowded into cheap Jettas and Civics, heading in early for the night.

"You shouldn't be out past dark, DG," a particular turd of a Tri Delt told me as she rolled by in her Honda Accord. "It's not safe for girls like us."

I wanted to point out that it had been two men who had gotten their bodies carved like ice luges. Instead, I sprinted off to run a second loop around the campus perimeter.

———

Stephanie was now at the psych ward of Atascadero State Hospital. She was technically a person of interest, but nobody really thought it could be her. Who would be stupid enough to kill someone and then fall asleep for three hours in his gooey afterdeath?

I didn't have to make an appointment with Slade this time: his office called me, two days after Jeremy's death.

His secretary handed me a water, flat, without asking if I'd prefer mineral or sparkling, lemon or cucumber on the side. Slade waited until she had closed the door to begin speaking.

"Another murder," he said.

"Another murder," I echoed, plucking at the bouquet of white roses on a side table, feeling the soft edges of the petals to make sure they were real.

"Didn't I warn you not to, under any circumstances, attend a fraternity party?"

"I don't think you realize the tradition that is Halloween in Greek culture. Everyone was there: jocks, nerds, virgins, randos. The murderer could be anyone."

I crossed my legs slowly. I had on a cherry-red dress this time. I wanted him to know I wasn't playing sweet with him anymore. A second bill for his services had arrived last month. I was dropping serious cash—and I expected him to take care of any complications discreetly and quickly.

"You may be questioned again."

I waved my hand. "Can't you make them go away? I have midterms and essays and stuff."

"A boy was found mutilated and dead. Again. You were in the general vicinity of the crime scene. Again."

"As I've said before, I have the worst luck in the world. And have you thought about *my* suffering through all this? The nightmares *I* keep having?" That part was at least true. "I get insane anxiety. There's no reason I should be subjected to any further questioning. I'm willing to double whatever it is you're charging me. Just for the peace of mind. For my mental health."

Slade sighed. The furrowed eleven lines on his forehead told me he knew more than he was letting on.

"I'll do my best. And remember, you get called in for any questioning, you contact me."

The police never called.

———

Two weeks later, I arrived at the DG house from a workout session to find a sorority meeting mid-session.

Camilla, who had been on a cleft palate charity trip to Costa Rica over Halloween, was back and front stage. I had completely forgotten that there was supposed to be a meeting that day, and I tried to walk right back out of the house, but I didn't catch the door before it slammed shut.

"Good to see you could join us, Tiffany," Camilla called out. "Why don't you take an open seat here in the front?"

My tongue instinctually slid over the crack on my lower lip, the only physical trace left from Halloween night. It was almost healed.

Camilla paused while I took a seat and threw my gym bag across a nearby chair.

"Back to business. Sorority safety update number three: We've now been assigned a guardian fraternity. If you find yourself alone on campus, drop a pin on Google Maps and share it with one of your assigned brothers at Pike."

The rest of the sorority was seated on folding chairs in the back. Most of the girls had their heads buried in their phones.

"In the unfortunate case you do end up alone, Fraternity and Sorority Relations has been kind enough to provide these whistles to serve as a deterrent to any would-be predators. I'll be passing them around."

I sighed and glanced at the clock.

I had come from a workout with a warm beef burrito from Chipotle that I had hoped to smuggle upstairs in my gym bag. My right hamstring throbbed. I had squatted too much weight, and I just wanted to put a pack of ice against my leg, chill with my burrito, and watch a new episode of *The Bachelor*.

Julie passed me the box of whistles going around the room. They were made of cheap metal, crafted into a necklace with just a piece of yarn. I grabbed one and blew into it, emitting a shrill scream as Ashley laughed behind me and did the same.

"Whistles are for emergencies only," Camilla said.

I should have just eaten at the warehouse. A few days ago, I had rented out a small space in Venice, a grungy section near Washington Boulevard where no college students would catch me. It was wide open and windowless. I hadn't been to a class at my normal workout spots—Booty Slut, Burn It, Get Hard—in weeks. I ignored calls from Sergio to conduct my monthly body fat percentage evaluation at Equinox. Instead, I had brought dumbbells and weights to the warehouse and had a high horizontal bar installed, which I had been working on today. I could barely do a couple of pull-ups when I first started working out on my own, but now I was up to seven.

"With Thanksgiving this coming week, we all recommend that you take this time to travel home as soon as your classes adjourn on Tuesday and spend the entire holiday with your family," Camilla said. "Here's a step-by-step guide on how to best explain the situation to your loved ones."

Camilla passed around a pamphlet from the Panhellenic Association titled *When Tragedy Strikes: Putting It All in Perspective.* I flipped through listings of hotline numbers, local shrinks in the area, support groups. There were crime statistics from East L.A. listed in red and a section titled "Why West L.A. Is Still the Safest Place to Call Home."

"And that concludes the safety portion of our meeting."

There was a long pause as the girls placed their phones across their laps and gave a tired clap. Mandy and Amy rose to sneak out, and I tried to join them.

"You're not dismissed!" Camilla called out. "Just one more piece of regular sorority business. Tracy has officially moved out."

Tracy was the second member in our chapter to leave the house after Jeremy's murder. She had gained ten pounds over the summer and had only three hundred followers on Instagram, so she wouldn't exactly be missed.

"As a result of Tracy's abrupt departure, we'll need someone to take Carrie, her little sister, who's moving in next year. Some of you already have two sisters, so I'll take a look at those who just have one."

She skimmed through a printed sorority roster and looked up at me.

"Tiffany, would you like to volunteer? You haven't been to a few of our past meetings. And by a few"—she ran her fingers down the laminated pink roster sheet—"I mean none. Wow. You haven't shown up to one meeting in the past two quarters. You must be eager to contribute."

"Hell no," I said. "I already have Emily, and you know how much work she takes."

"I'm sitting right behind you."

I turned to find Emily scowling at me two rows back. I shrugged. "No offense, of course. Love you."

"Fuck you," Emily said.

"I hear Carrie was on her cheer squad back in high school. She was a flyer, just like you, Tiffany," Camilla said. "And you're both from the same area."

"She's from Tustin," I corrected her. "I'm from South OC. That's like mixing up Bel Air and Compton."

Camilla pursed her lips but avoided confrontation. Passive aggressiveness was her preferred weapon. "I'll send out an email about it later this week."

Camilla wasn't getting me to do shit: my family donated way too much money for me to have to volunteer like I was some scholarship charity case.

"Let's end with a DG song." Camilla motioned for us all to rise, and I mumbled through the half-learned lyrics with the rest of the girls:

Our time for happiness is now,
because sisters will always
be forever.
When we chose Delta Gamma,
we did find
love and understanding
and friendships of every kind.

As soon as the song was over, I grabbed my bag and tried to blend in with the rest of the girls.

"Can I get a minute with you, Tiffany?" Camilla called out. "I know you typically don't even show, but we really need you to be on time for these meetings. You're getting fined each time you're late."

"Sorry," I said, keeping a forward trajectory. "Won't happen again."

"Can you not walk away while I talk to you?"

"Nope," I said, and ran up the stairs.

I threw my gym bag across my bed and grabbed the TV remote. Emily was trying her best to ignore me.

"Did I miss any other safety rules?" I asked.

She didn't say anything, so I unwrapped the burrito and threw a bell pepper at her head.

"Stop it, you idiot," she finally said.

"I'll give you half of this if you tell me what I missed."

She turned toward me, and I ripped off a piece of burrito.

"That's only a quarter."

"It's a third."

Emily sighed and took it.

I could take in hundreds more calories now. In addition to weight training, I was running every day. Not the light prance I usually assumed on the treadmill with my hair down in curls and full makeup applied in case any guys were watching, but actual runs, outside, until I was sweaty and overheated. I never used to exercise outdoors because of the uneven tan lines it produced. Yesterday, I finished a twelve-mile run.

Emily picked at the torn piece of burrito. "A security patrol is coming the Monday after we get back from Thanksgiving break. They'll be patrolling sorority row after curfew from now on."

"Great."

"And you got a Christmas card while you were gone." Emily passed me a red postcard.

"Really?"

"It looks like it's from your mom."

I snatched it from her. It contained a picture of Pam in a hoochie Mrs. Claus outfit. She was bending over, hands clutching two ski poles, and appeared to be skiing down a hill lined with palm trees. Todd was behind her shirtless, holding two Pomeranians dressed as elves.

> *Season's greetings!*
> *It's Thanksgiving in Cabo for us, then off to Capri for Christmas.*
> *Blessed,*
> *Pamela, Todd, and Santa's Little Helpers*

I noticed Emily peering over my shoulder.

"Is that your brother?" she asked.

"Stepfather."

She looked at me.

I narrowed my eyes. "What?"

"Are you going home for Thanksgiving?" Emily asked.

"No," I said. "I'm staying in L.A."

"You could come have Thanksgiving with me. It's just my grandmother and me, but we usually splurge on a whole turkey."

I imagined spending the day in some tract house with Emily and an old lady who reeked of mothballs and old skin. I shuddered. Besides, I didn't need any of Emily's sympathy.

"Thanks, but I already have plans."

I found *The Bachelor* on TV and turned up the volume.

"I have to study for an o-chem exam," Emily said.

"Multitasking has been proven to help your memory," I said.

"You just made that up."

It was down to the rose ceremony. I had missed most of the show. It didn't matter.

This coming break would be the last week before full-time patrols were rolled out on the row, before I'd probably have to start leaving and entering the sorority house by window on late nights.

I wouldn't be returning to frat row. I was over that scene. Driving back from the warehouse tonight, I had passed Wilshire Boulevard and caught sight of the condominiums lit up above: rectangular views of expansive living rooms, mahogany coffee tables, stainless steel kitchens kept spotless by entire cleaning crews, gourmet cappuccino makers, and large wall spaces filled with oil paintings in rich jewel tones.

It didn't matter that frat row would be closed indefinitely. I'd found a new playground.

11

"**O**N THE ROCKS OR NEAT?" THE BARTENDER ASKED.

"Rocks." I wanted to eat the ice after I was done, feel them crack like ribs breaking against my molars. I leaned over the bar and caught sight of myself in the back mirror. I was dressed in an azure velvet minidress that matched the cold front that had descended across L.A.

The interior of the bar was dark, a few lights casting red and purple beams across the room. Other women needed this cover, I reminded myself. I looked even better in the light.

The place was full, which was promising, and I could spot a few unattached men circling through the herds of women situated around the bar. I tried not to attract too much attention and took a spot at the far side of the room.

The change in routine was welcome. My days had been only slightly modified since the early fall. I still went in for manicures, blowouts, workouts. But everything was more intense, a little more meaningful. I had started boxing and weight training in my tiny warehouse on Washington. I ate. Full meals, every day.

I hadn't been near a man since Halloween. The closest I'd gotten to male flesh was waiting at a burger stand two days ago. I picked up a familiar scent before spotting the guy in front of me. He was sporting Tristan's Big Pony fragrance. Then I noticed the tailored jeans, the muscled curve of his ass. He turned, sensing my gaze.

"Hey," he said.

"Hey."

"You wanna hang out sometime?"

Hang. That word stopped everything. I was done with *hanging.* Going on another sad excuse for a date—a Starbucks macchiato followed by fellatio in the parking lot, a three-hour Netflix binge followed by a brief fuck on industrial-strength dorm carpet. I was done. Things would be on my terms now.

And so the day before Thanksgiving, after all the girls had cleared out of the sorority house, I slipped on my new dress. Putting on makeup felt like I was applying war paint. I left my iPhone on my bedside dresser and grabbed the iPad that Camilla had stupidly left in her room over the break, ordered an Uber from it, and found myself at the Whiskey Bear on Wilshire nursing a melting drink.

I used Camilla's saved credit card to shop online while I scoped out men. I told any losers who approached me that I was waiting for someone, which wasn't entirely a lie.

One hottie seemed like a potential match, and I invited him to sit at my table until I found out he lived in some shitty student apartment on Glendon Avenue. It took a good hour of sorting through the waves of men rotating past me before I spotted a dirty blond in a suit come in and take a nearby booth by himself. He made no attempt to flirt with the girl sitting alone behind him.

He was older, his skin showed the beginnings of sun damage, and his hair was a bit too brown for my taste, but he was well built. I spotted a Rolex on his left wrist. My eyes trailed down to a gold wedding band.

I waited to see what he ordered. It looked like whiskey on the rocks. He was definitely older than I would have liked. Then again, I figured I shouldn't be too picky. I wasn't dating him—I would most likely leave him gutted in an alleyway somewhere if the opportunity presented itself.

I took a closer spot at the end of the bar.

He was ordering his second round when our eyes met, just briefly. I lowered my gaze and stroked my finger against the tablet screen. I stole a glance quick enough to catch him slide his ring off under the table and slip it in his jacket pocket. I waited a few seconds, then I swiveled in my stool to face him. We made eye contact again, and I slowly un-crossed my legs. I moved back to face the bartender and waited.

He approached me within seconds.

"You've barely touched your drink." He motioned to the full tumbler in front of me. "I was waiting to order you a second round."

"There's time," I said, and took a long sip.

"I'm Keith."

"Camilla."

"That's a beautiful name."

"You think so?"

He grabbed another drink and eyed the people around us before finally leaning on a barstool next to me. "Cheers," he said. "So what's a typical night for you?"

I shrugged.

"You hit a lot of bars?"

"I'm not planning on leaving this one anytime soon."

"You live around here?"

I shook my head. "You?" I asked, annoyed with all the questions.

"I'm right down the street, a couple blocks over. The Arc Stone."

"That's a nice building," I said.

It was fine. The place was in the $5–$7k per month range. Good for people on the move, but nothing to feel particularly proud of. The building didn't have an on-site masseuse or an enema clinic, like the more upscale condos in the area, but security was also laxer. Other than surveillance in the front lobby area, I could expect it to be pretty clear.

"I have a great setup. You can see out to the ocean," Keith said, and swirled the ice against his glass with loud clinks.

"Are you on the top floor?" I asked.

"No, not quite."

Keith told me about his job: he was an exotic commodities importer, whatever that meant. He said he was back from South Asia this week, picking up expensive herbal remedies for all sorts of shit. He kept the topic of conversation on himself, stopping only once to comment on the classic simplicity of my necklace. I wasn't sure if it was even a compliment. Keith threw out these "look at me, I'm so awesome and fuckable" details, but then he'd pull back. There was a trace of hesitation to his flirting.

I finished my glass and let him buy me a second round when I figured it out. All the questions and uncertainty from my vague answers. He couldn't figure out if I was an escort or not. I didn't know if I was insulted or flattered.

"I'd love to see some of your latest imports," I said, nudging him with the tip of my foot.

"I could show you a few artifacts," he said. "I'm always in the business of buying beautiful things."

His Rolex cast beams of light across the counter as he moved to take another drink.

"I'm game," I said.

"Meet me at my place in, say, a half an hour? I need to get a few things in order. You don't have any other commitments?"

"Not tonight," I said.

"Here." He wrote down five digits. "Just type in this passcode at the door to enter the building. I'm in 921. I'll get something ready for you, too, if you just put it down there."

I looked at him. "Oh, right."

Fuck, how much was twelve years of dieting, sculpting, tweezing, and waxing worth?

I wrote down two grand. I could pull way more, but I couldn't risk scaring him off. In the entire time we'd talked, no one under the age of thirty had walked into the bar. I showed him the paper, and he nodded, so I slipped it into my purse.

"It's raining," Keith said.

I looked out one of the large slanting windows at the end of the bar. Rain flooded against it.

"Do you have an umbrella?" he asked.

I shook my head.

"I dropped one off at the front. You can have it."

Keith left for the entrance and came back with a travel-sized black umbrella. He offered it to me gallantly, like he wasn't a married john hiring a hooker before the Thanksgiving weekend.

"You're such a gentleman," I said, taking it.

"See you soon," he said.

I stood and watched Keith leave. He moved quickly but paused at the front entrance near the umbrella stand. A group of people came into the bar, shaking off rain. Keith leaned down and stole one of their umbrellas before leaving the bar and turning left onto Wilshire.

———

I arrived at Keith's apartment forty minutes later and entered the code without a problem. The hooker mix-up was a good thing actually, since it meant there wouldn't be any video of us arriving together. I took the stairs up the nine flights to avoid cameras in the elevator.

I knocked twice to no answer, before trying the doorknob and letting myself in. The scent of cigars and dust permeated the apartment. There was no clear coordinating pattern to the place, just a clutter of antiques and artifacts that made me feel like I was waiting in line at the Jungle Cruise in Disneyland. His wife had never set foot in this place, I was sure of that. There were tribal statues, a harpoon net hanging on the wall. I felt a sudden wave of disgust. I threw the umbrella into a corner.

"There's something waiting for you in the bathroom," Keith called out. He was rummaging through one of the cabinets in the hallway leading to the bedroom. He hadn't even turned to face me when I came in. Music was pounding in the apartment above us, an incoherent rhythm reverberating through the walls.

I found an envelope of cash on the counter of the sink. I flipped through the bills. He had given me half the payment. I stuffed the cash in my purse.

Keith finally greeted me.

"It's loud," I said, tilting my head up to the ceiling. No one would probably notice a few screams over the music and the rain.

He shrugged. "I'm only here a couple nights a week anyway."

"Yeah?"

"I've got a house out in Calabasas . . ." He trailed off. "But this is where I keep the real treasures. What do you think, Camilla?"

"It's definitely unique," I said, picking up some sort of dick-shaped flute.

"Let's get started."

Without a word, Keith headed into the bedroom.

I tried to feel the pulse of excitement as I followed behind, that tightening of my muscles and the rush of blood, but I couldn't get turned on.

I wasn't counting on such poor interior decorating choices. His bedroom was as ridiculous as the living room. A bearskin rug covered most of the floor, and he had what looked like a dissected octopus hanging on the back wall. The bedspread was red silk. The whole reason I had moved on from frat row was to get away from this shit.

"Just give me a minute," I said.

"Take the time you need, but I'm not paying for an extra hour," he said, unbuttoning his dress shirt.

I shuddered. I needed a knife or maybe just one of his heavier, sharper antiques. I could get creative.

But would I even be able to perform effectively without the appetite I'd felt seeing Tristan undressed, watching Jeremy's chest rise and fall? Was I just not in the mood tonight? Maybe I had put too much thought into something that needed to unfold naturally.

Having a weapon in my hand could help me decide. I thought I had spotted a dagger in the living room. I left the bedroom and noticed a stuffed wildcat crouched by the fireplace. It didn't look predatory, only sad. I stared into its creepy yellow eyes, noticing something strange.

A tiny green light glowed from behind its pupils. I leaned in closer. A camera.

I reached behind the animal, trying to figure out how it was hooked up. How many cameras did Keith have hidden around his condo?

It was sick. Absolutely sick. I thought of Chase after he punched me in the face when I wouldn't jerk him off. What was wrong with men?

I saw Slade reprimanding me again in his office. *Seriously, you murdered him in front of a bunch of hidden cameras?*

Then I thought about the door. I'd opened it with my bare hand. Was there a Ring camera in the hall?

I was learning quickly: murder was a hell of a lot tougher than getting laid.

"I'm waiting," Keith called from the bedroom.

I wanted to slit his throat just to teach him a lesson. But I couldn't risk it.

I slipped off my heels and hurried backward to make a run for the elevator before he noticed. I fumbled with the lock and had just opened the door when I felt Keith behind me, his fist reaching out, slamming the door closed.

"I get it. You're clearly not a hooker," he said. "What do I need to do to make you more comfortable?"

"Not be a fucking sicko," I said, trying to squirm around his outstretched arm. Keith pressed his body into me and stuck a slimy tongue into my ear. I pushed him back and hit him across the face with one of my heels.

"Feisty!" he said. "I like it."

I had enough space to kick him, so I aimed and hit him in the balls as hard as I could. He doubled over, and I jerked the door open and sprinted toward the elevator.

I pounded the gold metal button with my palm. Overhead, a number 12 flashed. I glanced back at the apartment. The door was still ajar. I hoped Keith would cut his losses and give up. I hated this feeling, this sudden sense of lost power, of vulnerability. This wasn't how I was supposed to feel. The entire night had been ruined.

The elevator reached my floor, and I rushed inside. I hit the L button and began the descent.

I put my heels back on and tried to reset. I could go home, finish my online shopping and blow a grand on some new clothes. I could order Thai, eat it all in bed, and then rub one out and go to sleep. It was basic, sure, but I was tired, irritated, and a little scared. I couldn't risk getting caught.

The elevator doors slid open, and I rushed out, only to be met by fluorescent lights and concrete. I was in an underground parking garage. I took a deep breath and reoriented myself. If there was a side exit that dumped directly out to Wilshire, I could get back on the street and order an Uber from there. I snaked around the entry, looking for an exit sign or a side gate, but there were no green lights anywhere. I'd have to return by elevator.

I came back and pressed the button, but it didn't light up. I punched at it harder. Nothing. I found the large metal door for a staircase nearby, but it was locked. I couldn't find anywhere to put in the code Keith had given me. I was trapped.

A sound echoed off the walls in the distance, coming from an unlit area of the garage. It was the type of unidentifiable, strange clanging that greets the lead blonde before she's taken out in a bad horror movie. I weaved through the maze of parked luxury vehicles, trying to decipher if it was a person or car, not fully sure if I wanted to follow and find out. There was silence for a minute and then the definitive sound of footsteps. I wound through the last row of cars toward the elevator as the footsteps grew louder, closing in on me. I tried to ask who was there, but my voice caught in my throat.

A man in a suit strode out from behind a row of matching white SUVs. He was young, and despite the unflattering lighting of the garage, his face glowed a healthy tan. His hair was dark. He reminded me of the dancer at the Strip-A-Thon, that brooding, methodical stripper who took the time to shed his clothing one piece at a time.

"Are you lost?" he asked, but he wasn't even looking at me. He riffled through a briefcase and pulled out what appeared to be a black car key.

"No. Yes. You scared me," I said, my voice cracking.

He glanced up, surprised. "What happened?"

I suddenly wanted to tell this stranger about the whole sordid night. That a prick with hidden cameras was stalking the halls of the ninth floor searching for me, nursing a bruised dick.

"I left my friend's apartment and got locked down here. The elevator's not working," I said.

"You need a key fob to get into the main building." He aimed it over the elevator panel, then pressed the button. It lit up this time.

"I was trying to find the lobby," I explained.

"You didn't try pressing the button that said 'Lobby'?" He gave a small smile.

I blushed. The doors opened, and he stretched out his arm, ushering me in. I glanced back quickly to see if he would check out my ass, but he was rearranging his tie. He took a spot close to me, though, and I noticed how broad his shoulders were. His suit was tailored perfectly. The elevator closed, and he reached his arm in front of me to press 14. The top floor. I inhaled his scent. Gucci. I tried to concentrate on my next move, but I couldn't think amid the cloud of cologne and pheromones floating my way. The fear from moments before mingled with another urgent feeling. I wanted him to notice me, to care.

"I thought you were going to press the lobby button," he said. "Isn't that where you're going?"

"Oh."

"It's my fault," he said. "I should have done it for you."

I pressed the button quickly.

"It's too late. We've passed it. We're headed to my floor," he said, and motioned overhead, where a digital light blinked 3. The elevator felt like a countdown. My time with him would soon be up.

I was conflicted. I knew I should get out of the building and cut my losses for the night, but there was something different about him. He looked like the type who would take me for a real date, at a place with a prix fixe menu where I could show off a pair of Louboutins without worrying if I might need to cross a deserted dirt lot late in the night to get back to his shitty off-campus studio. He might offer an umbrella that wasn't stolen and hold the door for me to an apartment that he wasn't hiding from a spouse or girlfriend. Regardless, he definitely didn't seem like the type who should be carved up and spit out in a single night, spent so easily.

I stole a glance, and he caught my eye.

"Hey," he said, and tapped a finger against my forearm. "Are you okay?"

Overhead, the number 9 flashed, and I held my breath. The elevator stopped. I imagined Keith strolling in, clutching his banged-up groin, ready to take me out.

The doors rolled open, and three people stood waiting in the hall. Keith wasn't among them.

"Down?" a girl asked.

"Up," I said, and clicked the DOOR CLOSE button.

"Pretty busy around here," I said when we were alone again.

"A lot of people stick around for the holidays. Not many families here," he said.

"I'm leaving tomorrow for Kauai with my family. We spend every holiday vacationing somewhere exotic," I said. None of this was true, of course, but I thought this would do a good job of showing him that I was a well-occupied, worldly individual. It also never hurt to drop money into the conversation.

He leaned back against the elevator wall and crossed his arms. "What's your name?" he asked.

"Tiffany."

"I'm Weston."

The elevator's ring interrupted us. We had reached the fourteenth floor. The doors parted.

"If I leave, can you figure out how to get down by yourself?" Weston said.

"*Yes,*" I said.

He let a tiny smirk slip. But there was more to the smile, some hidden knowledge. Like he knew what I was about to do, like he had a hidden passageway to my thoughts that no one had ever come close to accessing.

"Good night, Tiffany."

Then he strolled right out of that damn elevator without even a backward glance. I stared down at the panel, the burning red glow around the word "Lobby." The doors began to close.

I pressed the DOOR OPEN button before I could think. Weston already had turned around. He knew I'd stop him.

"It's still raining hard outside. You wouldn't happen to have an umbrella I could borrow?" I asked, hoping he'd pick up on the hint. I jutted my hips out at an angle, placing one leg in front of the other for a slimming effect.

"I came directly from one parking garage to another for work today." He paused. "I have an umbrella at my place. If you don't mind coming in for a second."

"Perfect."

I matched Weston's quick stride through the hallway. It was difficult since he was so tall.

Although the layout was similar, Weston's condo was twice as large as Keith's. He had two bedrooms, in addition to a bigger dining space.

"I've got an umbrella in the guest room," Weston said, after checking the front closet and coming up empty. He headed to the back of the apartment.

Weston's condo was a perfect masculine blend of deep colors, a model of utilitarian order, with a few personal touches thrown in. *Cosmo* would say he was a man of few words but resolute in his convictions.

Weston's open-concept kitchen was filled with expensive contraptions, all perfectly arranged around an expansive center island. I spotted a marble-and-pearl backsplash and got a little wet. I pulled out a few drawers, finding graters, wine openers, cheese trays. A twenty-four-piece knife set. I took one of the knives out by the handle and stroked my finger along its edge. Freshly sharpened. My kind of man.

I noticed photos casually cast around the living room in matching sterling silver frames. They were mostly pictures of Weston: in cap and gown at two separate graduations, at a football game. I scanned through them quickly to spot any potential competition, but there were no other young women in sight. I felt a pull, something deeper and stronger than anything I'd felt with Tristan or Jeremy. Maybe this would be a chance to find someone real, someone who was more valuable alive.

Weston came back to the living room, umbrella in hand.

"You have an amazing place," I said.

"You should have seen the apartment I had in Boston right out of grad school. Panoramic views of the harbor."

He held out the umbrella. I took it from him, my hand sliding over his briefly, feeling an electric jolt.

"Why did you move out here?" I asked.

"Job opportunity. I'm a financial manager."

"Nice."

He leaned against the counter, loose, at ease. He had taken his jacket off at some point, but I hadn't even noticed. "It's boring as hell. But I had the chance to work fewer hours out here. Work-life balance. I figured I might as well savor it."

"I'm majoring in business econ," I said. At least I was as of sophomore year. I think I'd had my tutor declare me a sociology major last quarter.

"You're an undergrad?" Weston asked.

"My final year."

"Sorority member?"

"Delta Gamma."

He nodded in approval. "SAE. Of course, that was a few years ago. And back east. So, when are you leaving for Hawaii? You said tomorrow?"

I had almost forgotten. "Yeah," I said reluctantly.

Under normal circumstances, I would have tried to seduce Weston right there, but I wanted to let him make the first move. I would take my time with this one. He was clearly not another dumb fuckboy.

When Weston failed to slide his hand up my arm or suggest taking a spot on the couch, I felt a mild sense of disappointment.

"How far are you parked from the building?" Weston asked.

"I was dropped off."

"You live close by?"

"Just over on Hilgard. It's not very far of a walk. Or I can call an Uber."

"In the rain? I'll take you back," he said. I let him lead me out.

On the elevator ride down, paranoia stabbed at me. I envisioned Keith, roaming the lobby looking for me. No other buttons on the door lit up, so it looked like a trip straight back to the car garage, until the LOBBY button glowed. The doors slid open to an old lady and her poodle.

I moved aside and gave her ample room to step in, glancing out to spot Keith. The doors closed without a sighting.

We returned to the underground garage. Weston drove a Porsche, which was a major plus, and we were silent as he accelerated along Wilshire. The city was dead. The rain cast blurred rays of red and green over slick black pavement. When we reached the sorority house a few minutes later, Weston draped his arm across the back of my seat. He hadn't asked for my number yet.

"So this is it," he said.

I nodded at the house and then motioned to the umbrella on my lap. "I guess I never needed this after all," I said. I felt stupid, transparent.

"Keep it. Just in case."

And still, no number. I stayed planted in my seat for another full five seconds, waiting for him to do something, to say anything. He wasn't going to ask. I couldn't believe it.

"Later," I said finally, and flung the car door open. But when I leaned back to grab my purse from the seat, Weston slid over and brought his face to mine. He moved his hand behind my neck and under my hair and went for it, full tongue. He was good: he allowed for the perfect amount of back-and-forth play, while still keeping charge with a light pressure of his hand against my head.

I licked my lips, ready for more, but he had already moved back to his side of the car, his phone in his hand.

"Your number?" he asked casually.

I gave it to him.

"You want me to call it?"

I said yes before I remembered that I had left my phone at the house and brought only Camilla's tablet.

"Did it go through?" he asked.

"Yeah, I felt it vibrate," I lied, jiggling my purse as I got out of his Porsche.

"I'll text you later. Have a good Thanksgiving, Tiffany."

I'd forgotten what day it was; his kiss had obliterated my memory.

I sauntered up the stairs to my room. I felt satiated like after the murders, along with another feeling. I was happy. I tried to remember the last time I'd felt this type of warmth, but no immediate memory came to me.

I pulled out Keith's wad of cash when I reached my room. I didn't want any of it. I wished I had never taken it. I'd almost blown everything—my cover, my time, a perfectly nice dress—all on a loser like Keith. I wouldn't be doing that again. I tossed the money on the bed and grabbed my phone. I saw the missed call from Weston, the 310 area code. It was just the cherry on top of a promising night.

12

THE NEXT DAY, I JOGGED ACROSS CAMPUS, SIDESTEPPING THE huge puddles left from last night's rain. I sprinted past deserted buildings. I tried to order takeout when I returned to the house, but the usual spots didn't deliver on Thanksgiving.

Pam and Todd were in Cabo. I had no idea if they had brought Celeste along. I'd stopped following my sister on socials long ago. My relationship with Pam was always "strained" (therapist's wording, not mine), but it became fucked beyond repair my junior year of high school when my father slowly began to die. I got used to the live-in nurse Lupita, the antiseptic smell that permeated the downstairs. That wasn't the problem. The problem was always Todd.

Pam thought I'd just let this interloper ransack our lives. She met him at the Strands, started taking private surf lessons from him, and soon he was over every night. My father could probably hear them go at it from his hospital bed on the ground floor.

Pam became obsessed with only two things: Todd and my college application. She insisted that I get into a top-tier California university, whatever it took. When she was done grinding up against Todd on one of our pool chaises, she'd meet with Mr. Pete, a creepy dude who made me call him "Coach," who stared at Pam's chest every time he came over. He grilled me about my interests and shook his head at everything I said. Cheerleading, trips to Tuscany, my intolerance for white rice. He said those topics weren't enough to write about in a personal statement, that they failed to fill out a well-rounded, complete person. What the fuck was he trying to imply? That I was half of somebody?

Mr. Pete wanted adversity, injustice, drama. He brought in a few tutors to mine for trauma and draft a suitable personal statement. But it was my father who helped land me into college. His drawn-out death was the compelling personal tragedy my tutors crafted into a proper college essay. The fuckton of money Pam donated to the school didn't hurt, either.

"Isn't looking at colleges so much fun?" Pam had exclaimed, dragging me across various sun-drenched campuses. All were pristine with manicured trees and clean redbrick buildings, but some campuses were situated near the ocean while others were a block away from payday loan kiosks and stacked freeways. I applied to them all. Why not?

Then one spring day I got a huge gold packet in the mail.

"We did it!" Pam screamed, grabbing my face and smearing lipstick on me, falling into Todd's arms. You'd think she was the one about to pack her bags and head to lectures. Sometimes I almost felt bad about her sad, small life. Then she'd cram her tongue down Todd's mouth, steps from my father's hospice room, and I'd want to slit her throat.

I didn't really give a shit about college, especially when I found out the sorority house's ban on single-occupancy rooms. A roommate? A shared bathroom? But it wasn't so bad in the end. It was never too hard to make friends, at least for long enough. And the thing about college was new people were always rotating in, girls who'd salivate for a pair of nice shoes and a designer bag, guys who got hard from one careless smile. You had to give people like that only a crumb, and they'd be yours forever.

The last Thanksgiving I'd spent with Pam was two years ago. I drove down to Orange County the night before and noticed the vomit of Christmas decorations covering the expanse of lawn, framing the palm trees on the edge of the bluffs. The inside of the house was the exact opposite: all white, devoid of personality or taste.

I arrived to a heated argument. Pam had found my sister's secret OnlyFans account. What surprised me was that it inexplicably drew a few thousand subscribers. Pam had discovered it only because she herself had joined. I wondered if Todd took her photos, if it had been his idea.

Pam had picked up a gluten-free take-out dinner from Café Gratitude and stayed on her best behavior with me that night, the words coming out of her mouth the exact opposite of whatever she really meant.

"We're so happy to see you, Tiffany!" (Translated: *Please stay a couple of days and then don't come back for another year*).

"I haven't had a drink all week." (*Maybe I've laid off the vodka martinis, but I'd inject wine intravenously if I could*).

"No recent work, just drinking plenty of water, staying hydrated." (*I've had enough filler and Botox to paralyze a rhino*).

When Pam was about three pinot grigios into dinner and pushing her meditation strategies on me, I finally punched back.

"Give me a break on the holistic stuff. You're about as natural as a three-week slice of bologna."

Todd cut in: "Tiffany—"

"You're not my fucking father, Todd."

"I know."

"Then shut your mouth."

By this time, Pam was crying into her plate of cauliflower stuffing and autumnal kale and cranberry salad.

"You do this to me every time, Tiffany. This is why I can't have you here. You're toxic," Pam said. She ran upstairs, leaving Todd staring at his plate and Celeste tapping away on her phone.

After her Thanksgiving breakdown, Pam stayed upstairs for the rest of the night. I had settled in the living room, looking over the dozens of portraits on the mantel, photos of her from at least twenty years back that took up every spare shelf space. I spotted a shot of her in a green one-piece bathing suit, high cut over her hips, low cut at her chest. Her hair was set in beachy waves, about my length. We had the same tan, the same cheekbones, the same legs. The only real difference were Pam's implants, her nipples jutting out against the tight spandex like sharpened arrowheads.

I felt Todd's presence behind me. I pulled the words he was thinking out of his head. "Looks just like me, right?" I said.

He fidgeted but had to agree. "You have a lot of your mother in you."

"And what do you know about my father?"

"I know he treated Pam awfully. She was a saint to put up with it."

"You know where they met?"

He motioned to the photos, one of Pam in a crop top and with a pre-contoured face, her foundation packed on like heavy clay.

"She was modeling," he answered.

I laughed. "Pam was a centerfold. My father picked her up at a strip club. But I'm sure you know all that, so why lie?"

"Sometimes you have to massage the truth a little."

I moved closer to Todd, and he almost flinched. I floated my hand over to his shoulder, pressed lightly, then harder, massaging his neck.

"I'm more the direct type."

I moved my hand closer to his throat.

"That's enough, Tiffany."

I brought my face to his. "Know your boundaries in this family, Todd."

I left the house the next day. I hadn't been back since. Still, it always felt like all of them—Pam and Todd and Celeste—were just borrowing the home. It was mine.

———

After a long online search, I found a Chinese restaurant that accepted take-out orders. I ate every bite, the glistening noodles and sugary glazed meats, washing it all down with ice-cold vodka.

Weston hadn't texted. I assumed he was with his family. I realized I hadn't asked what his plans for the holiday were. If his entire family was back on the East Coast, he might be alone too, maybe in his own bed on the fourteenth floor. Maybe his relatives were just as fucked up as mine. Maybe he also had a family estate he couldn't return to, a mother and a sister and a stepfather he fantasized about killing.

He texted the next morning. The notification woke me up from a blurry dream I couldn't quite remember. I was still slightly buzzed, used napkins and plastic forks scattered in a trail around my bed.

We agreed to meet after I returned from Hawaii. I'd have to post some old pics from my vacay last summer in case Weston started following me to cover up my digital tracks.

I rose unsteadily and checked my stomach in the mirror. Binging on takeout wouldn't fly anymore. It was too late to undo last night's decadent dinner, but I'd start today. I was going clean again.

I lost five pounds over the next week on a cleanse of cayenne pepper, lemon water, and laxatives. I dropped strength training from my routine, cutting out the curls, push-ups, and dead presses. I stood in front of the mirror and flexed, hoping for less roundness, searching for the jaggedness of bone. I checked each morning for another blue vein rising to the surface across my forearm.

The weight I had gained over the last month was shed one spin class at a time, every time my stomach twisted in on itself a little more. I was disposing of the extra fat as though each bit of cellulite was evidence, as damning as a set of fingerprints at the scene of the crime.

Whenever I felt hungry, I imagined Weston's tongue against mine and tasted whiskey, leather, and the hint of vanilla. He was better than food.

It was now December. The weather hadn't cooled much, apart from the rainstorms that had hit last month, but the sorority had put up a Christmas tree, and the smell of gluten-free cookies filled the downstairs. Everyone had returned from Thanksgiving break, and with the new curfew, the house was filled again with PMSing, party-starved girls.

A sizable number of the house's nerds sat in the dining room cramming for finals, while the normal girls watched the season finale of *The*

Bachelor upstairs. The conversation had carried into the bathroom as a group of us performed our nightly skin-care regimen.

"I feel like Vicky was on the show for the right reasons," Amy said. "I can't believe Tony chose Dana."

Mandy joined in. "I know, Tony and Vicky seemed like they could have had an actual future together."

It was hard to feel the satisfaction I once got from reality TV, but the girls were into it all; they ate up any form of drama, real or fake, murder or love. I tried to form my own outraged opinion of the show but found myself instead examining the curve of my stomach in the bathroom mirror.

I had worked to reclaim my online presence over the past couple of weeks, posting bikini shots at flattering angles, smoothie runs at Pressed Juicery, big-time purchases at the Grove, the receipts for $200 Nobu sushi lunches that I didn't touch. I watched the comments stack up hour by hour, letting the updates on my phone wake me from fitful sleep.

Emily had joined the girls in the bathroom after the finale. Mandy helped her apply an egg mask to her hair while they passed around a slender white bottle of Malibu. There was something different about Emily, but I couldn't place it.

"Does anyone recognize this number?" Ashley asked. "I keep getting dick pics from it, and I can't remember if I blacked out and hooked up with this guy or what."

I waved her away when she tried to pass me her phone and waited for a lull in the conversation.

"I met someone over Thanksgiving break," I said to Ashley, loud enough to ensure that everyone in the bathroom heard.

"Pics or it didn't happen," she said.

I showed a few photos I'd googled and saved from Weston's Instagram account. Then I gave the girls the rundown: that he was successful, *hot* Ivy League East Coast material with an eye for well-tailored suits and a sweet condo.

"How old is he?"

"Twenty-six."

"What does he do?" Mandy asked.

This was the clincher. I was sure they were expecting the typical actor-model-artist L.A. prototype.

"He's a financial manager," I said.

I wanted to add that he made me feel special, but that would be so cringe. Also, I couldn't risk articulating the main draw: Weston was the first guy I'd met since September who I didn't want to slaughter. I gave them the rest of the pertinent surface details: "He's tall, drives a Porsche. Lives over on Wilshire. He's taking me to see Wildebeest on Saturday."

"What's that?" Emily asked.

"It's a band. Of course you wouldn't know. Weston has excellent musical taste."

Up until yesterday, I hadn't known who they were either, but I'd looked up a few songs on Spotify and committed their key tracks to memory.

"How is the sex?" Mandy asked.

"Seriously? I just met him," I said.

"That never stopped you before."

"Choke on a dick, Mandy."

"You first," she said.

"If you must know, we haven't done it yet," I said. "I don't just give in to every carnal impulse that comes my way."

I left out that I had blown Weston in his Porsche on our last date. I had needed some way to know exactly what I was potentially working with. You can meet a guy with a great job, education, abs, and it all just becomes a sad consolation prize if he unzips his pants and shows you a two-incher. Luckily, Weston had proven to be the full package.

"So when do we get to meet him?" Julie asked.

"I don't know if the undergrad Greek scene is his thing," I said.

Weston and I had been on only three dates, so some of my boasting may have been a bit premature. I knew the girls would be texting about my relationship status as soon as we returned to our rooms and would look for social media confirmation.

"Where the hell have you been this week?" I asked Emily.

"My grandmother fell again last week. She's been in the hospital."

I immediately regretted asking about Emily's life.

"I'm sure she's fine," I said.

"No, she's not, Tiffany."

The polite thing would be to just say yes and move off this depressing topic of conversation. But Emily had gained the attention of all the other girls. They gathered around her. Amy patted her back.

"Your hair's going to look really great at least," she said.

While changing in my room, I checked to see if I had missed a text from Weston. Instead, I saw a calendar update from Camilla. It was another reminder about the Christmas gala later in the month. All Greek members were invited. It was the closest thing we'd see to a party for the rest of the year. Of course, it came with strict rules: security guards were being hired to search all guests, and alcohol was banned.

I scanned through the email. There would be a video tribute to Tristan and Jeremy. *Everyone, email me your best pics of our fallen brothers. No alcohol, drugs, or sexual content in any of the photos, please! xoxo Camilla*

That would be difficult. I caught Emily behind me, glancing at my phone. She had brought the Malibu with her. I hoped she had gotten all the sick-grandma talk out of her system.

"Are you taking Weston to the party?" she asked.

"I wasn't even planning on going," I said. "We both have better things to do than hang with a bunch of Tri-tards at a sober Christmas party."

She scowled. "You have to stop calling them that. People will find a way to sneak in booze. And I think the video tribute is nice. I'm sure Stephanie will appreciate it."

I almost dropped my phone. "Stephanie?"

"She's back in L.A. You didn't hear?"

"No," I said. "So Stephanie's been released."

Good for her. Whatever. I was over that drama. Jeremy, Tristan. They were so last season. I had Weston to think about now.

13

I PUT OUT THE NIGHT OF THE WILDEBEEST CONCERT. WESTON and I sat at the Greek Theatre for three hours on hard chairs in freezing weather. I resisted his offers to buy me a wine cooler. No more empty calories or empty boys.

When Weston and I finally got down to it back at his condo, it wasn't exactly earth-shattering. The sex was good. But it was normal, soft, and a lot quicker than I preferred. We barely disturbed the perfectly fitted sheets his housekeeper had folded for him. I didn't even have a chance to display my flexibility or dish out some of the dirty talk I had rehearsed earlier that day. It had just started to feel raw—I was beginning to smell Weston's Gucci-tinged sweat—and then it was over.

"That was really good," I said, after.

Weston reached for his phone and settled next to me. I was waiting, hoping for an invitation to stay the night, although I wouldn't take him up on it. Since I had brought a smaller clutch with me on the date, I didn't have the room to pack more than concealer and some lipstick. I couldn't sleep over without a properly stocked beauty arsenal for the next morning.

He finally asked, "Do you want to stay? I have to be up pretty early, though."

"No, I'd better head out."

I moved to get up, but he pulled me to him.

"Not just yet."

I felt his muscles relax. I had to bring it up before I left for the night.

"There's this holiday party in a couple weeks. With my sorority. Do you want to go with me?" I asked.

"God, all that Greek stuff was a long time ago for me," Weston said, rubbing his head.

"It won't be juvenile. I promise."

"Because I really don't know if I can handle a bunch of twenty-year-olds drinking Natty Light," he continued.

Weston wasn't biting, so I decided to play the murder card.

"The whole thing will actually be a tribute to the Greek members we lost earlier this year," I explained.

Weston just looked at me.

"You know, the two fraternity members who got butchered? It's all over campus."

"Right, I saw something on the news. Did they ever find out what that was all about?"

"Homeless people did it, I think," I said.

Weston stared up at the ceiling. He knew what I was really asking, what it would mean if he said yes and met all my other sisters in a large structured gathering. We'd be an official couple.

Weston got up and put on his boxers. I found my clothes. He didn't give me an answer until he was fully dressed again, back in jeans and a polo.

"Sure, I'll go," he said.

———

Weston and I had sex twelve more times in the two weeks after the Wildebeest concert. I logged each act in my iPhone notes. We followed each other on socials five days after the night we met, but he didn't tag me in a post until the concert (not a selfie, but a picture of the large theater stage, artistic and subtle). Our first public pic together came later that week (the Santa Monica Pier with the Ferris wheel behind us). He had cropped off my chin, and my hair blew in two directions, but I was too happy to remove the unflattering tag. He would learn to confirm all social media with me. I didn't want to appear overly aggressive in these opening months. In the meantime, I kept track of it all. The trajectory of his feelings for me was a solid climbing arc that I could chart and analyze on my phone.

At dinner in WeHo soon after, Weston began revealing personal details, about his parents' divorce when he was in middle school back in Manhattan, a real headfuck for an eleven-year-old.

"Split my younger brother and me up every week, sometimes every other day if one of my parents was traveling. I've seen couples arrange better custody splits for their dogs. I didn't know where I was when I woke up for a solid year, if I was uptown or in Tribeca."

He selected another oyster from the dozen that chilled over ice on the table between us. I tried to move a couple around, pretending to eat, but the oysters were hard to hide, trembling in their shells, fat and thick, and refusing to cleanly wipe into a napkin. I licked at the juice around each one, pairing a dab of the mignonette sauce with a swallow of vodka. I wanted to take the whole oyster in my mouth and chew it slowly, but I didn't.

I also wanted to tell Weston that my family was even more messed up than his. I wanted to tell him about my father, that he was dead, that before that my parents might as well have been divorced. But I couldn't. Back when we had first met, I had described my family as the intact nuclear type that took yearly beach trips and attended cancer benefits with wide smiles. I had said it to seem normal and balanced so he'd ask for my number, but now I realized it might have been better to have told the truth.

"Do you want dessert?" Weston asked before motioning for the check.

"Just you."

The sex was getting better and better. Weston took things slower, and when I directed his hands (or tongue), he listened. He could take notes. It was the little things, too. I respected the cleanliness he brought to the experience. The sheets were always washed that day, with towels nearby.

I'd gotten too used to stiff socks and twin beds at the frat houses. My favorite part, though, was directly after, when I could smell a little of Weston. I'd take a second to breathe in his scent, swallow it all in, before heading to the shower.

After sex one night, he pulled me in close for a kiss, his lips trailing lower to my necklace. He stroked my collarbone, touching the pearl of the necklace gently.

"Who gave this to you?"

"My father," I said.

"Daddy's girl?" Weston joked.

"Don't be gross." I felt uncomfortable suddenly, exposed, even though we'd spent most of our relationship naked in his sheets. My mind flashed suddenly to a gun, to the huge safe in my father's office where he kept it. Who was I kidding? I couldn't possibly tell Weston the real truth about my family.

"You're lucky to have him. And the sorority," Weston said.

"It's not all naked coeds and pillow fights," I said.

"Not because of that. It's like you get this whole second family. I miss that. L.A. can be lonely. More than I expected."

"What were you hoping for?" I asked.

"I thought I'd meet more people, go out more. It isn't anything like Instagram."

"Nothing is. None of that stuff is real," I said.

"You post all the time. Like today. I liked that photo at the beach."

I laughed. "That took me an hour of prep. And it was actually taken last summer." I spoke the truth before I had realized, quickly regretting it. The whole point was to make people believe the fantasy. Even my "vulnerable" posts were staged and crafted toward a particular end.

I changed the subject. "I'm happy to give you a tour of some legit L.A. spots."

"That would be nice. I wish I knew more people. After college, my friends all spread out."

"Well, I'm here now," I said.

"I know," he said, brushing back my hair before trailing his hand lower.

———

The day of the Christmas gala, Weston and I met beforehand at the campus rec center. It was an 80-degree December afternoon, the kind of day that had students posting shots of sizzling concrete and shade-less palm trees and sending them to the fucks who had left California for college with hashtags like #JealousMuch.

We shared a chaise longue, the press of Weston's skin sweaty against mine. The pool was filled with similar bodies: tan, lean, and nearly naked. Somewhere, a middle-aged celebrity occupied his own cabana, and texts had spread like a Malibu wildfire, drawing a large crowd to the pool.

Weston snatched my phone when I tried to broadcast the news, instructing me to live in the moment. He was a hypocrite; as soon as the slightest buzz rattled his own phone, I knew he'd glance down, but I didn't mind. The very fact that I knew these things about him, that I could start to predict even his hypocritical tendencies, excited me. I felt light-headed around him, weak at the knees, which was in part because I hadn't eaten in the past ten hours, but still. It was mostly Weston.

A few sorority sisters had arrived after hearing the celeb-spotting news, keeping a respectable distance from Weston and me. Emily had settled in her own chair a bit closer than I liked, a bottle of cheap wine next to her. I let her stay since Weston still kept in touch with his own fraternity big brother back on the East Coast. He emerged from the pool, catching the stares of every girl and a sizable number of guys. He captured Emily's gaze.

"This is your little?" he asked, nodding at her. I winced when I noticed Emily's saggy bathing suit short bottoms and the purple wing-tips across her lips. She was going to need to perfect her day-drinking skills if she didn't want to come off as the sorority's resident wino. If Camilla caught her in public looking like that, I'd get shit for it. I was already on thin ice.

I was about to direct a snide remark at Emily—which would be entirely deserved—but I knew before speaking that Weston would be nice. Sure enough, he settled into his seat without a rude word.

"God, I could die like this."

Weston's voice startled me out of half consciousness. I nestled closer to him.

He motioned to the burning sun directly above him. "California does have its perks. I could get used to this."

Emily offered her bottle, and I was surprised when Weston took it from her and drank the cheap stuff. He moved to hand it back.

"I'll take some," I said.

I could taste what I hoped was Weston's warm saliva on the rim. I settled back in our chair and let my muscles melt into the plastic. I felt a rare sense of calm. Maybe I could make some new L.A. friends with Weston, learn to engage in couples activities. Maybe I could slowly reveal more and more of myself to him. After the insomnia of September, it felt nice to fall asleep on a lounge chair right in broad, bright daylight.

14

THE CHRISTMAS GALA HAD ORIGINALLY BEEN PLANNED AT A trendy Santa Monica venue on Fourth Street, but so many people declined their Evites after learning there would be no booze that the Deck the Campus Committee moved it to the university's ballroom. I figured most girls would opt to wear Santa red, so I decided to go with green, finding a dress that matched my eyes.

I parked my Mercedes over at Weston's place an hour before the party. This would be the first time I was staying over for the night. I had three outfit combinations prepared for the next day and an entire line of cosmetic products stored in my makeup case. I would have to remember to set my phone to vibrate right next to my head, so I could get ready before Weston woke up tomorrow.

He met me at my car to help carry my stuff up. He looked like he had walked off a runway—it had been a while since I'd seen him in a full suit.

"You shouldn't be walking around out here after dark," Weston said, and hoisted my bag over his shoulder. "Jesus, what's in here?"

"Just a few things," I said.

In addition to clothes and toiletries, I had brought a hair dryer, a ceramic straightener, two pairs of heels, and my own wooden hangers, just in case. After I dropped my bag off and hung my outfits up in Weston's closet, we still had time for a drink before leaving, so I made myself a club soda and vodka.

"Is it an open bar?" Weston said, pouring a whiskey.

I rotated my necklace slowly around my neck. "No."

"I prefer cash bars anyway—shorter lines."

"I don't think there will be anything."

"No bar? We're going to a Greek party, and there won't be any booze? What type of college is this?"

I tried to defend our Greek system. "There's been some temporary suspensions on the parties because of the murders."

"That would have been a nice detail to include when you invited me."

He pulled two monogrammed flasks from a cabinet.

"Can you fit one of these into your purse?"

———

On the car ride over, I checked who had RSVP'd to the party. Tammy and a bunch of Pi Phis would be there. All the lame-ass members from houses like Tri Delta and Theta Chi would show up in droves since they had nothing better to do on the weekends. And, of course, Stephanie was set to make an appearance.

I had just posted a video with the caption *Party under the mistletoe tonite, bitches* when we arrived at one of the campus lots.

I led Weston down a flight of stairs toward the largest building I could see in the distance. We passed hordes of non-Greek losers in school sweatshirts and flip-flops, and I began to worry that we were heading to a library or study hall, when I caught sight of three girls stuffed into tiny red dresses.

"We're almost there," I said, and followed them through a gap in the buildings.

I was totally embarrassed upon arrival. The ballroom was decorated with a sad-looking Christmas tree and a bunch of tinsel. A menorah was shoved in the back on a corner table, most likely where the booze would have been if it had been allowed. Weston pulled out his flask two minutes in.

I spotted Amy and Mandy in a corner with three rival sorority members, passing around their own flasks. Mandy and I weren't on speaking terms after I had thrown a tampon at her for running her mouth off during a *Real Housewives* reunion. But I needed to introduce Weston to some of the other girls, otherwise he'd think I was at the bottom of the Greek social circle. Before I started dating Weston, I'd just walk up to the largest group of men I could find to receive immediate attention, but that wasn't going to work in this scenario.

A mixture of jealousy and intrigue hit the girls' faces when they saw Weston.

"Nice to meet you," Mandy said, her hand traveling up Weston's arm.

"So where's your boyfriend, Mandy?" I said.

She waved to a group of Sigma Nu members signing a huge memorial poster for Tristan. I couldn't read any of the messages, but I spotted a spouting dick near the bottom.

Camilla came up behind us. "Hello, alcohol is not permitted. Did we read the message on the invites?"

Mandy reluctantly capped her flask and stuck it in her bra, but Weston just smiled at Camilla and took a long sip of his whiskey.

"There was a memo about it—" she started, but Weston turned around on her midsentence.

I latched on to his arm, feeling immune from the dumb chain of command in his presence. We were both above it. Weston and I looked so good together. I wished there had been less tinsel and more mirrors in the ballroom, so I could see how perfectly paired we were throughout the night. This moment was far better than a movie, and we were hotter than the actors who could ever hope to play us.

Weston and I were soon separated by gender. I reluctantly let him mingle with the group of frat bros, calling him away when a surrounding pack of males contained more than three guys I'd slept with. He quickly settled in with the SAE cohort.

About a dozen Delta Gammas had filed in by then. Emily had arrived with Ashley, who was already drunk. Emily must have raided someone else's closet, because she was sporting a miniskirt rather than her standard prude attire.

"Slow clap for Weston. He's like a Grecian statue," Ashley said to me.

"Try not to drool," I told her, and left the huddle of girls. I had better things to do than sit around and gawk at my own boyfriend.

With Weston occupied, I set out to find Stephanie. I spotted her with two other KKG members. I watched and waited, sipping a Diet Coke. She was soon by herself, staring up at the pathetic Christmas tree. It made sense that people were keeping their distance; I'm sure everyone gave her a polite hello when she came in, maybe spent some time with her in three-minute cycles, but no one wanted to make small talk with a recent mental hospital patient.

I followed Stephanie's line of vision as she moved among the throngs of people, unaware of my presence. She stopped at the tribute stand in front of a large photograph. Stephanie was in this particular photo, alongside Jeremy at a western-themed SAE party, and the side-by-side comparison was pretty extreme. Gone were her pageant-style hair extensions and bronzed skin. Her clothes hung loose over her in a starved way that was beyond even L.A. standards of thin. Her hair was limp and growing out a dull brown color. I knew she wasn't a natural blonde.

Stephanie moved on to a portrait of Jeremy, alongside a separate one of Tristan. They both were clad in dress shirts and ties: their fraternity house photos. Looking at them, I thought of Jeremy after I had slit his throat, the blood soaking through his Romeo costume. I saw Tristan on that stained carpet, twenty-six seeping holes in his sculpted torso.

I moved beside Stephanie.

"They were so attractive."

I thought she'd be startled, but she didn't even turn to face me.

"Hi, Stephanie," I said, and got in front of her, so she'd be forced to address me.

Stephanie's gaze never shifted from the portraits.

Anger surged through me, starting in my stomach and moving up my throat.

"I heard they sent you all the way up to Atascadero for treatment. You still look unwell," I said, staring pointedly at her hair.

"Fuck off, Tiffany," she said in a whisper.

So there was still some venom left in her.

"I was just concerned about you. At least you're not a suspect anymore. Do they have any leads on the murderer?" I asked.

She barely shook her head. I was plotting my next dig when I caught Weston's eye. He had settled near a group of Sig Nus only feet away from me. I tilted my head for him to come over. He didn't need an introduction.

"Stephanie, I'm Weston," he said. "I'm so sorry."

He took her hand in both of his and squeezed it for a few seconds longer than I liked. I slid my hand up Weston's chest, letting it hook around his shoulder. Stephanie said nothing, but her eyes fell at the sight of us together.

"These photos of you two are really nice," Weston said, breaking the silence and motioning behind Stephanie. This was the first time I had ever seen him not at perfect ease, although he was putting on a good-enough act.

"They were so great together," I said. "Jeremy gave her this beautiful ring last fall. Almost three carats," I told Weston.

Stephanie looked down at her naked finger. I followed her gaze.

"You don't want to wear it anymore?" I asked innocently. "I can understand."

It took mention of her ring for the tears to finally run.

"He took it from me," Stephanie said, wiping her cheek.

"Jeremy?"

"The murderer, you fucking bitch." Stephanie spoke in a hoarse whisper, as though the murder had taken her voice, too. She still threw out barbs, but I could see it was only an involuntary reflex for her at this point, like the spasm Jeremy gave after he was already dead and gone.

My work was done. I hadn't just won this round. I'd won the entire game.

The music stopped abruptly at ten. I had forgotten we were expected to watch the tribute video for Tristan and Jeremy, that this was a memorial, not a victory party for Weston and me. I passed by the designated DG table and nabbed a couples table that was filling up with other pairs from the more popular Greek houses. I had motioned Weston over when Emily tried to join us.

"Couples only," I said. "You're going to make the seating uneven."

"I'm sitting with you," she said, defiant. She had snuck in a flask of her own and took a sip from it. I was surprised that a goody-goody like Emily would risk Camilla's passive-aggressive wrath.

Weston came up beside me, and I was confident he'd wave her off. But instead he moved past me and came back carrying a chair over his head.

"We can make room," he said. "You'll want to sit with your little sis, right?"

I frowned at Emily. "Yeah, I just thought she might be more comfortable with the other single DGs," I said. "Don't want her to feel like a third wheel."

Emily sat on the chair with a satisfied smile, and I thought about scrubbing the toilet in the communal bathroom with her toothbrush when I got back to the house tomorrow. Weston ended up between Emily and me.

Camilla, who had finally given up on her alcohol patrol, approached the front of the hall and took a mic.

"For those who have followed all the rules, thank you. I just wanted to send another quick reminder to be safe driving home. Not everyone respected the no-drinking policy."

The party had been unbelievably lame so far. There was supposed to be more music later, but I couldn't imagine anyone deciding to stick around much longer to dance amid crumpled tinfoil and depressing posters of dead frat bros.

"Tonight was meant to show that we as Greek members are about more than just tailgates and keg stands, that we have a duty to uphold tradition and honor. To celebrate our fallen."

Weston moved closer to Emily and poured some of the booze from her flask into his. It was low-end stuff, no doubt, probably from a plastic bottle.

After a few more minutes, Camilla retreated, and the lights dimmed. The opening to "What a Wonderful World" played, some of the lyrics projected over a grainy background.

The slide show started with a few recent photos of Jeremy and Tristan. I drummed the table, wondering how long this would take. The two became smaller versions of their college selves with each new slide. A gangly young teen with a football raced across a rectangular green lawn. I could see Jeremy's half-formed lean build, just on the verge of a growth spurt. There was a middle-school-aged pirate, one eye covered by a black patch, the exposed eye a light blue that told me it was Tristan. As they grew even younger, it became harder to say who was who. I saw a boy on a tricycle riding down a neighborhood street, a toddler covered in rainbow cake.

Then a newborn was cast up on the screen, swaddled in a cotton blanket and a beanie, followed by a sleeping infant cradled in some woman's arms. I saw the hemorrhage of entrails spreading out under Tristan's thighs, the jet of blood spurting up from Jeremy's neck.

Every girl in the room was sobbing. I shifted in my seat, uncomfortable, hoping nobody would notice my dry eyes, wondering if I'd have to put on an act soon. I didn't get the point of all this. Why meditate on a person's childhood when you've seen him blowing chunks in a frat house bathroom? It was too late for them to claim innocence.

Silence had spread across the room for the first time that night. Ducking under the table, I grabbed my purse. I pulled out a stick of gum and offered one to Weston, but he only shook his head. Everyone was focused on the images before them.

The song finally stopped, transitioning awkwardly into Green Day's "Good Riddance (Time of Your Life)." I refocused and saw some prom photos and shots of Jeremy moving into the SAE house with a suitcase and a giant keg. A picture of Tristan with a pile of girls around him, sneaking a boob grab that had gotten past Camilla. I felt better.

The video wrapped up with shots of the entire Sigma Nu and SAE classes in front of their respective houses. When the lights came back on, people stayed quiet and bypassed the dance floor, heading straight for the exits.

I had subjected Weston to a giant funeral party with no alcohol. I would need to perform a variety of uninhibited sexual moves on him to salvage this night.

"You ready to go?" Weston asked before I had time to adjust to the light. I nodded.

There wasn't much to say on the car ride back.

"What are you thinking about?" Weston asked, breaking a five-minute silence.

I had spotted a Carl's Jr. poster for a fried chicken and bacon sandwich on a soft pretzel bun. I was thinking about how nice it would be to order one and devour it alone behind the tinted windows of my Mercedes on the drive back from his condo.

"That I'm really glad you came with me," I answered.

Of course, I wouldn't be eating any burgers tomorrow. I had kelp chips and tofu blocks waiting for me at the house. I had found what I was looking for in Weston, and I wasn't going to fuck it all up by growing cellulite on my ass.

"The girl, Stephanie, seemed really unwell," Weston said. "It's too bad," he added.

"She was sort of messed up to begin with," I said, ready to forget the Christmas party. I had made my point by showing off Weston: to Stephanie, to my sisters, to the other sorority houses. We were official now.

As we headed up to Weston's place, the elevator stopped on the ninth floor. I felt a sudden stab of nausea. I wanted this night to be over.

And then it happened: my worst nightmare was realized. The doors slid open, and Keith stood there, his hair disheveled, his eyes shifty. I quickly hung my head, hoping he wouldn't catch a glimpse of me, wouldn't recognize me from the month prior.

"Camilla?"

My mind ran one thought on loop—*shit, shit, shit*—and I reluctantly looked up.

He was confused, unsure. I'd play dumb, feign an angelic innocence that made him doubt his own reality. I'd done it before.

"I beg your pardon?" I said sweetly.

"Camilla? We met at the Whiskey Bear. Thanksgiving."

Keith's expression was changing, a scowl forming, tightening his features. He was angry. And he knew exactly who I was. Now Weston was the confused one, glancing back and forth between us.

"You!" Keith sputtered, stepping into the elevator and jabbing his finger in my face.

I mustered a look of outrage. "My name's *not* Camilla. And I don't know who you think you are, screaming at me like this."

"You hit me in the fucking balls! I had to get my prostate examined because of you!"

I turned to Weston, my hands raised. My eyes smarted with tears. "He's scaring me, Wes."

Weston stepped in finally and shoved Keith back into the hall. He was bigger, stronger.

"Get the fuck away from her."

"You don't—"

"Back off." The words came out as a growl, and I suddenly wanted to fuck Weston in the elevator, right on the spot.

Keith had lost. He stumbled backward. He was clearly drunk. He'd wake up tomorrow and wonder if he'd dreamed it all.

"You better watch this one," he said, pointing a final time and stumbling off.

The elevator doors closed, and Weston turned to me, the hero.

"You okay?" he asked.

"I think so. Thanks for stepping in."

"What a creep," Weston said.

"The city's full of them," I said.

"This *building* is full of them. I'm getting out of here."

Weston had mentioned he was looking to buy property, a house somewhere near Century City, closer to his office. I had told him I thought it was a great idea, a smart investment move. He was serious about it, I realized happily.

We arrived on the fourteenth floor. Weston threw off his jacket and tie as soon as we entered his place. He headed over to the bar and poured himself another drink before I could take off my heels.

"You want your flask back?" I said, sliding the zipper of my purse open and pulling out the silver container. He turned to wash it out in the sink, and I moved toward him, pressing my hips against his back and reaching my arms around his waist.

Weston had the foresight to dim the kitchen lighting before turning around. He pushed himself into me, forcing me against the kitchen counter, so I could feel he was hard. He had never acted this aggressively before.

He lifted me onto the edge of the countertop, between his knife block and a row of wineglasses hanging by their stems. As he stripped off his shirt, I noticed for the first time a small arrowhead tattoo on the inside of his right biceps.

I leaned backward as far as I could against the overhead cabinets, as Weston worked my dress up my thighs and unzipped his pants. I pulled on a cabinet door to steady myself, and it flew open, almost hitting Weston in the face. He pulled back just in time, but his elbow collided with the row of wineglasses, sending them shattering across the tile.

The sounds of glass breaking and Weston's yell sent me reaching for the handle of the butcher knife perched beside me. I was clutching it tightly in front of me, heart pounding, before I knew what had happened. As Weston crunched through the glass, kicking some of it aside, I thought for a moment how vulnerable he was with his head tilted to the side and his neck exposed. I slid the knife back in its holder before he could see what I had done. Weston had moved away from the counter, and I took the opportunity to jump off, away from any dangerous kitchen utensils. I shoved him into the kitchen island.

"Get on this," I told him.

"Why?" he asked, hesitant.

"So I can fuck your brains out."

He climbed up onto his back, no further questions, and I sprung up beside him. It was only after I had settled on top of him and started riding that I noticed droplets of red forming across his arm like ruby raindrops.

"Keep going," he said, like I would have let some blood stop me. I sped up, pushing my hips into him harder, digging my hands into his chest until I felt him come.

When it was over, I tiptoed around the shards of glass littering the floor. I stopped to pick up the lingerie that I had shed in the act, and Weston mistook the action for me attempting to clean up.

"My housekeeper comes tomorrow morning," he said. "Just leave it."

We did it once more, this time back in Weston's bedroom. He was still feeling kinky, even in missionary on his king-sized bed, and went at it so hard he knocked me against the headboard a couple times.

When it was over, he passed out without a good night. He was sprawled out naked, in the blissful non-caring that must come from being male. I usually liked to change into lingerie or at least underwear afterward to help combat the effects of gravity. But that night, I settled next to him naked.

It was a restless sleep. I kept thinking about my close call with Keith, about what would happen if Weston found out the truth. I wound my bare legs around the sheets and then kicked them off, over and over. Finally, I got up and took a shot of Weston's whiskey, then returned to bed. I rolled around until I felt myself falling into oblivion.

———————

I woke up to a slight chill. I spread my arms, and the bedsheets were smooth underneath me, like I was gliding on my back across a shallow pond. It felt cool, almost comforting, since the room had been so stuffy before, and I let myself sink into it for a few seconds. I was still drowsy, probably from the alcohol. Then I looked at my arms.

In the dark room, with only a slant of moon through the window, I couldn't see much, but I spotted the blackened streaks. I was covered in it, what looked like ink or oil, black and heavy, until I slowly realized what it was. I felt my chest, my legs, in a panic. I was drenched in blood.

I felt sick before I even turned to face the body to my right. Weston was split open across his neck from ear to ear. It must have been hours ago, because everything had emptied out of him. I scooped some of the blood around his face, puddles filling his pillows, and frantically tried to push it back into him.

It was all a mistake. I couldn't remember anything. I wouldn't have let this happen, I couldn't have; this was completely unlike the other times, when I had remembered it all, *savored* it. A blind panic hit me, and I had no idea what to do other than try to splash the blood back into him. I was scooping it frantically across the bed when my left leg spasmed. Then it was my stomach, twisting in on itself, sending me keeled over across the mattress.

I woke with a start. I was in bed, drenched in a finer liquid, one that didn't leave streaks of black across the bed. It was sweat, running down my chest, along my back, soaking the sheets. I turned, and Weston was beside me, intact, his neck solid and strong, his chest moving slightly up and down, his arm curled under a pillow. I collapsed onto my back.

I steadied my breathing and stood up. I had to check and make certain the knives were all in their place in the kitchen, run my fingers along each handle in its appointed slit of wood.

When I was sure everything was normal and untouched, I found the refrigerator. I started with a wedge of Parmesan and gnawed at its sharp end until it turned to flaky mush in my mouth, and I spit it out into the sink. I didn't stop, though. I gave myself five chews for each bite I took, then spit the remnants in the sink.

I used to get strange nightmares all the time in high school—never this vivid, but close. They would come on nights I was gearing up for a cheer weigh-in, the product of an empty stomach most likely. One time, I heard the screams of a random woman being split in two and woke up to silence. I walked downstairs to investigate and found only cold marble and empty space.

Weston didn't keep any unhealthy foods, nothing I could really sink my teeth into. I would have settled for any type of meat, but the only stuff he had was raw chicken breasts sealed in tight plastic. I settled on more cheese and some walnuts. I ended up with a pile of chewed-up food in the sink. I ran the faucet to cover up what I'd done but didn't want to risk turning on the disposal and waking Weston. I could imagine him coming in, finding me naked and bent over the counter with the masticated contents of his refrigerator.

My ears had started ringing, first a buzzing hum and then a steady beat. I searched the condo for the source of the noise before I realized what it was. It was my heart, pounding, though it seemed louder than just mine alone. I moved to the full-length window that faced the city, overlooking the buildings, and wondered at how many men were housed in each one. It was as though I could hear the hearts of all the men down on the street, beating in rhythm. Wilshire was one giant artery, pulsing below me.

15

FINALS WEEK ARRIVED, AND THE GIRLS BEGAN TRICKLING OUT of the house for winter break. Security on the row was reduced to two chubby guards scootering around on Segways. I told Weston that I would be gone for a week to celebrate the holidays with my family after he announced he'd spend Christmas on the East Coast. Instead, I booked a seven-day stay at a spa in Malibu. Pam and Todd were in Italy as far as I knew, probably riding a Vespa around in matching red Uggs.

The sorority had implemented quiet hours every night starting at nine. Emily and the other nerds took over the living room, our downstairs flat screen was disconnected, and the rest of the house had to watch TV shows on their laptops with headphones. Camilla made sure all the rules were enforced, at least until she left for the inner-city charity trip she had planned to help renovate houses in Detroit. With any luck, she'd get herself shot.

When it was unbearably quiet in the house, and I could only hear a faint grumble from deep in my gut, I found myself driving to the warehouse on Washington. I wasn't training but usually performed a round of sit-ups and some plyometric drills, just to fill up the time and feel a burn in my thighs and core. I was restless. The nightmare I had at Weston's kept worming its way into my head.

Everyone did stupid shit in their twenties. Every girl had her story: threesomes during a drunken blackout, leaked sex videos. And there were girls who hid worse habits than that, chicks who spent nights alone eating entire cartons of ice cream while shopping online in their sweatpants until they finally found themselves a boyfriend. The right guy could turn everything around. I could be satisfied. Happy.

———

I stopped by Slade's office on my way out to Malibu. I brought him an organic fruit basket since I wasn't sure what else an attorney would appreciate other than money, which I already provided him in plentiful amounts. He seemed flustered to see me without an appointment. He smoothed his tie across his chest and slicked back each side of his head. His hair was definitely his worst feature. It made him seem more like a used-car salesman rather than a $500-an-hour attorney.

"Tiffany. Didn't take time off during the holidays to spend with your mother?"

"No," I said. I didn't elaborate and instead thrust the fruit basket at him. "Merry Christmas."

"Why, you didn't have to."

"I know."

He stood there holding it awkwardly until his secretary took it off his hands and out of sight. "So how are things going for you, Tiffany?"

"I'm seeing someone."

Slade raised his eyebrows. "Lucky man." He started to say something more but stopped.

"Anyway, I just wanted to bring a gift, as a token of my appreciation," I said. "I don't think I'll be making an appointment any time soon. So I guess this is a sort of goodbye."

I waited for him to say something.

"Goodbye, Tiffany." He hesitated over his next words. "Be careful."

I smiled. "I'll be fine."

I wanted to believe the words. I wanted to believe that this would be the last time I'd ever see the inside of Slade's office. When I left, I deleted his office number from my phone and told myself the murders were officially over.

———

Then I spent Christmas alone in Malibu. After New Year's and several days of exfoliating mud baths, deep tissue massages, and chemical peels, I returned to the sorority house in a town car, hoping to make a grand arrival. I was in the middle of posting a photo of the ocean view from my suite when I was interrupted by the sound of the glass partition lowering, the driver turning in his seat, telling me that all of Hilgard Avenue was coned off. I spotted an ambulance parked a few houses from the sorority.

No tip amount could get me closer than two blocks away. I lugged my Louis Vuitton down the street and up the front steps, through the common room and around to the dining area, but the rooms were all empty.

It didn't make any sense. It was the night before a new term, and the driveway was filled with cars. I made my way upstairs, threw my bag in my room, and checked the halls. Nothing.

"Hello?" I said, and the only answer I received was creaking above my head. I followed the noise to the end of the hallway, out to the balcony of Camilla's bedroom, where a ladder had been propped against the wall.

I climbed up and found five DGs reclining in lawn chairs on the roof, surveying the crowded street below with Coronas in hand. Mandy wore binoculars and dangled a leg over the side of the building ledge.

"How'd you get through? No one's allowed to drive past Westholme," she said.

"I had a car drop me off a few streets over in the neighborhood," I said. "What the hell is going on?"

Mandy pointed down at two ambulances and a row of police cars. "It's an active crime scene. They just loaded the body."

"We don't know if he's dead," Amy said.

"They put a tarp over his head. I saw it with these. That fucker's dead as a doornail."

It was way too early in the quarter for an accidental alcohol poisoning, especially with all major parties still banned.

"Give me that." I motioned to Mandy.

She handed me her beer.

"The *binoculars*."

The activity was all concentrated in front of Triangle. The fraternity was widely ridiculed for its proximity to sorority row, as well as its status as a math and engineering frat.

"Some nerd probably blew himself up doing science experiments over the break," I said, but the knot in my stomach told me this was no accident. "When did this happen?" I asked Amy.

"A couple hours ago maybe? We were getting ready for the SKIMS sale late this morning when the ambulances started blaring. They blocked it off super quick, they wouldn't even let us cross the yellow tape on foot. We came up here to see what was going on."

"I think it's pretty obvious what happened," Mandy said. She slashed her hand across her throat. "The Greek killer's struck again."

It felt as though the sunken plaster of the roof had given way under me. There was another killer on the loose. What kind of weird fuck would want to kill an *engineering* fraternity member? Our school offered more than two dozen Greek societies, and the killer picked off a science frat boy? It all made zero sense.

"Maybe they'll cancel the first day of class," Amy said.

"You wanna hit the rec center if they do?" Mandy asked.

The girls had already moved on, but I was still reeling. I ran through the consequences of this latest development. At least I had an alibi in case the cops swept through the row again to investigate. I'd been miles away from the scene of the crime. Though I doubted they'd even question houses like Delta Gamma—girls like us never spoke more than a few words to Triangle members, and we purposefully left them out of Greek activities.

I took another look through the binoculars, but the EMTs were gone, and there were only cops milling around at this point. How had it been done? A clinical incision across the throat, a straight stabbing, or a gun blast through the chest? And who had done it? Was there another vicious bitch running around? I felt a sudden pulse between my legs. I handed off the binoculars.

"What other news did I miss over the break?" I asked Amy.

"Let's see," she said, tapping a turquoise nail on the glass of her beer bottle. "Julie got her breasts done over Christmas."

"You're shitting me," I said. "How big?"

"Full C's, silicone. They went up through the belly button so there's no scar. They look really good."

More bad news. I needed to sit down, take this in by myself. The roofing felt unstable beneath my feet as I stumbled back to the ladder and climbed down.

I returned to my room to regroup. The murder didn't mean anything, I told myself. Los Angeles was a dangerous city, people died every day from bizarre accidents.

I needed a distraction, a release to let my mind run on autopilot, so I opened my closet and ran my fingers through silk, cashmere, and leather. I put my bundled energy to good use and began coordinating, pulling clothing I had already worn once on dates with Weston and placing newer items to the front. I was stumped on whether I had worn a white Givenchy dress out with Weston for tapas, when the sound of roller wheels lumbering across the wood of the hallway told me Emily was back from break.

"How'd you get your car through?" I asked, not bothering to look up. I suddenly laughed when I remembered Emily was poor and didn't even own a bike. It felt nice to laugh at her expense—this was the first time I had smiled all day.

"The bus wouldn't take me farther south than Sunset. I had to lug this nearly a mile."

I ignored her and moved a miniskirt over to the virgin section of clothes.

"What's going on? Where is everyone? Why are there cop cars down the street?" she asked.

At least I could scare Emily a little with the news. I turned to face her. "Someone's been murdered."

The words barely left my mouth before catching in my throat. I took in the angular slope of her jaw, the sharpness of her collarbones across her shoulders. Emily had lost a good fifteen pounds.

"You're skinny."

All I could do was state the obvious. The hangers of clothes in my hand fell to the ground.

"There was a murder? Near campus?"

"How did you lose so much weight?"

"Who's dead?"

I had to sit down on my bed, ignoring her questions. The entire sorority house had been turned upside down in a matter of weeks. Emily's lips curved into an O, but I couldn't hear anything coming out of her mouth. The bedspread I sat on seemed to be sliding down to the floor, bringing me with it.

"Who's dead?" Emily repeated.

"A Triangle math geek. It's not important."

I hadn't popped a Xanax since last year when Pam tried to lower my credit limit, but I left immediately for Julie's room to steal a few from her dresser before the girls came back from the roof.

In a medicated haze during dinner, I caught a glimpse of Julie, who had arrived late. Even with a slutty corset top, there was no denying it, her breasts *had* been tastefully done, by a real professional with some artistic flair. Once seated, she made a big show of refusing the vegetable lasagna for a single-serving tray of high-protein soy steak and flaxseed.

"Your body depletes so much energy after surgery. It's really important to take in plenty of nutrients and protein."

"You're the expert on plastic surgery," I said under my breath.

"I'm one hundred percent natural, Tiffany," Julie replied. "Besides the breasts and lips."

Amy had baked vegan brownies for dessert, but I couldn't eat, not with Julie's new implants staring up at me like that. I brought a small brownie square back upstairs with me and sat at my desk mashing it with a fork, until the stuff turned to sodden brown pulp.

"It's my grandmother," Emily said. I hadn't even realized she was in the room with me. She was on her bed, in pajamas that now hung off her frame, a travel-sized bottle of Barefoot wine in her hand. "She's dying."

I thought Emily was smart enough to realize I was the last person she wanted to pour her heart out to. I had washed down the Xanax with a glass of wine at dinner and could barely keep my chin from hitting my chest.

"I can't seem to keep food down," she continued. "But it's not because I'm sad. I'm just tired. I feel like I'll be relieved when she does go at this point. Is that horrible?"

I was ready to go to bed and pretend this day had been another dream.

"Try to look on the bright side," I said. "I wished I had dropped major pounds when my father died."

I saw the flames from the bonfire I lit in the backyard the night he died, the screams of Pam's Pomeranians filling the air. I glanced out the window, expecting to see another police car, its siren on, coming for me.

But there were only empty streets, evenly spaced rows of lampposts shining out against the dark.

16

I SOON HAD TO PUT ASIDE THE CHANGING DYNAMICS OF THE
sorority house for other practicalities. Weston's birthday was only
two weeks away. Mine wouldn't arrive until August, and it sucked
that his would come so soon after we had started dating. We were
over a month into our relationship, long enough that I'd need to do
something to celebrate, but short enough that it couldn't be too ex-
travagant or it might make me seem desperate. TikTok devoted whole
tutorial videos to this delicate balance.

To put even more pressure on, Weston had informed me over dinner that three of his fraternity brothers from back east would be visiting for his birthday weekend.

One of my favorite things about Weston (right below his chiseled
cheekbones and *GQ*-quality physique) was that he didn't have too
many friends. He was still new to L.A. I kept forgetting until he'd
drop some bombshell, like that he'd never been to Coachella.

Weston spoke often about the members of his fraternity and his
business school classmates, but here in L.A., he caught only the occasional round of golf with a small group of doughy work colleagues.
There was no question that I'd ever be superseded by any of those guys.

I had enough to stress out about at the sorority house. This new
complication was the last thing I needed. I wanted Weston's old
friends to stay in their own city. I tried to be nonchalant after
his announcement at dinner. We had taken a tiny two-seat table that
spilled onto the sidewalk just a couple feet from the traffic on Santa
Monica Boulevard.

"Didn't you just see your friends? Over Christmas?" I had to yell over the roar of a passing motorcycle.

"No, they don't live in Manhattan anymore; they're in SF. Entrepreneurs. They've got like a dozen different projects on their plates right now."

"Oh. They sound great."

Weston's last sentence just made me think of food, raw steaks bleeding onto a tray.

"We should get the check," I said. "I have to be back at the house by ten."

"Ten?"

"It's a weekday."

The Triangle murder down the street had the row on lockdown again. The news vans were back, taking up the street parking and occasionally blocking off the sorority driveway. Reporters were circling closer to the truth, that the other Greek murders might not in fact be connected to this one. I caught up on all the intel, even the boring shit. In recent weeks, a group of chem students had taken to carrying pocketknives with them and cutting out pages of the library's science books to sabotage their other classmates. Knife fights had broken out in the soundproof reading rooms. It turned out there was a hidden, violent underbelly to every segment of campus, even the socially inept circles. There was an edge of suspicion to people on the streets when I walked by on clear afternoons. Everyone seemed to suddenly wonder what they were capable of. The thread that kept us from giving in entirely to animal urges was thinning.

———

Two days before Weston's birthday, his friends all bailed on him. The news had bummed him out bad, but I was ecstatic.

With Weston's friends out of the picture, I could plan something romantic for his birthday. What that would be, I had no clue. I decided to take a leap and make it big, expensive, something that would remind Weston that I was well worth a dozen of his no-show Ivy League frat brothers.

Worrying about Weston's birthday, I let other things slip. My tutor had spent the day figuring out my class schedule for the next term. She'd managed to salvage my grade by finding some nerdy blonde to take my finals for me. I also had to deal with another probation notice from the sorority—this time, it wasn't my grades but missing service hours. The notice had been signed by Camilla, a fucking heart over the "i" in her name. I had almost missed both my waxing and mani-pedi appointments.

I told myself the recent lapses were the worries of a diligent girl-friend amid the obligations of sorority life, but I knew why my head was all jumbled. On the car ride to the salon that day, I had spotted a shirtless college boy crossing the street, clad only in loose gym shorts, his core muscles rippling in beautiful concert, and my hands clenched the steering wheel so hard I was sure it would disconnect with an electric snap and smack me in the forehead. I imagined pulling alongside him, rolling down the window, and offering him a ride to his apartment or dormitory, then veering off course, finding the nearest restaurant alley, and taking a blade to his stomach, watching his skin as it relented to sharp metal.

Daydreams like these were what kept me going during the days when Weston was working, and I found myself driving down deserted streets. Who else thought about what they might get away with? There was a brawl in the middle of a biolab, an assault on a campus security guard the day before that. Every time I saw a vulnerable boy on the street, I repeated to myself that Weston was enough.

Emily was constantly distracting me now, her general skinniness serving as a good-enough annoyance by itself. She'd begun working out for the first time only *after* losing all her recent weight. She had even tried to tag along on one of my runs, but I warned her that she wouldn't even begin to keep up. She accompanied me anyway one afternoon, and I prepared to leave her in the dust, rounding the steep incline on Hil-gard. I was practicing my sprints, short intense spurts of power. I had a lot of pent-up energy that needed to be let loose, even if running was a weak substitute for what I really craved.

But the power I felt dripping off me evaporated quickly when Emily met me pace for pace up the hill at the initial start. I pulled away from her eventually, my heart racing and my thighs burning as I entered the downhill stretch.

"I'm faster than I thought," she said when we had slowed to a panting walk.

"Not as fast as me," I returned.

"Barely."

I scowled at her. But she was right. So it only took losing fifteen pounds. Who would have guessed it was as easy as that? Emily could smell it too, the upper hand she might finally gain over the whiskey dicks and sixth-years of the neighboring fraternities, the shift in the scales. She was peaking while some of the frat bros were already balding and growing beer bellies.

I had first felt it years ago, when I was a preteen, walking the streets near the pier: the shouts and honks coming from both beat-up and luxury cars. There was only a brief period I didn't understand it, maybe a couple years before I realized what the catcalls meant, what they could get me.

We had almost reached the sorority house. Emily had stripped to a sports bra. Her next words made me stop in my tracks.

"I just want to run until I explode. You know the feeling?"

Emily had the itch too, the desire to release all tension and go wild. I turned to face her. "Maybe. But what would you do then, Emily?"

"What do you mean?" she asked.

"If you could explode, who would it be on? How far would you go?"

I half hoped she would share a violent fantasy, that there would be a knife's edge she also thought about crossing. But she shook her head, confused.

"It's just an expression."

"Be careful what you wish for," I said.

After I had stripped off my sweaty clothes and showered, I found Emily on her bed, a wine cooler in hand, with a huge pink card that had scattered glitter over the hardwood and gave off the disgusting scent of Juicy Couture.

"What's that?" I said.

"A sympathy card from the other girls."

"Did your grandmother finally die?"

"No. She fell again."

Her grandmother had been dragging her death out the entire school year. No wonder Emily was getting antsy.

"I'm sorry to hear," I lied, remembering that I needed Emily on my side if I was going to reinforce my legitimacy during spring rush in March. I placed my hand on her shoulder, but I had nothing else to say, so my hand just hung there, deadweight on her frame. I lifted my arm and walked over to my closet. I had dinner with Weston in an hour and still had to moisturize and dress.

Emily watched me sort through the color-coded minidresses in my closet. I settled on something in the red-to-coral spectrum.

"Spending the night at Weston's?" Emily asked.

"Most likely," I said. "Why? You planning to finger yourself tonight or something?"

"What is wrong with you?" she said.

I noticed my pack of birth control pills had spilled out from my purse on the dresser. According to the row of white, it should have been Monday. I double-checked my phone. Thursday. I popped out three.

"Are you supposed to take that many?" Emily asked.

"That many what?"

"Pills."

"It's fine."

"I don't think that's exactly how it works."

"If you're so fucking smart, why are you asking me?"

"What does it feel like?" she asked as I grabbed a towel.

"The pills? They're really small. I don't even need to wash them down with water."

"No, your first time."

"It sucked. Like it's supposed to."

I had given it up at thirteen in a San Clemente lifeguard tower over splintered wooden slats so sharp they left indents on my ass. I remembered those markings more than the act itself.

Of course, Emily was too inept to pick up on all the nuances of her newfound weight loss. But the dynamics around the house were shifting. She didn't understand why Mandy was dropping by, asking to borrow a hair dryer when she probably had seven of her own. She was eyeing the competition, too.

Explaining to Emily the delicate, dirty process of getting laid for the first time would take an entire night, and I still had to find the appropriate thong to wear under my dress for my date. I slid onto the bed next to her and gave her the condensed rundown.

"If you're scoping out possibilities, your first should be slightly below you, because you're gonna be horrible. So since you're like a six right now, start by finding yourself a five."

"I'm a six?" Emily asked.

She was a seven, but I wasn't going to tell her that.

"You were a four back when you were fat," I said.

"I just want to get it out of the way. Maybe that would be easier."

It was cute that Emily thought losing her virginity would tie up things, when sex was a beginning, never an end. I thought about what it felt like to still have an appetite for missionary, a hunger for regular sex.

"So I guess the next question is what's your type. Good boy or bad guy?"

She took a moment to consider. "Bad guy."

She was fucked.

I could give Emily pure gold, but none of it would matter. She'd probably swoon over the first eight who paid her any attention. He'd crack her open for the street cred, talk her into anal on the second date, and then ditch her midparty once he found a KKG with better extensions and a bigger rack.

"Just listen to what I'm saying: I've slept with a lot of guys . . ." I started, but as soon as I said it, I realized the statement hadn't come out right. I tried again: "I currently have a serious, healthy relationship built on both physical and emotional intimacy. I know about these things. And I'm your big. Don't make any decisions about who's going to swipe your V card until you confirm with me."

But I knew Emily wouldn't listen to a damn thing I said. That was the problem with virgins. Emily would need to learn on her own the normal, hard way.

17

T HE THING I WAS DISCOVERING ABOUT THIS RELATIONSHIP
business: some of it blew. I could plan the perfect evening, starve
myself for twelve hours so my ribs poked out just so from my crop
top, and one false start, one offhand remark, could scatter the night
to pieces. Once we got past the phase where Weston and I spent 90
percent of our time straight-out fucking, I realized it was a much more
nuanced game. Keeping a relationship steady had nothing to do with
seduction. It required other knowledge, deeper and more complex. I'd
find it, though, eventually, and master it.

On Weston's birthday, I ended up surprising him with a couples
massage in Beverly Hills, the spot I always frequented after a bad hookup or intense catfight. Then we headed to Sunset Tower, where I had
booked a two-bedroom suite for the weekend. It took over an hour to
drive over—it was a late January evening that matched the season for
once—and heavy rain had reduced Sunset Boulevard to a slow crawl.

When we checked in, the room wasn't as large as I had assumed
based on the four-figure-per-night price tag. Champagne and straw-
berries also weren't waiting upon arrival as I had requested. While
Weston took a birthday call in the bedroom, I dialed downstairs asking
them to step on it.

"Hey, gorgeous," Weston said, lips immediately on mine, after he'd
emerged from the bedroom, phone in hand.

He didn't tell me the news of his phone call until we had done it
across the bar, then on the bed. He waited until I was sprawled naked
on top of the comforter, my thong stretched over his head and a dumb

look spread across his face. It was only then that he mentioned off-hand, as if it were only a minor alteration of our plans, that the three of his fraternity members who had canceled on him had only been messing around. It was an elaborate prank; they had booked flights and had already touched down at LAX. It was all some sort of grand surprise, seemingly meant to butcher my careful plans.

I stiffened in his arms at the news. His friends had carved themselves into what was supposed to be *our* evening. When I thought it couldn't be any worse, Weston added that two girlfriends would also be accompanying the guys. The five of them had rented a house in the Hollywood Hills.

"But I booked this suite already," I said.

"It got its use, if you ask me. I'll pay you back. Just tell me the amount."

That's not what I wanted to hear. For him to assume it was an issue of money was fucking offensive.

"I wanted something special, just the two of us," I said, making sure there was no whine to my voice.

He relented a bit. "Well, we can play it by ear and see where we feel like sleeping at the end of the night. The option's open."

He came up behind me as I put my clothes back on, and I froze.

"Thanks for the effort, Tiff," he said. "I'm just so happy they're coming. You get to meet Dean."

"Can't wait."

Dean could suck my imaginary dick as far as I was concerned. The night was ruined.

From then on, it was nonstop chatter about SAE and the guys, as if their announcement had opened the floodgate on long-lost memories of elephant trunk circles and ass-paddling. And Dean seemed to be the main perpetrator. *He* was the only one Weston had bothered to individually mention again and again.

"Dean. Is that even a real name? Sounds like a porn star's alter ego," I said.

"Of course it's real," he said. "What's wrong with you?"

"Do we really have to drive all the way into the hills tonight?"

"They wanted to have drinks over at the house, but the hotel is closer to the club. It probably makes more sense to pre-party here. I'll text them now."

I realized this meeting would be inevitable. I could peg the guys, but I had no idea about the girls.

"You said girls were coming, too?"

"Yeah, only two, with Harrison and Brad. Dean always flies solo."

"What are they into?"

He seemed bored. "No idea—I've never met them."

At least I wasn't up against any certified seniority-status girlfriends.

"I need to get ready," I said.

"You look good to me."

I glanced down at my flimsy sundress, not even designer, and the flat sandals I had paired it with to look California chic. I had spent the day freezing in the icy weather, and it had dropped another 15 degrees at sundown.

"I have a whole other wardrobe of club clothes."

I also needed a night layer of makeup, but I didn't want to draw attention to the fact that I had multiple forms of cover-up, that some nights required repeated applications of foundation and gloss. We weren't ready for those truths.

I went into the bathroom and selected a sequined Dolce and Gabbana top in pale silver to contrast against my glowing tan. I slipped on a pair of leather pants sans underwear, since the material hugged so tight around my ass even the thin string of my thong would show. I paired the outfit with five-inch stilettos and minimal jewelry. When I walked out, Weston circled behind me like a vulture sniffing carrion, and I smiled.

"Let me get us some champs," I said. "You need to hop in the shower."

I had taken a solid forty-five minutes in the bathroom, yet the hotel staff still hadn't delivered the champagne. I called downstairs, furious.

"Who do I need to blow down there to get a little service?"

"No one, miss."

A bellboy rang a few minutes later with towels, no alcohol in sight.

"What the fuck am I supposed to do with these?" I asked, throwing the towels back at him. Repressed bloodlust made me want to break a champagne bottle against the soft skin of his neck and let him bleed out on the tacky maroon carpet. But I was empty-handed.

"*Champagne,*" I said. "I wanted champagne."

"I was told extra towels and shampoo. I'll check downstairs and be right back."

"Forget it, I'll go myself. You're a fucking moron, you know that?"

I glanced back toward the bathroom. Weston was still in the shower. I had a solid fifteen minutes of him preening in the fog of the bathroom.

I grabbed the key and headed to the hallway. The towel boy had already pedaled away in a semi-run. We probably wouldn't even have time to drink the stuff at this point, but it was the principle now. I was heated, angry.

I took the elevator down to the front desk. It was swarming with people running in from the rain. I slipped on a slick spread of tile, almost landing on my ass.

I bypassed the line and hooked my fingers over the edge of the mottled marble of the front desk, launching right into it: "Is it because I'm a woman I can't get any decent service?" I shrieked at the nearest twat wearing a blazer and name tag.

"Excuse me, name please."

"Tiffany fucking Ames."

She typed furiously on her desktop. "Someone should have been up with the order. I'm so sorry. I'm not sure why there was a problem. It might be the rainstorm."

"How does that make a difference? We're inside!"

Some douche in fitted cuffed jeans was behind me, looming in my periphery.

"You have ten seconds to get your shit in order. I mean it," I said.

The tool behind me suddenly reached for my forearm.

"Back off!" I screamed, finally giving him my full gaze.

He opened his arms. "Just thought you needed to calm down a little."

"I just think you need to mind your own business a little."

I glared at him. His brown hair was swept up in a loose top knot. He looked like he had rolled in from Intelligentsia.

My eyes traveled a little lower. Peeking out on the inner flesh of his biceps was an arrowhead tattoo, the exact coloring, size, and placement of Weston's. My stomach dropped. I glanced again at his hipster regalia, unable to believe it.

"We've fixed it all up, ma'am," said the woman at the desk, motioning to a man carting out a bucket of champagne.

"Thanks" was all I could muster as I left. The intruder's arm was down, he was turning away. I was already questioning if I had imagined it.

———

"Champagne?" I asked Weston.

Weston had emerged from the mist of the bathroom, showered and groomed, in slacks and an unbuttoned Hugo Boss shirt. He reached for his iPhone.

"Shit, Dean and the rest are here. They couldn't get the staff to reveal the room number," he said as he buttoned up.

"Oh really?" I asked, feeling nauseated.

"What's the number? Can you check the door?"

"Sure," I said as dread filled my body. A whole facet of Weston's history had emerged out of thin air, taken all the oxygen with it, and left me gasping. I was trapped in a cheaply furnished semi-luxury suite. I gave Weston the room number, sat on the sofa, and waited, my mind fighting against the inevitable, willing myself to believe it was only coincidence, a trick rearrangement of inked colors and shapes across a stranger's arm.

There was a knock. He stepped in first, flanked by two girls and two guys behind him. When he spotted me, brief recognition passed across his face, replaced quickly by a closed-lipped smile and an outstretched hand, that tattoo returning to taunt me. I placed my hand in his, unable to look anywhere but down at that marking.

"Dean," he said.

"Tiffany."

18

I WAS TEMPORARILY DISTRACTED FROM DEAN WHEN I GOT A look at the girls. One wore neon harem pants and a feathered turban, while the other channeled her inner old lady with a tunic dress and combat boots that chopped off her calves. Even their names were weird: Lydia and Tabitha. I was commando in skintight leather and a top that revealed a well of cleavage, and they were in contradiction of every slimming principle in the fashion canon. They didn't even tan.

Lydia sported a purple armadillo tattoo on her shoulder. Tabitha's tattoo just read LATEX in cursive across her forearm. And I was supposed to hold a conversation with these boho clowns? They were wearing eyeglasses on a Friday night, for fuck's sake.

"I wish you had warned me," I said to Weston, slipping in between him and the others when he turned to refill his drink. We had decided on staying in the suite, for now at least, and pre-partying before going to the club.

"Warned you about what?"

"About the dress code. I'm clearly out of place."

"You look fine."

I look more than fine, I wanted to snap. I had meant the fact that his friends were members of a completely inverse category of rich from us. How could he leave this detail out?

"Just relax and have some fun," he said. I could tell he was annoyed, so I bit my lip and joined the group.

Harrison and Brad were easier: they spoke to me in a slow singsong that might have been directed to a three-year-old. But at least they paid attention to me, appreciated my body with the occasional roving glance. Dean avoided eye contact and kept away.

I returned to the girls, and they continued talking, not bothering to turn in my direction. I tried to form a triangle to include myself in the conversation, but they repositioned their bodies away from me.

"Where did you get your top?" I asked Lydia in the ridiculous pants.

"Hand sewn by a local weaver outside Portland," Lydia replied.

"We believe fashion is more than the designer you wear," Tabitha said. "It's an expression of your creativity, your art, your respect for your body, and, through your sustainable choices, a reflection of your ultimate commitment to the earth."

She glanced down at my leather pants, eyebrows raised.

"I hope that's not leather."

"Everything has to die at some point, right?" I said.

I downed my tumbler of Red Bull vodka in one long swallow. I had ordered zero-calorie and zero-sugar chasers (an absolute rule at the sorority), but Lydia and Tabitha quickly informed me that wasn't good enough. They couldn't drink artificial preservatives or caffeine. Their bodies were sacred, chemical-free zones, even on Friday nights.

"Isn't most of it going to get thrown up by the end of the night anyway?" I joked, still trying to remain on my best behavior. Dean was on the opposite end of the room, his back turned to me.

"Bulimia isn't a punch line," Lydia said.

After rejecting every single chaser the hotel minibar had to offer for health reasons, Lydia and Tabitha settled on straight vodka over ice and took the drinks to the balcony for a cigarette.

I stayed inside, exhausted already. Weston called me onto his lap. He reeked of whiskey, and it masked the scent of his cologne and fresh aftershave.

"We're leaving for the club in a few minutes," he said.

"Whatever you want."

I tried to play it off like I was low maintenance. Like I was happy and chill. Like I didn't want to kill someone.

I learned more about Brad and Harrison, and the pieces fell together. The guys all had their own companies, ventures supported by sizable trust funds. They owned tech apps, all cutting edge, while the girls had taken the opposite route and sold products only available during the time of primitive man: hemp, jams, crystals, beads. They took bikes to work, grew their own fruit, got on buses voluntarily. They seemed to do everything possible to mock their wealth, and I hated them for it. I couldn't understand why Weston didn't also despise them.

I broke my one-drink minimum and downed two Red Bull vodkas in the space of an hour. I felt loose, shaky, which was better than the tightening panic I felt around Dean.

At ten, we headed over to the Colony, a club set up like the East Coast Hamptons even though the Pacific was ten miles away. Bartenders with collared polos, fitted shorts, and slicked hair beamed like sunny mannequins as the rain continued to pour down. It stunk of early '80s L.A. or maybe Miami—decorated like the book jacket for some horrible teen series.

None of it made sense: I couldn't figure these people out. I had no idea how Weston had lived with them throughout college—if they had changed, or if it had been him. Maybe I didn't really know him at all.

We had bottle service, thank God, and the pounding club music took away the need to talk, so I settled into the plastic sea-green booth and tried not to drink myself into oblivion. I hunted around for familiar faces, but I knew no one from the Greek crowd would be around. No one from the in-crowd of any L.A. scene would be caught dead here.

The girls were on another smoke break, talking shit on L.A.—the usual suspects: pollution, the traffic, the lack of culture. I didn't want to stay alone with the guys, so I told them I was headed to the bathroom and submerged into the crowd. I was desperate enough to join the clubgoers, the sad amalgamation of bandage dresses and stripper heels that filled a Hollywood dance floor.

I made my way to the front and leaned against the bar, spreading my arms out to block a group of girls attempting to weasel their way forward, until my chest grazed the black granite of the bar top. I got the bartender's attention immediately. He was blond with a swimmer's body, and my pulse picked up.

Then I spotted a semi-familiar face alongside me, the first of the night. I usually would never give a second glance to someone like him—dressed in an overly large dress shirt that still couldn't conceal the bulge of his gut, unbuttoned too low at the top. It took a second glance to recognize that the ill-fitting clothing was designer, that he was sporting thousands of dollars that hung on him like a tarp.

His name was Malcolm. He wasn't fraternity material by any stretch of the imagination, but he managed to get into most of the major parties through connections. And it was common knowledge that Malcolm was rapey. He was currently embroiled in a case with a KKG. Spiked drinks. He could get away with it, he was that rich. He'd either burn out in five years and move into his parents' guesthouse or go to law school and become a Supreme Court justice. It was a toss-up with those kinds of guys.

Malcolm caught my eye as I was receiving my vodka Diet Coke. He let out a low whistle and tilted his head to check out my ass. "Excellent wardrobe choice. Next drink on me," he said. He exhibited an un-earned confidence that made me want to get him alone and undressed, just so I could laugh at his dick. Girls found him charming somehow. I didn't get it.

"We'll see," I said, and decided to rejoin the group, forced back into their shitty company by the creeper next to me.

"That wasn't a question. I'm here all night, and I've got my eyes on you," he said as I returned to the crowd.

Back at our private table, Harrison and Brad were flirting with girls in two-inch miniskirts who looked like off-duty strippers. I felt a stab of jealousy, then noticed that Weston wasn't anywhere near them. He was in rapt conversation with Dean. I couldn't even get his attention. I gave up and watched the two of them. I wondered if Dean would reveal our earlier meeting, what Weston would think, if he'd believe him, if it would really matter, me hassling a couple of nobody front desk workers. I had done it all for him, for his birthday.

I'd never seen Weston this drunk. And he looked so happy, so much younger, wearing a puppy dog grin that I could only get out of him through vigorous fellatio.

I'd need to talk to Dean, alone. Figure out where we stood. If that was even possible, with Weston clinging to him like a long-lost twin.

I kicked back my drink.

Tabitha and Lydia returned from outside.

"She's from the OC, the shitty Republican part," I caught Tabitha say.

I bristled. "What are you talking about?" I asked.

"The refugee crisis in Eritrea. Stuff you'd probably find boring."

I had no idea what Eritrea was, but fuck those girls.

Lydia's face was red as a beet, a worse shade than the mozzarella white of earlier in the night. The rosiness could have been from being outdoors in the rain, but I guessed it was the alcohol. There was a fresh bite to them—they were getting drunk.

"How'd you meet Brad?" I asked Tabitha, hoping she'd get sloppy with the details.

"I'm dating Harrison," she said curtly.

"Right. Do you go clubbing a lot?" I asked.

"Not really. The scene's different in SF. The guys said this place would be more Weston's thing."

"What do you know about Weston?" I asked.

"Shouldn't I be asking you that? You're dating him."

"You're a real shithead," I said, my head turned away from her, so the words poured right into the speaker.

"That fraternity stuff is just so third grade," Lydia said. "And the sororities are even worse. How can you be a feminist if you insist on dressing everyone in the same size two miniskirts? The gender dynamics of the whole thing are frankly reprehensible."

"That means bad," Tabitha said to me.

I visualized shattering my drink across her cheek.

"Where's the nearest bar?" Lydia interrupted, leaving an empty tumbler at the booth beside her. "It's been ten minutes, and I haven't seen one server."

I looked back at Weston. He was still talking to Dean. It was Dean who mattered. Dean, the one who had caught me off guard.

———

Another ten minutes passed with no service. Lydia and Tabitha thought it might be amusing to walk among the Angelino peasantry. I lingered behind, following them to the upper bar.

We had squeezed up to the bartender when Malcolm materialized again.

"You girls need a drink," he said.

"We're fine," I said.

"I insist. You already escaped once."

The tool wasn't giving up. Malcolm had the bartender make something simple: cranberry vodkas. I was sure this would violate one of Lydia and Tabitha's hippie rules, but they accepted his offer.

They turned from Malcolm, who had cashed out at the bar. He hunched over the drinks, his wallet in hand. But I realized he had something else in his palm, I wasn't sure what.

It was only three seconds, and then he turned around to pass Lydia and Tabitha their glasses.

"Cheers," he said, handing me the last drink. I didn't touch it.

I stood there staring at the drink, Malcolm oblivious to me for those few seconds, talking to Lydia. Then he came over and pulled me by the wrist. I fought the urge to break his nose with my fist.

"Come back to my table, meet some of my friends," he said. There were no people waiting, I knew that.

"Later," I told him, snapping my wrist against his thumb and out of his grip.

"Just sit down for a minute. You don't want to get overheated," Malcolm said. Tabitha and Lydia were already following him.

I started to say something to them, to give out some sort of warning, but I stopped. They were right: I was no girl's girl. They were on their own tonight. They knew all about international news, but they hadn't read the local crime headlines. Murder had become L.A.'s newest sport.

"I'm going back to the table. You two stay safe."

They didn't even hear me.

I returned to check on Weston. I was going to stop at the nearest planter and pour the drink out, but there wasn't the usual outdoor vegetation; it was all neon lights and bright aluminum. Our table was empty.

Where are u, I texted Weston, and sat by myself before getting a kiwi emoji in reply. Things were disintegrating quickly.

I snaked my way around the club into every nook and cranny, all the places money was supposed to keep me out of. I finally spotted the four guys out back, smoking cigars. Weston was leaning on Dean, practically attached to him. I still had Malcolm's drink in my hand—it was melting, diluting, and the cold was burning my hand.

I watched them. I was the only woman in the vicinity, glimmering in my top like a siren call, exposed flesh and tightened muscle against sequin and leather. And yet he never saw me. He suddenly grabbed Dean's head and touched foreheads. I couldn't hear what they were saying. A flame ignited within me. I didn't even think.

"Weston!" I shouted as if I had just spotted him.

"Hey, babe," he said sheepishly, finally pulling away from Dean.

I let a smile stretch tight across my face. I thrust the drink at him, its glass dripping with condensation, almost slipping out of my hand. "I got you a drink."

"Cranberry vodka?" he said, scrunching his nose.

"I forgot you prefer Scotch," I said weakly. "I went to a lot of trouble to get it, though, and to find you. You didn't answer my texts."

He didn't want it, I could tell, but he knew he was in trouble.

"Thanks," he said, and took the drink like a shot, ripping the straw out and kicking it back.

One of the others, Brad, began a weak conversation with me, but my eyes were only on Weston, traveling over his body, looking for signs of weakness, trying to gauge if my instincts about Malcolm were indeed true. I wanted this night over, and a roofied birthday boy was one sure way to call everything off. But Weston was back with Dean, leaning on him, whispering.

"They're close," Brad told me.

"How close?" I asked.

"They were an institution at the frat. Legends."

"That was a long time ago."

"That stuff stays forever."

I thought about how Weston had assumed I was close to Emily. I had nothing like that with anyone. What would it feel like, to be able to share every secret and sin with someone?

———

Weston finally showed signs of deterioration a half hour later, when he fell onto a side table and broke three martini glasses. He'd had at least ten shots, so I wasn't even sure if it had been Malcolm's drink that had done him in. Dean came over and spoke his first words to me since arriving at the club.

"I'm calling an Uber."

It was that time. Lydia and Tabitha had disappeared, but the other guys didn't seem worried.

"Shouldn't we find them first?" I asked.

"I'll text, and they can meet us at the house," Brad said.

"But all my stuff is back in the hotel," I said.

"You can pick it up in the morning," Dean said.

And like that, it was decided. I didn't even have a chance to prepare a night bag. I just happened to trail along, attached by a flimsy string to Weston. I'd wake up tomorrow morning with mascara running like lane dividers down my face and be expected to leave. I offered a silent *So long* to Lydia and Tabitha as we exited the club and felt the chill of the night. The boys and I took an Uber Black north across Highland Avenue and up into the hills.

The house was old Hollywood cool: four stories, the floors stacked on top of one another at odd angles. Some obscure silent film star had once owned the house, according to Brad. Marilyn Monroe had nannied for the owners, back when she was Norma Jeane.

We settled on a black velvet couch on the ground floor, facing a vast windowed living room, the open space below a set of claustrophobic bedrooms piled on one another like a Jenga tower. The boys still weren't worried even though neither Lydia nor Tabitha had texted in over two hours.

"They do this," Brad explained. "The silent treatment. When they're mad or whatever."

He had become my translator for the evening, ever since Weston had started fading. Weston could barely sit up at this point; he was slowly sliding off the velvet chaise onto the hardwood.

"Sexy time," he whispered, as I pulled him upright. He must have thought we were alone, he was so smashed. I felt a little bad about giving him that drink when he started drooling.

"I think we're tapping out for the night," I said, and tried to lead Weston away to our bedroom. He was too heavy, though, and Dean had to help drag him to the room. We were at the very top, which required ascending a narrow, enclosed staircase. Weston kept ricocheting off the walls. He would have fallen backward if Dean hadn't been planted firmly behind him.

"Where's your room?" I asked Dean.

"I'm right below you," he said.

The others would be sleeping in a separate wing of the house.

"I'm glad to have you close by," I said with a smile. "You know, in case there are problems."

"Weston's fine," Dean said. "He just needs to sleep it off."

We reached the room and threw Weston onto the bed. I was inches from Dean on my knees across the mattress.

"Thanks," I said in my highest, sweetest register, arching my back a tad as I crawled off the bed. Dean said nothing. "Can we talk for a sec about earlier?"

Dean wouldn't even give me an answer. He walked out and shut the door behind him.

I fought the urge to chase him down and tried to smother my ballooning rage. Who the fuck did he think he was?

I flipped onto my back and let out a long scream into my pillow, then another and another, until my voice was hoarse and my throat burned. I kicked at the bed so hard I managed to wake up Weston. He attempted to pull off my pants, but the heat of the club had plastered them to my thighs, and his drunken pulls weren't nearly strong enough to budge the leather against my skin. Weston gave up and entered a sleep so deep, I had to roll across him and place my ear to his chest to catch the faint beating of his heart.

I stayed straddled on top of him, remembering Jeremy in the same position on Halloween. That had been almost three months ago. It felt so far away, yet when I closed my eyes, I could replay each step in that night so easily, recall the electricity in the air, the sense of possibility. The cool metal of the scissors in my hand, guiding me along.

I stroked Weston's bare arms, bringing my hands up to his face. I leaned down to give him a long kiss. He was sprawled out, helpless. I settled into the crook of his arm and waited for the noise downstairs to dim and fade, long enough to hear Dean settle in through the thin wood floor below me. I breathed slowly and tried to calm down. I told myself I should fall asleep, call it a night, but sleep wouldn't come. I kept my ears tuned, my hand on Weston's chest, counting the beats of his heart.

When the music had been cut, the footsteps dispersed, and a door opened down below, I rose from the bed. I touched Weston one more time. I remembered the last words he had whispered in a bout of semi-coherence, about birthday sex. But it was past midnight now. His day was over.

I stopped on the stair landing to look out the low, square windows at the illuminated houses on the hills beyond and hear the wind banging against glass. It had begun to rain again. The trees swayed outside, sending shadows up and down the walls.

I walked downstairs. I stepped through the sliding door of the living room and walked around the patio, checking for an alarm system. Nothing sounded. The house was vintage chic, a party spot where dozens could stretch across the hardwood on long weekend nights, too cool for security systems. Places like this drew danger to them—not often, maybe once every few decades. But when it came, the violence was deep, brutal. Manson family bad. Blood-splattered front-page news bad. I looked up to the back wing of the house, to the single light still on. Dean's room.

It was time for us to have a chat.

19

FLUNG THE PATIO DOOR OPEN AND STEPPED BACK INSIDE. The storm had picked up. I watched rain pellets spackle the living room floor. The room would be a complete mess in about an hour. I smashed a glass tumbler of whiskey onto the hardwood. I missed that lack of control, the frenetic feeling of not knowing where the night might take me, what I might sink my teeth into. I needed this. I headed to the kitchen and rooted through drawers until I found a pointed boning knife. I slid it into the band of my bra, snug between my cleavage, and climbed the stairs.

When I reached the second landing, I put my forehead against the door to Dean's room and leaned my entire body against its weight, pressing into it so I could feel the cold wood on my skin. I swore I could hear a beating heart on the other side. I reached for the doorknob. He had locked it.

I knocked gently.

"Yeah?" Dean said, yanking the door open, a look of surprise on his face when it was just me before him.

"I feel like we didn't get a chance to talk at the club. About the beginning of the night. I need to explain—"

"We'll talk tomorrow," he said, and moved to close the door.

"We might not get the chance. Why not here? Now? While we're alone." I ran my hand up the doorframe.

"I have nothing to say to you, Tiffany."

"You don't know me." I leaned slightly in. "Let me in for a second."

"Go to sleep."

And in one definitive move, he swung his arm and let the door fly. Without thinking, I thrust my right leg out, catching its heavy weight with my thigh and letting it slam against my muscle.

I screamed, falling forward, fighting through the sudden surge of pain. Dean bent to help me up, and I took the opportunity to plunge into his room. I let him drag me over to the couch by his bed.

"I'll need to sit for a second," I said, limping over to take a seat. "You really hurt me."

"Sorry," he said reluctantly. "But you just stuck your leg in the door."

"I didn't think you were slamming me out."

I massaged my leg slowly and counted out a full minute, letting Dean's discomfort grow.

"So Brad and Harrison are asleep?" I asked.

"They're gone."

"Gone?"

"They took a car back to the club. Lydia and Tabitha never answered any of their texts."

"They said not to worry about that."

"Well, they're worried now."

I let that sit until the silence was something palpable, heavy. Then I got down to it.

"Dean, how long have you known Weston?"

He sighed, seeing I wasn't going anywhere. "Long enough."

"Long enough for what?"

"You're not going to quit, are you? Fine. You want to know him? Really know him? Here's a fun fact: He has the worst taste in women. Never picked anyone remotely worthwhile. Gets devastated by the truth each and every time, becomes an inconsolable wreck for a couple weeks. And then he's in love all over again when another self-conceited blonde walks his way. Has he told you he's in love with you? Has he gotten that far yet?"

He looked at my face and laughed. I couldn't hide the truth from him.

"No, he hasn't. Maybe Weston's starting to learn a little."

"What, I'm not pretty enough?"

"What I'm talking about has nothing to do with looks. It's the opposite. He only sees the outside. He can't ever get a feel for what's behind the extensions."

"My hair is real, as is everything else on my body."

"Oh, I saw the real you. Downstairs in the lobby of the hotel. You're nothing but a shallow, fake fucking narcissist."

I leaned toward him. My knife was waiting, but I couldn't use it even if I wanted to, I was shaking so hard in fury.

"You tell Weston about that? About what happened in the lobby?" I finally said.

"Tiffany, I won't need to."

I leaned even closer, picked up the scent of Gucci, the same as Weston's, a slightly saltier smell mingled on Dean's skin. I tried to calm down. I reached to touch him, to lick the scent off my finger and see if he tasted like Weston, too.

Dean smacked my hand away. "Tell you what? I'm going to give you one minute to collect yourself, stand on your own feet, and walk the fuck out of here. Ice your leg back in your own room."

Then he turned his back on me, like he was the principal dismissing an unruly student. That would be the last time he ignored me.

"I need to go to the bathroom," I said.

The look on Dean's face told me he would carry me out if he had to.

"I'll leave right after. Promise," I said.

I walked the few feet to a tiny bathroom that was carved into a spare space against the wall of the bedroom. I locked the door and hit the light switch. One bare bulb flashed bright. I could feel its heat, and the blood rushed to my face. The ceiling was so low it seemed to be caving in. I hunched over the shell of the sink and splashed cold water across my cheeks, letting any remnants of makeup wash away. I could feel my heart, my head, pulsing. My leg was pulsing too—all these pressure points feeling like they might explode.

I pulled out the knife and turned off the light. I waited for my eyes to adjust until I could see the faint outline of my body in the mirror. Then I took off my top, letting the sequins scratch against my chest and arms. I peeled off my pants like they were a second skin. I unhooked my bra and stood naked, wearing nothing but my necklace, the light catching only the broadest curves of my body. I grabbed the knife and opened the door so that the darkness could no longer hide me.

Dean was startled. I had the knife behind me, and it took a second to realize it was my nakedness, not a weapon, that had him casting his gaze downward, sideways, everywhere but my waiting figure.

"Okay, you're having a rough night," he said. "Let's just get you back to Weston."

"I'm not ready to go yet."

"Look, this is not going to happen. You've clearly had too much to drink."

"Can you make me a whiskey?" I had him on the defensive now. He wasn't just going to dismiss me.

"Absolutely not. Put your clothes on. Or look, just leave, go to bed. I can walk you." And he came closer, looking at me for the first time, realizing what was behind my back. "Why do you have a knife?"

I glanced at it, feigning surprise.

"You're going to hurt yourself, put it down."

In lightning speed, I dodged his advance and aimed the sharp point of it at my throat. "Don't come any closer," I said.

"Look, I know your existence is pretty vapid, but this isn't the answer. Please don't pull a Valerie."

I bristled. "Who's Valerie?"

"Never mind. Just take a deep breath and give me the knife."

"What were they like?"

"I think you're in the middle of a mental breakdown. Just give me the knife."

"The ones that came before me, what were they like?"

"Weston's girlfriends? They were like you. Almost. Blond, skinny, a bit taller."

I brought the blade in closer to my skin, pretending it was Dean's throat. "Can I tell you a secret, Dean? You and Weston seem to have a lot of them, so I'll share one with you. I've never had a true purpose.

I've always been what you might call a bit *basic*. I'm good at plenty of things, sure, and I'm rich as fuck, which is always helpful, but I've never held a real passion for anything. Until now. Do you know what it feels like to realize what your calling is, what you were meant to do?"

"Sex is hardly a calling," Dean said.

"Do you think I'm trying to seduce you? Is that why you think I'm naked?" I laughed and brought the knife away from my neck. "I'm naked because I don't want to spill blood all over my clothes."

I waited a few seconds for the words to sink in, so I could see the full recognition across his face before I lunged at him.

I had starved myself these past couple months dating Weston. But it all came back to me—a rush of wild instinct.

I aimed and hit Dean's throat, the knife entering cleanly. When the blood bubbled out, warm and strong, we both knew he had no chance. I fell on top of him as a manic fury rose in me, my body tightening, making me impenetrable. I could no longer feel the pain in my leg. I could feel nothing but the reckless desire to kill. Dean screamed—and I went ahead and screamed with him.

I was back in the shadows of the club. Malcolm was there, laughing at me, his cigarette-stained teeth gleaming yellow. He was shoving neon pills down my throat, until I crumpled to the dance floor. Then I was in Dean's bedroom, stabbing him, until there was no flesh left to puncture, just an open wound, intestines spilled out like the soaked wreckage of a capsized boat. The roar of noise filled my ears: drums, music, and then the flash of a brush fire. I could smell the smoke rolling in from the hills. The fire was coming.

I woke, burning with fever, head pounding. I was wrapped in black sheets, naked. I took in my surroundings. Weston was warm beside me, snoring. I saw the strange angles of early-morning light against the window, the hillside in the distance, and realized I was back in our bedroom on the top floor of the rented mansion. Had the last part of the night been a dream?

The drumming from my nightmare turned out to be the beating of door knocks. They continued, frantic, loud. Then there was a crack and a rush of wind. People were in our room, yelling. Brad and Harrison.

The first wave of nausea hit while they were shaking Weston awake, screaming Dean's name. I caught mention of an ambulance. I rolled off the bed and almost puked over the side onto the hardwood. I had to drag myself on hands and knees naked to the bathroom.

Last night could have been a dream, but I knew it wasn't. It was all coming back. I had returned to Weston's bed, naked and wet, after taking a shower. After I had stabbed Dean, stabbed him over and over until there was nothing left of his chest. When there was nothing more of him to ruin, I had lapped up some of the mess, swallowed down his warm blood.

A sickening realization had come over me after the killing, the remembrance of the aftermath of previous murders: the questioning, the waiting, the visits to the lawyer.

And now: Weston's reaction when he woke up to the news.

I threw up.

I had wiped down everything that I'd touched in Dean's room, including the knife that I had left standing upright in him. I had returned from the shower, still frantic, until I settled for the spread of goodies downstairs, the bottles of Vicodin and Ambien. I had counted them out, still naked: three pills washed down with a heavy pull of Glenlivet. Then I had crawled into bed with Weston, ready to flush away the consequences.

I had welcomed utter oblivion—and it came. I could barely move my body apart from the uncontrollable spasms of nausea. I had completely wrecked myself.

The police arrived along with the ambulances, and Weston was questioned while I kept retching. It wouldn't stop coming. Things I hadn't remembered eating surfaced until it was just the clear burn of alcohol hitting toilet water. I missed the whole process of Dean being carted away. I would have liked to have seen how they got him on a stretcher.

The police had me wrap myself in a blanket before questioning me. They had more to talk about than just Dean. Lydia and Tabitha were still gone. Missing persons officially. Brad and Harrison hadn't found them.

They'd returned from the search in the early morning and noticed the wide-open patio door. Gone upstairs to check on Weston and caught the blood oozing out from Dean's room.

I didn't have much to say. I could barely tell how many cops were in the room; I could barely decipher what they were asking me. They suggested maybe I had been drugged at the club, and I agreed. I wanted the questioning to be over. Then I spotted Weston crying in a corner, hunched over, and I would have rather faced five more hours with the detectives than sit next to him, see his face twisted like that.

It was dark again when I finally could pull myself back into last night's clothes. I had refused to go to the hospital, barely allowing the EMTs to check my vitals. I was disoriented, hazy, weak. A completely different person from the capable, skilled killer who had murdered Dean. I had given my most believable performance yet. With Slade's help, hopefully it would be enough.

***

There wasn't much to say in the aftermath when the investigators finally left, and we'd been instructed to return to Weston's since the rented house was a crime scene. Weston was pretty much comatose that night, slowly rocking in his bed.

"It's not real," he whispered. "It didn't happen. Did it?"

"No," I said, and took the moment to sit beside him. I leaned into him. He was freezing. "It's all a dream," I said, stroking his hair.

What else could I tell him? This murder was going to have consequences. Why couldn't I have taken out a random loser at the bar? But just like the previous murders, I didn't regret it. I had done this for Weston. It would be impossible for him to understand. But I could fix this. He could get over it.

Two days after Dean's death, I drove Weston to LAX. The funeral would be on the East Coast. It was the first time I had ever driven someone to the airport.

At each red light, I searched Weston's face for any knowledge, any suspicions.

We arrived at his terminal.

"You have everything?" I asked.

Weston nodded. He hadn't spoken more than five sentences to me since that morning.

"I guess I'll see you in a few days. Just text me to let me know when to pick you up," I said.

I turned to unlock the car door, and Weston clutched my wrist.

"Wait," he said, so forcefully, so violently, that I feared the worst. They say liars never look you straight in the eye, so I willed myself and looked up, stared straight into his blue-gray eyes, waiting. Finally, he grabbed me in a hug, so hard and desperate it hurt. "Don't leave me."

He pulled me in, tightened his fist around my hair, until I feared he might rip it straight from my scalp. He finally leaned back.

"I love you," he said.

"Me, too," I said.

Then I watched Weston disappear into the airport security line. His broad shoulders and his tapered waist. I wanted it all. I circled my car out of the terminal and pulled over on an empty street off International Road. I picked a random plane starting its ascent and pretended it was Weston's, saw him rocket toward the sky, his words nestled in my memory, safe. He was leaving me, only for a time, but then he would be back, right where he belonged. He was mine.

20

"**Y**OU SURE YOU WANT TO HEAD THIS WAY?" THE UBER DRIVER asked. We were passing graffitied brick, barbed wire, muddy encampments. "You're well out of the Arts District."

I knew that. We'd crossed Skid Row a few minutes ago, past the craft breweries and organic coffeehouses that skirted the periphery of Downtown L.A.

Weston had been gone for a week now. In that time, there had been three more mystery murders. Mariposa Avenue. Abbot Kinney. Robertson Boulevard. An innocent-looking actress at her slummy studio, a bartender in a back alley, and a middle-aged investor in his Lexus. I wondered how many like me were out there, on our separate L.A. hunts. If we drove past each other at night.

"Keep going," I told the blond, leaning forward in my seat, my face inches from the back of his head. I could smell his shampoo, the clean scent of his aftershave.

Seven days had been the length of time it took for Dean's murder to stop marinating in my system, for the memory of that night to cool and leave me hungry for more. I was ready again.

Tabitha and Lydia had turned up two days after Dean's death, right after I'd dropped Weston off at the airport. They were found on the side of Sunset Boulevard near the 101 on-ramp. They couldn't remember any clear details, just that someone charming and complimentary had offered them drinks. The description of this blurry, irresistible suitor with no name would never match up to grease-dolloped Malcolm.

And if he was ever implicated, it was a fair bet he had more than enough money to take care of it. He was like me, in that way at least.

A narrative emerged, one Slade's legal team encouraged: that someone had been watching us at the club, had roofied the girls, and then had followed us into the hills. I was brought in for questioning again, but Slade was present every time after that first morning when I was barely coherent.

I had fucked myself up good on whiskey and painkillers. I looked frail, confused. I didn't even have to fake it. I had figured out my defense, the persona I needed to adopt for these questionings: the drugged-out, 110-pound girlfriend, confused, weak, just another version of Tabitha and Lydia with better hair and clothes. As soon as the cops had finished calling me in to the station, though, I knew I had to get strong.

Earlier in the night, I had parked my Mercedes off Seventh and Wilshire and snaked my way east on foot until I had found an Uber driver in a Prius parked next to the pressed crowd of an after-hours Mexican cantina. He had asked me if I was Melanie, and I had smiled and nodded. I hadn't even brought my phone.

I told him to ignore the destination routed on his app and directed him down Industrial Way to the city's edge. It took two sentences to convince him to park. He shivered in the cold, struggling with my skirt, bunching it up against my thighs in such a desperate, clumsy way that I felt oddly drawn to him, almost protective. I stopped him when he felt for my panties. I pulled him down to the sidewalk and told him to close his eyes as I felt for his belt buckle. I made sure he was relaxed, smiling, before I slit open his throat.

It was nice to have a murder off the radar this time, a clean kill like an impersonal business deal, no loose ends. I wouldn't even have to visit Slade afterward.

I was getting sick of his calls, his worries. His admonishments that I was putting myself in harm's way. Flying too close to the sun. He didn't understand that was what gods did, that I wasn't just a mere mortal anymore.

On my last visit, Slade had closed the steel door to his office, had me move from his behemoth marble desk to the leather chairs by the window so we faced each other, our knees almost knocking.

"I'm a bit troubled by the coincidences occurring in these cases," he started.

"Bad luck," I answered. "I was born with it. My father had it, too."

"You've got to be more careful, Tiffany. You're putting yourself in dangerous positions. Out the same night Tristan was murdered. In the same house as Jeremy."

"So?"

"There may come a time the detectives propose that it is more than coincidence, even though we both know that's ridiculous."

I had teachers who had told me the same things all through high school, that I wouldn't be able to cheat my way out of this one, that I couldn't have my nerdy little tutor take my SATs for me or bullshit my way through an interview. And sure, occasionally I'd be caught, and they'd gloat as they wrote their flimsy pink slips and sent me over to the administrative office, informing me that justice would be served on swift wings. And then what would come of it all? Not a goddamn thing. One call from my father's office, and I never heard about it again.

"You'll want to start thinking about your boyfriend," Slade said.

I ignored his concerned look and stared out the window, to the streets of Century City, all the glistening cars down there, driven by glistening men, waiting and ready.

"You know Weston is a person of interest. You said you care about him."

"I do."

"You might consider that next time you find yourself in another compromising position."

So I'd be more careful. I'd sharpen my craft and calculate every kill. I had the entire city to hide behind. I'd made my decision—I'd have Weston. And I'd have my murders when he was gone. Who said women couldn't have it all?

The sorority house didn't give a shit about the slain Uber driver when the news broke; they were more enraptured with another recent murder, one that had occurred in Malibu off the cliffs. An aspiring actress, clothed only in sand when they found her. It was better than any of the reality shows on Bravo. Death and sex only five miles away, where they could check out the crime scene and then get a tan.

Ashley and Julie were watching a press conference with the police chief on their phones when I returned from Century City. I heard words like "law and order" and "vigilance" and "justice." It was the same spiel that we had sat through back in the fall after the first murders on frat row. Only now the violence had spread, broadcasted to all the city. Good luck trying to contain the heat of whatever was igniting.

The girls were downstairs prepping for some sort of semi-casual event with tight jeans and school sweatshirts thrown over bare shoulders. Probably a bonfire or basketball game. I hadn't kept up with sorority activities since I started dating Weston. And I hadn't stepped foot in a frat house since I had killed Jeremy.

"Where are you going?" I asked.

"Stop the Stabbings," Ashley said. "A bunch of student groups are holding a vigil in the middle of the quad."

I hadn't heard about the event. I knew the school's Wikipedia page was continually being edited to "University of Strangled Los Angelenos."

The girls had moved to the kitchen, where Emily was filling up water bottles with vodka and shoving energy drinks into a backpack. I picked up pieces of the conversation.

"It's not safe here anymore."

"I'm looking to transfer. San Diego."

"That's just as bad. Too close to the border. Santa Barbara, that's where it's at. Better party scene anyway."

"There are triple the number of murders only ten miles south of here," Emily cut in, zipping up her backpack. "It happens every day. We're just hearing about it because it's on the Westside."

"That's the whole point," Julie said. "Celebrities live in this neighborhood. A-listers. That sort of thing isn't supposed to happen here."

Camilla had materialized behind the refrigerator like a magic leprechaun. "When I was volunteering in Detroit, I met a five-year-old who had been shot—twice," she said. "He had a wonderful attitude about it, though."

Camilla put on a brave act, but the word in the house was that even she was trying to transfer. The plus was our chapter had thrown out all volunteer requirements for the spring semester. The Panhellenic Association was desperate to keep students from leaving. We'd lost three-quarters of our new pledges, all the sad misfits who I knew couldn't last out a real hazing.

That night, alone in bed, I thought of Weston, his words before he left for Dean's funeral. I had so much to be happy about. But I couldn't be fully satisfied, not with the questionings and the mask I had to put on every day for my lawyer and the police, for the sorority house, and, especially, for Weston.

———

Then he returned, lighter and heavier at the same time. Weston barely spoke on the way home from the airport, and I worried he was stuck in some sort of morose daze, but when we got to his condo, he pulled a bottle of champagne from his wine rack. He announced that this was the first day of the rest of his life. I was all in.

To my relief, Weston never even mentioned Dean that night. Instead, he said he planned to get rid of his condo, quit his job. He said he was ready for some major changes. That worried me a little.

We had quick, serviceable sex after we had drained all the champagne. In the minutes before he fell asleep, Weston asked me random things: about my day, what I'd do after graduation, how my roommate was.

"Emily's not fat anymore."

"Good for her."

Weston played with my hair for a while, but he wouldn't sleep. He asked me strange things. "If you could go back in time to any place, where and when would you go?"

I didn't know if it was a trap. "Where would you go?" I asked.

"Medieval Ireland."

"I guess that would be cool," I said. "Me, too."

"I don't think you'd go for that type of thing," he said, looking at my transparent bra, my silk thong.

I shrugged. I couldn't share what was really on my mind, what consumed my thoughts through breakfast, through workouts, on my drives across town. I fed off the news reports, the deaths delivered by my hand and even the ones caused by the other nameless killers across the city.

I had hoped my murders would get more coverage, but Dean was already old news, and the blond Uber guy I had butchered downtown was out of the headlines, too. The women always got more press. Everyone liked to imagine them dead, what they were wearing, what they weren't wearing, if their dress was bunched up, their top pushed down, their tits dumped out of their bra cups. Dead guys couldn't compete with that sort of thing. I would never get the glory earned by whoever was stabbing young, soft women.

On Wednesday, I came home to roses leaned against my bedroom door. A bouquet of two dozen, a deep scarlet, so lush and full I could eat them. I plucked them up and headed to the kitchen for a vase. Finally, Weston was doing the things that went along with "I love you," inserting a little more romance into the picture instead of asking me about theoretical time travel.

I was cutting the stems over the kitchen sink when Mandy appeared behind me.

"What are you doing?"

"What does it look like?" I said.

"You're cutting those for Em?"

"What are you talking about?"

"Did you even check the note?"

I hadn't seen it. I snatched at a tiny rectangle of paper, just a simple ivory card with a typed note: *To Emily, the cutest DG.*

"She's not *that* cute," I said.

"Someone begs to differ," Mandy said.

"Is this just encouragement from the girls for her to stay skinny? A pity gesture because of her dying grandmother?"

"We didn't send it," Mandy said. "Came from a secret admirer. So I'll just take the flowers back."

"I'll give them to her," I said, clutching at the stems. I waited until Mandy had left the kitchen and reread the note. Then I crumpled it up and tore the petals off all twenty-four stems. I washed the remnants down the drain and let the disposal roar.

21

THE FOLLOWING WEEK, I RECEIVED TWO GOOD PIECES OF NEWS.
Camilla's transfer request had gone through, and she was off to
Utah. I came home one day to find Amy and Mandy setting up a fluffy
hammock chair in her bedroom. I let them take Camilla's old room. It
was a free-for-all, no more rules, and I loved it.

The second victory was that Weston had finally acted on his promise
to move out of the condo complex and into a three-bedroom Spanish-
style home in Mar Vista. We'd have more privacy, and I wouldn't have
to worry that Keith would spot me in the lobby and throw a shit fit
again. And first-time home ownership in this economy was a promising
sign pointing toward Weston's increasing financial worth. He was
feeling better, finally.

I told him I'd help coordinate the furniture. He'd need a longer
sofa, a couple of ottomans. He'd have an entire extra bedroom that I
was hoping to fill with some of my workout equipment. I wondered if
I could buy a Peloton to use in one of the spare rooms and pass it off as
a belated birthday present.

The next day, Weston drove me to check out the place after work.
The neighborhood was well maintained, though I noted the tricycles
and plastic trucks scattered across approximately half of his neighbors'
front lawns. When the wind blew in just the right direction, I could
hear the strangled screams of a toddler in the distance.

Domestic chaos aside, the house was fully worth the $2 million ask-
ing price. The kitchen was newly remodeled with granite countertops
and recessed lighting. The master bedroom could easily fit three cars,

and the backyard was large and manicured. There was no swimming pool, but the former owners had constructed an outdoor cabana, bar, and fire pit. I could get used to this. Maybe I'd start spending entire weekends over.

"You like it?" Weston asked. He already had a whiskey in hand even though I had brought champagne.

I wrapped my arm around his waist, felt the firmness of his side, and inched my fingers around his stomach. I felt rooted, not just by holding him here, but by the land underneath me. The entire place would be ours to fill.

"I love it."

We went through two bottles of champagne with dinner, though I barely had two glasses, and settled on the couch for an HBO binge session. Weston stroked my hair during the third episode, and I took it as the cue to swivel around and straddle him. He smelled good, that scent of man that I had missed when he was gone. The tingle of a few days of growth across his cheek. But he didn't kiss back.

"After the show," he instructed, pointing to the flat screen.

It was the first time Weston had ever turned down sex.

An hour later, we got ready for bed. I removed my eye makeup—I was slowly taking off more and more of my face each night, easing into greater intimacy—and was finding a spot in the new house to hide my makeup wipes and coverage, when I spotted pill bottles in Weston's bathroom cabinet, more than I remembered. I read through the familiar labels. They had tried to prescribe some of the stuff for me when my father died.

I thought Weston was already asleep when I returned to bed, but he grabbed my hand. He was hard, barely enough that it'd work, and I remembered back to when we'd first started dating, how strong and unmistakable his desire had been. I wanted that Weston back, the one ready to pounce on me, the one who took in every detail on my body like a starved prisoner. Even when I was on top, he'd meet my thrusts under me, then flip me over and finish me off no matter how many whiskeys in.

I wondered how long a thing like getting over a best friend's murder would take. My thoughts were interrupted when the bed started shaking. One of Weston's books rattled off the dresser. He shot up next to me.

"What is that?" he asked.

I yawned, ready to go to sleep.

"Your first earthquake."

———

The next day, I caught up on the local crime bulletins. Not much, just an old-fashioned rape, but it had happened in Bel Air, right outside the gates off Sunset, so people were in an uproar.

I was watching reports on Amy's tablet in the common room when Emily came down the stairs, clutching a bunch of chrysanthemums.

"Have you been taking flowers from me?"

I looked around. She was talking to me. Someone must have ratted me out.

"Why would I do that?"

"Mandy said three deliveries have come for me—and I've only gotten the one!"

All the girls were staring now.

"Look, I'm sure it's just a miscommunication or something," Amy said, stepping in between us. "You ever find out who Romeo is, anyway?"

Emily smiled, calming down. "Not yet. We've been messaging online."

"Sounds like true love," I said. "He'll probably turn out to have a family of five or be a twelve-year-old girl."

"Fuck you, Tiffany!" Emily said.

I jumped from my seat, ready to tear the flowers from her and hit her on the head with them, but Amy blocked me, and Emily ran back up the stairs.

"Be nice," Amy said. "Her grandmother is dunzo."

———

I dropped Weston off at LAX the next week. He was leaving again, this time for a conference in Omaha. He had protested, saying he could easily take a car, but I had insisted on driving him. I hadn't seen him in days. An undercurrent of dread had been building in me every time he texted that he was still at the office, that he was too tired to hang out.

"You have everything?" I asked, when I pulled my Mercedes up to Terminal 7, the same terminal where Weston had first told me he loved me, right after I'd slit Dean's throat.

"It's too late anyway if I didn't."

I took in Weston's sculpted jaw, the veins straining against the tan skin of his neck. He was as gorgeous as ever, even if his gaze had grown vacant.

I brought him into an embrace, locked lips and slipped my tongue into his mouth. He'd been smoking, I could taste it. He didn't even try to hide it anymore. I saw him slouched on his couch back at his place, cigarette lazy in his hand, not giving a shit. He was young and male, still at the age where letting everything go only made him hotter, James Dean deadly. His kiss was missing the emotion that he'd had that day he first told me he loved me. I wanted it back, even if it had sprung out of desperate, frenzied grief.

Weston pulled away.

"I better go."

Weston removed his compact black suitcase from my trunk and dissolved into the crowd of travelers.

On the drive back from the airport, I eyed every lone male under thirty on the street. The day was early, far too early to kill. My room was empty when I returned, and I remembered that Emily had mentioned visiting her grandmother in the hospital.

I locked the door of my bedroom before opening my safe. I'd built up a small collection of items in recent weeks: a class ring, a watch, a couple of nice wallets—all from my victims. I had nothing of Dean's, though. It was one of my greatest regrets.

I touched each valuable before settling on Stephanie's diamond ring, my most prized memento. I slipped it over my finger and waited for the wash of calm I usually felt when I wore it. It wasn't coming, so I slipped the ring off and put it in my mouth, rolled it around, feeling its crevices with my tongue.

I should have had a productive day applying a sheet mask and deep conditioning my hair, posting a few videos. I should have been brainstorming possible monochromatic color combinations for Weston's new house like a devoted girlfriend.

Instead, I lay in bed for most of the day, watching the sun slowly descend, not even bothering to check my phone for updates. When night came, I changed into dark jeans and a tight black tank. I pulled a black sweatshirt over my head and made sure I had my gloves. I tied my hair back and left through the bedroom window.

It took about twenty minutes at a crowded dive bar in East Hollywood to find the right guy. He was blond, as usual, but a little more slight than normal. I waited to catch his gaze and held it, before glancing to the exit. He was already tailing me as I got up from my seat, ready to follow me into the dark.

I ripped the blond open across the stomach in a narrow alley behind a deserted carpet store. I'd underestimated how quickly it would begin smelling, when you tore straight into a person's intestines with a long blade. I only had time to rip the silver Saint Christopher medal hanging from his neck before the stench overwhelmed me.

I had returned to the sorority house in a trance, my victim's necklace in hand, and had almost gotten to my safe when I tripped and fell hard to the floor. I had stumbled over Emily. She was back, sitting in the middle of the floor between our beds. She held a fresh bouquet of flowers as though she were clutching a baby. A bottle of rum was by her feet.

"What are you doing in the dark on the floor?" I asked, slipping the medallion into my jeans pocket, checking for any blood I might have missed. It had been a clean kill, and I had left my gloves in the car, but still, I worried. "You were supposed to be gone for the night."

"She's dead."

I froze on that second word. "Oh. Your grandmother. Sorry."

"Thanks," she mumbled.

"You wanna talk about it?"

"No."

As my eyes adjusted to the dark, I could see the hurt written all over Emily's face—not just anguish, but a hunger. I pulled out some Percocet from my dresser and started to tell Emily to take one every few hours, but she swallowed both pills dry.

"You're welcome," I told her.

"Who do I have to thank?"

"*Me.*"

She laughed. "You never gave a shit about her or me. Don't pretend to now."

"I know plenty about you. And I *am* sorry about your grandma."

"What's her name?"

"Who?"

"My grandmother."

"Trick question. You don't call her by her first name."

Emily took a pull from her rum bottle. I'd never seen her like this. She was being downright mean.

"You left your phone."

"Excuse me?" I said.

"Your phone's on the dresser. You've been gone all night without it."

"I'm on a tech detox." I glanced at her bottle of booze. "You should try a real detox."

Emily just laughed. "Maybe you're right."

———

The house had a meeting the next day to deal with Emily. I wanted to skip after her little tirade, but I got sucked in. Emily had left to take care of the funeral preparations. In Camilla's absence, Mandy led the meeting.

"Girls, Emily is an orphan now. A real one. And she's poor. Things are bad. We should do something special for her."

"What does she like to do, Tiffany?" Amy asked.

I shrugged. "She basically just hangs out at her grandmother's every weekend."

"She had started coming out to parties the last couple months after she got skinny," Ashley said. "She loves Captain Morgan and cat videos. What else? She's really good at math."

"Maybe we should look at donating some money for the funeral expenses," Mandy said.

"Her clothes suck," I said. "We can offer her a makeover, a new ensemble."

"That's a good idea," Amy said. "I like that."

"No shit, it's a good idea," I said. I needed to leave the house soon. I was headed to Weston's.

I had an overnight bag already packed. I was about to head up the stairs and grab it when I spotted the bunch of white orchids on an empty dining chair. I swiped a glance at the card, the swooping black calligraphy on pure white stationery addressed to Emily. It had been signed this time. *Malcolm.*

22

EMILY WAS GONE ALL WEEK. I USED THE OPPORTUNITY TO HAVE the safe in my room moved. My closet wasn't secure enough, not with the collection I had accumulated in the last few weeks. I had a new titanium safe placed under my bed, which I then bolted to the wall. I had three workers install it on a Monday afternoon when the other girls were in class.

The safe was now impossible to spy and could be accessed only by sliding beneath the two feet of space under the bed. I fell asleep that night curled in my comforter, secure in the thought that all my mementos were resting directly under me.

I had planned on staying at Weston's for the upcoming week. I didn't want to see Emily and that pained, angry expression on her face. I didn't make fun of her anymore, but I also couldn't muster the strength to pretend to care. So her grandmother was dead! I had lost a father, and my only regret was I still had a mother and sister. I thought of my stepfather. Death was nothing: it was far worse when you gained family members.

But Weston was barely back from his business trip when he had to leave again. Boston this time. He still hadn't trusted me with keys, so I'd have to remain at the sorority house.

Weston told me I didn't have to drop him off at the airport, that he was leaving at dawn, not on the usual red-eye. I was secretly relieved. LAX was a nightmare during rush hour, and since I'd already murdered someone nearby, I couldn't kill in the area again. I was trying to space the murders out geographically, to follow Slade's directions to stay inconspicuous.

I had told Weston to call me when he got in that afternoon. He finally rang around 5:30 P.M., well after I'd worked out and moisturized twice with shea butter and self-tanner. I was taking my late-afternoon nap in my room. Naps had become necessary on the days he was gone. I'd be up all night. The sun cast a hard ray of light over my bed when my phone vibrated.

Weston didn't have much to say.

"Business class was a joke. They sat me right behind a baby. A six-hour flight listening to the sounds of a screaming, rodent-sized human is a unique type of horror."

"Aren't you going to ask about my day?" I asked.

"Of course." He sighed. "What did you do?"

My weekly exploits didn't sound so interesting when I removed murder from my inventory of activities. I realized that sense of pride I wanted to share came from the twenty-year-old I'd killed on the beach last night. The stuff I *could* share didn't seem like much in comparison.

"Spin class. Then I found this stupid hot clutch."

"Good for you."

"Listen, I'll be free to hang out Sunday evening when you get back."

"We'll see. I'll be coming straight from a meeting, landing at ten at night. I've been feeling pretty tired. Jet-lagged, I guess."

It was true that Weston didn't get a lot of sleep. Some nights, the rare ones when I slept over at his place, I'd wake up to feel the bed shaking. I had first thought it was another earthquake. Then when I discovered it was coming from Weston, I assumed he was jerking off. The truth was even more uncomfortable. I heard a choking sound and realized he was crying.

It happened more than once. I'd lie there, not risking moving to reveal I was awake, and I could hear his sobbing. *You're a man,* I wanted to say. *You smell like leather and feel like stone. Why are you letting yourself do this?* I'd wait for the sounds to die out, until I'd hear his soft cries transform into ragged snores. Then I could finally roll over and get some sleep.

Other times, Weston would be angry, when he was between his fifth and sixth whiskey. That was an emotion I could deal with; that was something I understood.

"If I ever find out who murdered Dean, if I ever get alone with the guy who did that to him, I'll staple his fucking balls to his forehead."

"What good would that do?" I'd ask.

"I'm not kidding. I'll do it."

I'd try to change the subject, find something to watch on Netflix.

"Do you think he suffered?" Weston would ask on dinner dates while I was trying to enjoy a perfectly nice overpriced plate of sashimi.

"Why would you think about stuff like that right now?"

It didn't matter if I was wearing a low-cut dress or if I was standing over him in a thong. There was nothing I could do, no scanty clothes I could wear, to influence his train of thoughts when he was trapped in one of his moods.

"Do you think Dean suffered?" he'd repeat.

He was obsessed with re-creating those final moments. I wanted to tell him the truth: *If you want an answer, yes. He did.*

I saw Dean on the floor, his windpipe ripped straight open, incapable of making a sound, the pain all escaping out his eyes.

"So we'll meet on Sunday, if you're not too tired?" I reminded Weston, grabbing a knife from my desk drawer and settling back onto my bed. "Let's go on a date. In Westwood. Like we used to."

Weston was probably also in bed, settled on a starched comforter right now, looking out at some good-enough view of the Boston skyline, nursing a beer and the idea that I was touching up my nails, not heading out once the sun had stopped tracing its red path down the streets.

I wanted him to be like he used to be. How long would it take for things to go back to normal, for everything to settle down?

"Yeah, we'll do it," he said.

"I thought more about what you said a couple weeks ago. The time period I'd pick if I could go anywhere, any time."

"Yeah?"

"I'd stay right here, by the ocean, the studios," I said. "The twenties. Gold and art deco, champagne."

"That sounds like you." His voice was distant. "I'm driving back to the hotel now; I should go."

"You're not in your room?"

"No. And no driver this trip. I had to rent a car. The sun's in my eyes. I probably shouldn't be talking."

"Yeah, it's wicked right now," I said, realizing his mistake a second later. I jerked my head toward the window. "Where are you staying again?" I asked.

"The Hyatt. Lame."

"Okay. Be safe. I'll see you soon." I could barely get the words out.

I stood up and walked over to the window. The sun was almost down, sending its last lethal rays through the room. Weston had claimed he was in Boston, yet here we were, sharing the same sunset.

I tried to calm myself by holding Stephanie's ring in my palm, but even that couldn't soothe me. I slipped it into my mouth, letting my tongue run over its rough ridges. Nothing.

Then Ashley barged through, dressed in a cheap H&M top and cutoffs.

"Emily's coming tomorrow to pick up some clothes for the funeral. I need to go through her closet."

I motioned behind me to her tiny wardrobe, unable to speak. She rattled open the sliding closet door.

"Could she borrow a purse?"

"Sure," I said in a daze.

"I thought you'd be at Weston's. So where's he gone to now? East Coast?"

"Here," I said, a fury building inside me. The sun had burned down to darkness. "He's right here."

I watched the sky turn from gray to black. I waited for the tightness in my stomach to ease, but it only grew worse. My body was hardening, muscles straining against the weight of air. It was the feeling I got right before a kill.

The initial surprise that Weston had lied about his current location faded, and the question of why he needed me to think he was in Boston took over.

There was only one answer. All the crying, the histrionics, wasn't just about Dean. It wasn't just about a dead best friend. It was another woman. Women, maybe. That would be the only reason for pretending to be out of state away on business.

I spotted myself in the full-length mirror of my closet. Weight had started to creep back; muscle had slid over to replace the sharp angles connecting my thighs and pelvis. I wanted to punch my reflection, but I settled for tearing apart another one of Emily's flower arrangements. I dumped the ripped stems in the trash.

I changed into black jeans and a tank. I took the knife I had stabbed Tristan with and slid it under my right back pocket. I thought the weapon would be fitting.

I drove my Mercedes to Weston's ranch house, the place I'd helped decorate, where I thought I had finally marked my territory. I flew down sleepy side streets, crossing south of Santa Monica Boulevard. My mind raced through images of the slut Weston would be having over. I wanted to catch them red-handed in the act. I hoped they were fucking, right on the granite kitchen island. I'd douse the place in their blood and then set it all aflame.

I approached the house, turning my lights off when I was a few blocks away. Sure enough, Weston was home. The lights were on in the front of the house, the shades barely drawn. My hands tightened around the leather of my steering wheel.

I parked. I pulled the knife from my jeans, not bothering to keep it hidden. I didn't care if people saw; I didn't care what happened afterward. I'd only need to get into the house, past the front door, and surprise whoever opened. No innocent pretenses, no time wasted to ask questions, to find out why. I didn't need answers.

The grass was moist under my feet. I settled by the side window, facing the wide expanse of the living room. Weston was seated on the sectional we had picked out together. Alone. Something wasn't right. The TV was on. He was wearing a ripped college T-shirt and the flannel bottoms I had hidden in the back of his closet because they made him look like a middle-aged man. They were one of the few mistakes in his wardrobe. Maybe he was calling over a prostitute, so he didn't need to worry about his clothes. He didn't seem the type, but guys could be real fucks.

I needed to see the bedroom. I circled around the house to his window. He really should have installed the security system I had suggested.

No one was in the bedroom. The bed was unmade on Weston's side, and his room was full of clutter. None of it made sense. My instincts had been off.

I returned to the front of the house and settled in the bushes near the side gate, so I could watch Weston undetected. I stared at the back of his head, waiting for a doorbell, the sound of a car, a phone call. Something. Anything.

I moved into the shadows when he got up to make popcorn. Then he left for the guest bathroom and came back sans flannel pants, with a dab of wet on the front of his boxers. I watched him sprawl open-legged back onto the couch. I saw it all in the exquisite spot lighting of his living room.

Slow nausea crept over me as an hour passed, and I realized no one would be arriving. He was alone. Another hour went by, a World War II special, a motorcycle show. I had spent most of the night watching him from the window.

My rage became something else, something much worse. I tried to tell myself this was good, he wasn't going to have a gonorrhea-soaked orgy with a hooker, but I knew that would be better than the truth. I wanted to wash the scene I had just witnessed out of my head, the tableau of Weston arranged sloppily on the couch, preferring to munch alone watching car shows rather than spend time with me. I realized I wouldn't have minded as much if he had a whole menu array of side pieces. If he ate them out in bed, or literally impaled and ate them. The real secret he was keeping from me was much worse than either cheating or murder.

I still hadn't bothered to put the knife down and could barely feel my hand, I was so cramped from sitting crouched outside in the dark. I was hoping I'd still have some reason to use it. But there was none. My back was sore, my legs numb. I rested my forehead against the cold glass of the window. Weston was only five feet away. He hadn't moved in the past hour. He must have fallen asleep.

I had to leave. I got up slowly, my muscles tight, and crossed the lawn back to my car, quickening my pace. Then I slipped on the wet grass, falling hard onto my side. My hands flew down, and I rolled to avoid the blade underneath me. I landed right next to the knife, barely feeling the slice of its end across my thumb. I stuck my hand in my mouth and swallowed down the blood. Dazed, I stayed on the ground. I sat there on Weston's front lawn, bleeding, almost impaled by my own knife.

My memory flashed back, like a slice across my brain, to my father and his .357, practicing with him on the spare land over the cliffs behind our house. Shooting that gun was one of the few times I had spent time with him alone that he talked to me like a person.

While reloading, he had said one day, out of the blue, "I never loved your mother. That's a good thing, in the end."

The statement hadn't come entirely out of nowhere. He'd been home for the week, and the nightly screaming had been particularly bad, accompanied by shattered glass, the sound of flesh being hit bare-handed. I'd blasted music through my headphones and fallen asleep to syrupy pop each night.

He looked me over before handing the gun to me, barrel down. "You don't seem like the romantic type, either. You're like me."

I remember I had scoffed at the statement, taking in his leathery skin and age spots and crooked nose. *I'm* nothing *like you,* I had thought.

I'll marry the captain of the football team. We'll have everything to-gether, and he'll lick the ground I walk on. I won't make your dumb mistakes. I'll have it all on a fucking platter.

A thin line of blood rolled down my thumb across my wrist. I ripped a piece of my tank top off and wrapped it around my hand. I had to get back to the car. When I finally returned to the Mercedes, my grip across the steering wheel felt slick, and I saw blood streaked across its leather.

I had my answer. It was time to go. I headed east on the 10. I settled for a busy sports bar on the outskirts of Hollywood, just outside the moneyed boundaries of the luxury high-rises.

I found someone suitable immediately, a boy who could take my mind off Weston for a brief moment. He looked like he needed some-one to save him.

When we were alone outside in the dark, I let his hands stumble over my body, under my sweatshirt. I let him kiss me in the shadows, let him push his tongue into my mouth, detecting hints of citrus and cream, a softer taste than Weston's. Our lips finally parted, he took a breath, and I shoved the knife into his throat. With both hands, I ripped it across the width of his neck. It was a familiar motion, a tech-nique I had perfected completely.

Afterward, though, I felt sick. Dirty. I wanted to get rid of every surface we had shared, so I carved out his tongue and sliced off his lips, throwing the gelatinous remains into a dumpster.

I was choking, unable to take a breath. I realized I was crying, and that made me more nervous than the trail of blood I had left behind, the blood that had sunk into my clothes, turning everything a deeper black.

I calmed myself and walked the entire two miles back to my parked car, head in a daze, my thoughts back on Weston. He had lied to me who knew how many times, and yet I was the one who now felt guilty.

Guilt. Was that it? Was it that brief kiss I had shared with the boy before I ripped off his lips? Could it be cheating if I stabbed someone to the cadence of Weston's name, if I thought of him the entire time?

No, it was something else. The word fluttered in my mind, finally no longer out of reach. The thing that had led me to guard a window for four hours, that drove me around the city all through the night. The very thing my father had warned of.

I was in love.

23

Two days later, I stopped by Weston's place after his supposed return from his business trip. He had a gift from Boston waiting for me on the kitchen counter: a snow globe with a tiny city inside, tissue wrapped in a duty-free airport bag.

"It's still snowing over there," he said when he handed it to me.

I looked at it and fought the urge to shatter the thing against the wall.

"Are you okay?" he asked.

"I'm fine. How was your trip?"

"Boring. I'm glad to be back."

"Is that right?" I asked. I felt hopeful when I heard those words from him, ridiculous as it was. I alternated between anger and desperation. *Just tell me what I can do,* I wanted to insist. *Tell me what you need in order to forget Dean, to come back to me. To look at me the way you did before.* I shook the crystal ball and watched the snow fall down in tiny, endless flakes.

We ordered in for dinner. Chicken moo shu. We both didn't mention the past few nights, what we had really been up to.

Weston was reading all the time now, filling his library with stacks of books: compilations, histories, autobiographies. I tried to read a few selections to gauge where his mind was at, his current interests, but every title on his coffee table seemed to be more than four hundred pages, way too long to sift through for clues. He couldn't possibly hope to finish them all.

The CliffsNotes I found online told me nothing useful. The people and places blurred together; there were no love stories in the books I pulled off his shelf, mostly descriptions of valleys and hills, of brothers, of family betrayal and manhood. I thumbed through them, trying to start one with a thinner spine, but they were all about men: lost, beleaguered, boring men.

I went out a lot now. Every night I wasn't with Weston and even some nights I spent with him, those early nights when he was passed out on the sofa by ten.

I learned to never take chances. I had tempted fate a few times, played around with some of the boys a bit before the kill. But that shit didn't work when you were a woman. I couldn't afford to wait a beat too long.

I learned the hard way in a dingy, deserted bar bathroom one Tuesday night. I was taking my time, attempting to strangle a young bartender with his tie instead of the usual stabbing, until his left hand was suddenly free, and he punched me in the throat, knocking my breath away. I gave him a kick, and he threw me against the mirror so hard it splintered. I managed to land a fist to his temple, hard enough for him to stumble and give me time to find my knife and finish him off.

From then on, I was smarter. The element of surprise was my secret weapon, my advantage over muscle and weight. There was no shame in kicking a man straight in the balls each time; there was no room for waiting around for him to keel over, no stab too many.

My father had told me something similar, one night when I was off to a pep rally in my cheer uniform. He usually never said anything those rare nights he was home. But he had stood in front of me in the living room, looked over my clothes, and asked, "You know how to knee a fucker in the groin?"

"Sure," I said.

He smiled. "What about if someone grabs you?" he asked, and his hand was suddenly tight around my wrist.

I recoiled, almost panicked. He never touched me.

"Don't fight it like that. You stay calm, figure out where the thumb is and pull against that, quick and smooth. Try it."

I twisted my wrist against his thumb, a little jerky at first, but it worked.

My father taught me to escape. He had surprising skills like that, tricks he passed on to me even when I didn't want to listen, even when I didn't think I cared.

———

It was true that men had the advantage on me, but I had put on my own muscle in the past month. And I was fast. I was in top form now.

"Goddamn," Ashley said one day when I was heading for the shower in a sports bra and bike shorts, a towel tossed over my shoulder. "You're like 1999 Britney Spears. Where the fuck did you get those abs?"

I hummed now. I felt so tightly bound I might snap, so electric someone's finger might get zapped if they touched me. I fucked Weston hard on the few nights I stayed over. I'd swing one leg over him on the couch, grab tight around his neck, and thrust against him so rough I'd accidentally knock my head against his. He wouldn't finish much of the time, which was fine with me because it meant I could move on my own schedule. I'd get off him only after I'd gotten off myself. Then I'd go into the bathroom, splash cold water on my face, and try to slow my racing pulse.

I was realizing something powerful. The violence gripping the city, the growing headlines: I was a part of it all. I lived in the bloodred twilight of these crimes, even after dark when I was alone and the city was quiet.

———

After her grandmother's death, Emily pretended like nothing had happened. Denial was fine by me. She was back to her alcoholic ways, flask in hand. Everyone noticed she was plastered by 5:00 P.M. most evenings. What had started as normal college experimentation was turning into full-blown substance abuse. She almost had Smashley beaten. She was one meltdown away from her own nickname.

March came, and the end of another quarter approached. One evening, I walked in on five DGs sitting cross-legged on the floor of my bedroom, Emily in the middle like a sacrifice. My gaze darted to my bed, the safe, but everyone was on Emily's side of the room. There was no way they would be able to notice it under the bed beneath the floorboards. Still, I felt naked, vulnerable, with them so close to my hidden stash.

"Can you go to another room?" I said.

"No," Emily said.

"Excuse me?"

"We're hanging out here. Join or leave."

I sat down reluctantly, leaning against my bed.

"Tiffany," Amy said. "Fuck, marry, kill."

"Kill," I said immediately.

"No, you idiot. I have to say the names first."

She listed *Bachelor* contestants. I hadn't seen any of the new season. Julie gave me the new pledges from SAE instead, but I hadn't been to any recent frat parties. I couldn't answer.

"What's gotten into you, Tiff?"

"Nothing." I'd need an excuse. "I've been busy this year, getting ready to graduate. I have other, more important things on my mind."

"Like Weston?"

My stomach dropped. I had left him last night passed out, whiskey in one hand, book in the other.

"Relationships take up a lot of time. They require work."

"If it means missing *The Bachelor*, I'll stay single," Amy said. Everyone laughed.

The girls didn't leave until past midnight. Emily was piss drunk by the time everyone finally packed it in for the night.

I climbed in bed and tried to read one of the novels that I'd pulled from Weston's library. I couldn't get past the second page.

"You ever read this book?" I asked Emily, motioning to the cover.

She stopped and focused her eyes on the title. "Yeah, senior year. It's pretty famous."

"Well?"

"They all die at the end."

I took one more glance at it and threw it onto the bedside table.

All the girls were still doing nice things for Emily, making her cards and baking gluten-free pastries. I ignored her previous meltdown and let her borrow some of my clothes—out of season, of course, along with the outfits I had worn twice with Weston and, as much as it pained me, a couple of pieces that no longer fit across my thighs and ass.

Emily was trying on one of my skirts, admiring the high cut against her legs. "I think I might wear this on my date with Malcolm Thursday."

It was the first time she'd mentioned him. I had never told her I'd found his name on those orchids. I'd forgotten all about Malcolm in the weeks following Weston's lie. How they had connected online beat me, but I didn't care enough to ask. Still, I thought about that night at the club, how easily he had wormed his way up to Lydia and Tabitha. Emily would be an even cleaner target.

"Why are you interested in Malcolm?" I asked her.

"Look at all those flowers." She motioned to the greenhouse on her side of the room. She had refused to throw out any of the arrangements, so half were dead, dropping dried-up petals over her dresser.

"Tell the truth: You're not interested in him. You're just interested that he's interested in you."

"What's the difference?"

"Let's be real here: you're not a ten by any stretch of the imagination, but he's way below you attractiveness-wise."

"He seems nice."

"I thought you said you wanted a bad guy."

Emily shrugged. "And I don't care about looks."

I laughed. So she had fallen into that trap.

"You do realize that ugly guys can also be total shitbags. I hope you don't think, 'Oh he's got a potbelly and bad hair, he'll be so grateful if I let him stick it in.'"

Emily was shaking her head. "What's wrong with you?"

"I'm warning you: Malcolm's not a nice guy. And he's not the kind of bad guy you're looking for."

"It sounds like you're jealous."

"Don't flatter yourself."

I had performed my big sisterly duties. My obligation was fulfilled.

"Stay out of my life," Emily said.

"Done and done," I said. "Learn the hard way."

———

Weston had a thicker book now at his bedside, tattered and yellowed from the first time he read it in high school, two men on the cover, locked in a fatal embrace.

"Looks boring," I said.

"Hardly," he answered, and kept reading.

I left Weston's early that night. He had a morning meeting the next day in Burbank, or so he claimed. I was forced to admit that I had no idea what he was really doing or thinking half the time, if it was a mindless wall of silence or intricate avenues of activity racing through his brain.

I had planned on setting out for Hollywood, but hunting on weekdays had been slow. Nobody worth killing found himself alone at a bar on a Thursday at eight.

So I was back at the sorority house with nothing to do. The girls were getting ready for a party at Pike. There was a time I would have been with them. Only last year I had gone the entire school calendar without missing a single rager.

Things were different now. For one, we couldn't publicize any of the parties. We couldn't post a single photo. We couldn't invite non-Greek members to the fraternities, and the total head count had to be under fifty. That just made it all the more closeted and crazy, according to reports from Ashley. Themes were gone, not because they were against policy, but just because no one wanted to pretend that these parties were anything other than reckless drinking and fucking. Without documentation, it no longer really mattered. No rules, no limits.

Ashley asked to borrow my straightener during her pre-partying. She reeked of weed and Smirnoff.

"You coming out tonight?"

I considered the offer. The alternative would be sitting in my room alone, watching Emily's flowers wither, waiting for Weston to text.

"I think maybe I will," I said.

"Shit, that was a joke. Well, toast to that. Vodka?" she motioned to the handle next to her.

"Champagne."

"I hope you like Roget."

I hadn't set foot in a frat house since Jeremy's demise back on Halloween. I wanted to witness the ferocity of a party again. I hadn't worn something slutty in weeks. I settled for a red micro-mini Versace dress. I headed to the bathroom to shower.

When I returned to my room, I found Emily on her bed staring at herself in the closet mirror. Something was off. I started to make out the lines of her dress: chic, fitted, designer. It was obviously mine, but not from the set I had let her borrow. She stood up, and I realized what was wrong. Emily was in my black-and-white Dior dress, the one I had worn the night I murdered Tristan. Her skin stood a shade in between the two contrasting colors, and it hugged the jagged curves she'd developed from a liquid diet of booze.

I searched for blood on the dress, across her chest, down the body of it, though I knew I wouldn't find any. I hadn't been wearing it when I had slashed Tristan open; the dress had already been flung onto his bed by the time I had found the knife. But all I could see was bright, screaming red.

"Take the dress off." The words came out in a whisper.

"It was at the bottom of your closet. You haven't worn it in months."

"You're not wearing that to the party. Take it off."

"I'm not going to the frat party. I have a date with Malcolm tonight, remember?"

"Take it off."

Emily didn't move. "It wouldn't fit you anymore, anyway."

I lifted my arm, closed my hand into a fist, and swung hard at her dresser, shattering one of her flower vases.

"Why can't you let me have this? You have everything!" Emily motioned around the room. "Why can't you just say 'Have a nice time?' Why do you need to ruin everything for everyone? Do you understand how much people hate you?"

"It's not your dress. Give it to me. Don't make me say it again."

Emily was undeterred. "What's your plan, Tiffany? Who are you going to take your venom out on after you graduate? When you're not top bitch? Your entitled bullshit won't work in the real world. It barely works here."

"And who do you think you are? At least I have a boyfriend."

"Do you?"

I caught her knowing look, and my stomach dropped.

Emily kept going. "You listen to me for once: I'm keeping the dress on, I'm going out, and you can just do whatever weird shit it is you do alone all night. Yeah, you don't think I notice you leave almost every night? I don't butt into your life. Stay out of mine!"

She didn't even wait for an answer. I listened to the clumsy racket of her heels on the stairs, the slam of the front door.

"Your funeral," I whispered.

I was frozen for a second until Ashley burst in with a bottle of Malibu.

"Is the catfight over? It's party time."

———

I hadn't missed much, I quickly realized, after arriving at the Pike house party. I found myself upstairs immediately, since the prohibitions had sucked the money for a DJ dry. With no themes, no DJ, no crowds, everyone filled up a Solo cup and set off for a bedroom. Amy and Ashley had joined me, but they quickly paired off with second-years. I was left with Jimmy, a third-year econ major from Ventura with nothing to his name but top-shelf liquor and a BMW. That was good enough for tonight.

"Where's your roommate?" he asked.

"Off making horrible decisions."

"Sounds awesome."

Maybe I was wrong about that night at the club on Weston's birthday. The drinks, Tabitha and Lydia's disappearance. Predators were everywhere. It was in the news each morning. Maybe Malcolm had nothing to do with it at all.

"Don't you have a boyfriend?" Jimmy asked me, starting to pour me a cup of Tito's.

"No vodka. I'll take whiskey, your most expensive stuff. And yes, I have a boyfriend."

"Then why are you here?"

"It's not cheating to go to a party, to sit and talk," I said. *Or to gut you later in the night after you pass out.*

"Sure. But you haven't been to a Pike party this year. I'd remember. We're not baking cookies around here. We rage, and we fuck. Are you lonely or something?"

His question threw me a little, and I answered honestly. "I guess."

He felt for the nape of my neck, rubbed my shoulders, massaged the back of my scalp. It felt nice; I couldn't remember the last time Weston had touched me like that. I closed my eyes. Then I felt my head slowly sinking. I realized what was happening as his hand tightened around my hair and he pressed my head toward his lap. I spotted the hard-on stretching his jeans.

I jerked upright.

"Cut it, Jeremy."

I should have known better in a frat house.

"Whoa, I was getting all the signals. And it's Jimmy."

"What?"

"My name is Jimmy."

I looked for my purse. I was stupid to come to a party in the first place. I couldn't murder Jimmy anyway; there were fifty people all sardined in the upstairs rooms and hallways.

"Wanna see something cool?" Jimmy asked.

"Your dick doesn't deserve that descriptor."

"No, something else."

He grabbed for one of the top shelves, where most members stored their choicest weed. He pulled down a small wooden chest and opened it, revealing a pistol.

"This is a .44."

That got my attention.

He moved his red cup to his left hand and balanced the gun in his other.

"What do you think?"

"What's it for?"

"Protection. These murders, this shit, it ain't happening here, not in this house. We all have guns."

"We?"

"The brothers. There's one gun in every room."

My heart skipped against my chest.

"Have you ever fired one before?" I asked.

"Are you kidding me? Of course I have."

He aimed the pistol at his window, then at a Playmate poster, pretended to blow out each tit. Then he turned toward me. His hand was curled tight around the trigger as he leveled the barrel directly at my head.

"Don't do that," I said.

"Don't be scared," he said, and laughed. "The thing's not loaded. I'm not stupid."

I kept my eyes locked on him, body frozen, until he finally lowered the gun.

"See?" he said, popping the chamber open and holding it upside down. Two bullets bounced onto his bed. "Shit, my bad."

I got up to leave.

"Trent must have reloaded it or something," he said.

"Nice meeting you." I dropped my drink on the floor and was out the bedroom door before he'd put the gun back in its box.

I jogged home, thinking about every Pike member with a loaded gun. It was only a matter of time. This city was about to explode.

24

WHEN I RETURNED TO THE SORORITY HOUSE, I FOUND Emily blocking the doorway into our room, curled up on the floor in her underwear, and I knew I was right—about Malcolm, about everything. Little did she know she was lucky just to be alive, to be deposited back in the house and not thrown out by an underpass.

Still, I knew what it felt like, that first night when you stumbled home unsure of what had happened hours before. Every sorority member had her own version of the same story, her own morning after to deal with. I remembered that first week as a freshman. I had met a Malcolm, had had to trek back in last night's clothes, wondering if the blood collecting between my legs would reach my thighs before I arrived at the dorm. It was typical first-year stuff. You wised up and moved on.

I sat down on the bed and faced Emily. "You know, the same thing happened to me."

Her shadowed form moved slightly, but she didn't speak for a minute. "Was it Malcolm?" she said finally.

"No, someone else," I said. "I can't remember his name anymore. You'll forget, too."

"I don't think so. And don't pretend you're like me. We have nothing in common."

"I was just trying to help," I said.

"None of this helps, if you're actually trying to be nice. But I don't care anymore. I know the truth about you."

My stomach dropped. "And what would that be?"

"You're just a giant fake. I figured that out a long time ago."

Emily spent the entire night on the floor in our bedroom. I didn't want to see what she looked like in the morning light, so I stayed in Mandy and Amy's old room. I never saw my Dior dress again, but I didn't imagine I'd want what was left of it.

I could have stayed with Weston, but I wanted to be close by, just in case Emily got it in her brain to snoop around the unattended bedroom, hunt among my things. I ran through the inventory: I had a knife stuffed in a dresser, some rope in the back of my closet, a pair of pliers behind the overhead mirror. None of the weapons had been used, of course, so they were untraceable. I was leaving in the night so often it was convenient to have spares close by to save me shopping trips.

I entered my room a couple times each day when I was sure Emily was in the bathroom to grab my clothes and quickly dart my head under the bed. It was killing me, being away from my safe, but I also couldn't be in the same room as Emily.

Four days passed, and I returned to my room to find Emily dressed in knockoff sweats and a school sweatshirt. Mandy was talking to her, patting her on the back.

"Love you, girl," Mandy said.

Emily brushed past me, silent.

"She doesn't want to see you," Mandy said.

"Yeah, because I told her the truth about Malcolm. She should have listened to me." I paused. "What happened?"

"What do you think?"

Mandy spread the news in greater detail that night, when the girls were herded into the living room after Emily had stumbled back to bed.

"She wants to press charges," Mandy explained, "drag the whole house into this."

"I mean is that necessary, though?" Ashley asked. "We barely get to party as it is. She technically doesn't remember any of it, so how does she know? Every frat is blackballing Malcolm. He won't ever step foot in a party again."

"What Emily needs is a romantic comedy," Mandy said. "And ice cream."

———

Weston came over to the house the next evening to take me to dinner. We hadn't seen each other in a week. He arrived in his Porsche fifteen minutes early, and I wasn't close to ready.

"Can you give me a few minutes?" I said, when he called from the driveway.

"You know, I've never seen your room."

That seemed impossible. He'd picked me up from the house dozens of times, but it was true. He had never been upstairs.

I told him no problem, come up for a second, but I didn't like it, seeing him enter the sorority house, cross my room, and sit on the bed, right over my safe. Weston didn't belong among all the plush pillows and mirrors.

He clearly felt the same way.

"Will you be ready soon?" he asked.

"Yeah."

"Is that my book?" he said, glancing at the bedside table.

"Oh, yeah. You let me borrow it."

"I did?"

"Of course. Don't you remember? You had been drinking."

It was so easy to pull out a lie like that. Weston's slushy memory was the only alibi I needed.

"How do you like it so far?" he asked.

"Like what?"

"The book."

"It's interesting."

I left for the bathroom to finish straightening my hair. When I returned, Emily was in the room on her side of the bed, facing Weston, both their hands on their laps.

"Will it get any better?" Emily asked.

"I don't know," Weston said.

I felt a drop in my stomach. Were they talking about me? Did they ever speak when I wasn't around? I remembered when I had watched Weston and Dean, their sweaty foreheads touching at the club. Like I was a million light-years away.

I stepped into the room. "Let's go, Weston."

He shook his head, as if coming out of a dream. "I'll get the car started."

"What were you saying to him?" I asked Emily.

"He's missing something. Weston. He's lost."

"Thanks for the tip, Emily. How about you worry about your own life? Have another drink."

"I'm not drinking anymore." Emily motioned to the lime-green Gatorade in her hand.

"A bit late for sobriety, isn't it?"

"It's my first week."

"How do you feel?" I asked.

Emily put her Gatorade down and settled on the bed. "Like road kill."

She looked up at the ceiling.

"You think Malcolm will ever be punished?" she asked.

"He's pretty rich," I said.

"Right. So no chance in hell. That's what I thought."

I shrugged. It was the truth. What more was there to say?

25

I HIT A NEW BAR THE NEXT NIGHT, IN A GAUDY PART OF HOLLY-wood south of Sunset. I told myself it was necessary, that I had to visit a different part of town each time for safety, to remain unrecognized. It was only a coincidence that it was one of Malcolm's usual spots.

I took the bus over and watched the streets get dirtier as more and more bodies crowded into crusty carpeted seats. There were three of us when we began the route in Westwood. By the time the bus reached Cahuenga Boulevard, it was standing room only. It would be best to get off a few stops early and walk the rest of the way.

I glanced at a warning sign on the window: SEE SOMETHING, SAY SOMETHING! Everyone around was on guard, suspicious. I fingered the knife that sat under the waistband of my jeans and wondered if he'd be there.

When I arrived at the club, I ordered a vodka soda at a bar with glitter embedded in the counter. The place was decorated in all gold: curtains, tabletops, and gilt picture frames empty of photos. I was still nursing my first drink when I spotted Malcolm. He was dressed in a silver button-up that looked like scales on a fish. I imagined he smelled that way too: the scent of sardines and spoiled, soft flesh.

He saw me minutes later after I had settled behind him, just far enough back that he could think he had spotted me, that he was the one out hunting tonight.

"Tiffany," he said, proud of himself.

I pretended to be flattered he knew my name, the whole time thinking, *This can't possibly work. How could someone like him think I'd be the least bit interested?*

Malcolm was used to getting what he wanted. And he could be nice when he tried, sending flowers, cute notes. This was one of his mean nights, though; I could tell already. He snatched my vodka soda and placed it on the counter, still half full, and then thrust a new drink in my hand. He ordered me to drink up. I clinked my glass against his, and I drank it right down, in two hard swallows. It tasted metallic, not quite right.

"Whew," I said. "Went right to my head."

"That shows it's working," he said, his tongue sliding out for just a second across his front teeth.

"I need to pee. Be right back."

He grabbed my arm suddenly, before relaxing his grip and letting me go. "Make sure to head right back. I'll be waiting."

I slipped off to the bathroom and found the last gold stall. I didn't bother politely masking the sound I made when I pressed my index finger against the back of my tongue, the splash against the side of the toilet bowl. I needed to make sure I had vomited out every ounce of his deadly brew. When I was done, I checked for my knife and moved it from the elastic of my waistband into the inner pocket of my leather jacket.

When I emerged from my stall, the girl at the sink stood so close she could have been my shadow. She handed me a toilette to dab at the mascara that had pooled at the corners of my eyes. She put a mint into my palm. I gave it one strong suck and then cracked it into tiny pieces.

"There you are," Malcolm said when I returned. He took my hand in his and gave me a forced twirl, eating up my figure with his eyes. I pretended to be off-balance like he expected.

"You wanna go on a moonlit drive?" he asked.

He pressed his hand against the small of my back before I could answer, and I let him propel me through the crowd to the exit.

"Car's parked around back."

He opened the passenger-side door of his black Lamborghini and helped me inside. All these gestures of what might be interpreted as chivalry by a naive girl were just reassurances that he was in control of the situation. He would have strung me up like a puppet if he could.

He slammed the door and took his place behind the wheel. I noticed how far he needed to pull up his seat to reach the gas pedal, his gut folded into the underside of the wheel.

"Where are we going?" I asked.

"Surprise."

He accelerated in one startling push and began weaving across two lanes on Sunset.

"I've seen you around at parties," Malcolm said. "I feel like I already know you. What year are you?"

"Fifth-year."

"Almost out of here. Me, too."

I leaned against the headrest to avoid having to see that stomach, squished into the angular lines of the car's interior. Malcolm took it for fatigue.

"You look tired. Let yourself rest."

I had gloves tucked inside my leather jacket, and I worked my hands into them.

"What happened to those short, skimpy dresses from last year?"

"This is a little subtler."

"You look like a dyke. No offense."

There it was: that edge. I looked down at my dark Levi's jeans, my black Calvin Klein V-neck tee. I enjoyed dressing this way. I could move with freedom, second only to when I was wearing nothing at all. I thought of when I approached Dean that night, naked and glowing, a little drunk.

"I get it," Malcolm continued. "You put on a few pounds between school terms. Can't wear those micro-dresses anymore."

He had no eye for detail. He couldn't see the muscle hiding under the fabric, didn't notice my body tighten as I bit the side of my cheek.

Malcolm was driving north, toward the hills. Close to where I had killed Dean, but farther east. We passed a sleepy neighborhood, and I realized he was taking me to Griffith Park. He took the tourist route, right below the sign, residential houses within easy earshot. He was doing it all wrong.

"You want to stop here?" I asked. "What about farther out? There's a fire road that takes you right to one of the back gates. It's secluded. Romantic."

He glared at me, no doubt furious I was still conscious. I couldn't help myself. I didn't want him to ruin everything by picking a busy location.

"I hike near Canyon Drive all the time," I said.

"Hey, how about you shut the fuck up and let me drive?"

"Okay, I can do that."

I put my hands up, helpless, confused. Like I wasn't used to harsh words, like I hadn't been raised on the screams of men. I settled back onto the leather headrest.

But Malcolm took my direction, turning off the busier street and heading slightly east, into the darkness of unlit roads.

He was getting nervous. I could hear the creak of leather as he clenched the steering wheel tighter. Good. I let his feelings excite me, since his flaccid body sure wasn't going to. I knew he wanted me quiet, but I wasn't ready to let him off so easily.

"There's a mountain lion roaming around here," I said. "It crossed the freeway over six lanes of traffic."

"I don't think we'll have to worry about him tonight."

I wanted Malcolm to think he was still in control.

"You really fucked up my roommate," I told him.

"Who?"

"Emily."

"Oh, her. I didn't do anything really. I don't know what her problem is. No sense of humor. I was just playing around."

Malcolm turned toward me and squeezed my thigh.

"You like games, right?" he asked.

I looked around. We had finally pulled away from the glowing tower of houses in the hills.

Malcolm was smiling, squeezing my leg hard, trying to gather courage. I could read his face so easily.

"I barely touched Emily. What do you think I'm going to do to you?"

I shrugged.

"Are you scared?"

"Extremely."

"You're pretty stupid, coming out here with me. Of course you are, look at your face. You made a big mistake. Daddy's little checkbook won't get you out of this one."

"My father's dead," I stated flatly.

Malcolm attempted to pivot. He was still nervous, but he was starting to get that angry rush. I felt it, too.

We arrived at the gates, ten feet high, set up against a sloping valley of brush guarding the entrance to the park. Its doors wouldn't reopen until sunrise.

I continued to hold it all in, feign fear. I had come so far, suppressing my urges for the proper moment. I wondered if I could do everything I wanted with Malcolm while leaving all his clothes on. I wanted none of his fleshy gut and stray hairs.

I waited until he parked. When Malcolm unbuckled his seat belt and started fumbling for the belt of his pants, I figured that was as good enough a time as any. I didn't want to press my luck. Any sane, defenseless girl, however stupid and oblivious, would flee at this point, so I opened the door and ran, but not too quickly, toward the park's interior.

"What the fuck do you think you're doing?" he called. "Where do you think you're going?"

"Get away from me," I yelled half-heartedly. I stopped at the gate as if unsure if I'd climb over it. I took the time to tighten my gloves. I had to pretend like I didn't know exactly what was about to unfold. Maybe I should trip, sprawl out on all fours for a second, to let him catch up.

I lifted myself up and began scaling the gate, intentionally sloppy, as if I couldn't just vault over the final portion. Even going my slowest, I dismounted easily onto the bed of dirt below before Malcolm had even scaled the top. His flashy dress shirt caught on the top spire. He tore the shirt loose, slipping and landing hard on his back in the dirt. He didn't get up for a few seconds, and I checked to make sure he was still conscious.

A guy like him should have used a gun. Lucky for me, it was just the two of us and my blade. Looking at him bent over and coughing up the pack of cigarettes he had smoked at the club, I decided this must be his first time with a conscious victim.

"Where are you, cunt?" he screamed, stumbling to his feet.

"Over here," I helpfully offered, walking backward slowly, carefully, toward a nice open clearing deep within the park. I pulled out the knife, practicing the clean slice I'd deliver to his stomach right below the fold of fat. He jogged right to me like a filthy animal.

The truly amazing thing was that up until the end, the very end— after I had led Malcolm a half mile deep into the park, disarmed him, taken out both his kneecaps, and ripped off his pants, gotten him stripped and naked—it wasn't until those very last moments, flat on his back, that he finally realized he hadn't won.

26

THE NEXT MORNING, I WAS IN SUCH HIGH SPIRITS THAT I bought Sephora samplers for the entire house. It was easy to be benevolent, to share my wealth, when I had everything. I hadn't felt this good in weeks. I always felt better the day after a kill.

I gave Ashley the Clinique and Yves Saint Laurent, the best of the bunch, so she offered to make me breakfast in return. I settled at the head of the table in the dining room. Camilla's old place.

Ashley served me a plate of poached eggs over toast with a side of spinach. No bacon, but I could handle it. I dug in.

The news came sooner than I expected, brought by Amy on her iPad.

"Another murder. Guy this time, young," she announced casually, until she began skimming the details. Then she put down her avocado toast. "Fuck me," she said, and started reading the police report aloud. This wasn't another run-of-the-mill murder.

I stabbed the egg on my plate with my fork, letting the yolk spill over the bread and soak through. I took a bite.

A hiker had found the body. Or smelled it, to be more precise. The descriptions were graphic, and some of the details surprised even me when articulated in raw, clinical terms.

"They say he may have been conscious while he was tortured," Amy said, finishing up the article.

"That's impossible," Mandy said, pointing at her phone. "No one can stay awake, much less alive, while having his dick and balls shoved down his throat. I accidentally kicked Dan in the nuts one time during foreplay, and he was out for like ten seconds."

Ashley joined in: "TMZ is saying it was the coyotes that killed him, technically."

All the girls were fixated on their phones, finding their own sordid addition to the story, tapping furiously on their screens. Every major newspaper and tabloid had picked it up in a matter of hours. Finally, a kill worthy of national attention.

The girls were transfixed by the varying accounts, all the possible scenarios of torture. I had to bite my lip; I wanted to tell them there were no competing theories at play, whether he'd been raped, stabbed, or strangled. I'd done all those things during the course of the night.

I wondered how long it would take to ID Malcolm. Even though I'd cut up most of his body, I'd taken care to leave his face largely intact. I'd had to break his jaw to get his mouth open wide enough, but I took care to do little else to his face. I wanted his parents to see what I'd done to their little prince. I wanted them to have to confirm the slab of meat left of him.

I finished my eggs, and Ashley took my plate. I had a day of business ahead. Self-maintenance had taken a back seat over the past month. I now consolidated all my cosmetic endeavors to just one day a week. I drove out to Brentwood for a nail appointment first. I had split the side of my thumbnail and broken two nails last night. They'd need to be kept short, no acrylics, but that didn't mean they couldn't still be feminine. I settled for a lilac gel, something soft for the approaching spring.

Next, I had a waxing. I had started rotating appointments at spas around the Westside. I didn't want too much attention drawn to the various marks and bruises that kept appearing on my thighs and shins.

The aesthetician at a small shop off Sawtelle Boulevard had me take off my pants and get on all fours across the table, and I thought of last night when Malcolm had been on his knees, right before he'd given up his last piece of dignity and started to beg.

He had rattled on, still thinking I might turn him loose because of his parents' money, not understanding my family's net worth was more, that him thinking money could be any enticement only made me angrier. I easily sidestepped his attempt to grab my ankle in the darkness of the park. I hit him hard against the side of the head and rolled him onto his back, ignoring his screams.

"Could you quiet down? I need to concentrate," I told him.

"What are you doing?"

That was the moment the terror had set in, that look that made it all worth it.

I ripped his pants off and spread his legs. I hadn't anticipated the growth of hair burrowed down there—it stretched down half his fucking legs. I had to rip some of it out with a pocket knife just so I could find his excuse of a dick.

His screams had turned guttural at that point in the night, gurgled, like he was swallowing down blood.

I told him, "I have to be delicate about this. You need to be silent."

He had quieted for only a moment, until I brought out the scalpel. He screamed the rest of the way.

I was on my stomach now, just finishing up the procedure, the smell of hot wax tingling my nose. The aesthetician spoke for the first time in the last hour.

"You take pain well."

"You have to, if you want to look good," I said, as I bent to slide my underwear back on. A candle nearby gave off the scent of mandarin and rose. I spotted blood on my panties, tiny pinpricks rising to the surface of my skin.

———

When I returned to the DG house, everyone knew the corpse was Malcolm. I hadn't been keeping track of the news during my errands. I'd accidentally left my phone in my bedroom again. The last time I had scrolled through my socials was earlier in the afternoon, when #DeadCoed had popped up on my feed as trending. The story had already gotten twelve thousand views.

"How did you not hear about this?" Mandy asked. "It's blown up across socials. There's even a hashtag for it now."

I glanced at her phone and spotted it: #HeAteHisOwnDick.

"I left my phone in my room," I said.

She looked at me like I'd just admitted to eating a dog. "How could you do something like that?"

Of course it hadn't been an accident. I couldn't take my phone with me when I left most nights; I couldn't risk the GPS tracker, any chance of surveillance that could be blinked on in a second by investigators confirming my alleged alibi. Phones never lied.

At first, leaving without my iPhone had terrified me. I felt stripped down, more bare than the hundreds of times in my life when I had actually been naked. Just a year ago, leaving my phone over in the next room would have been unfathomable: the potential for missed texts, refreshed videos.

Then something started to change on those nights when I was out by myself. I began to pick up the sound of my heartbeat, my internal rhythm, and tried to listen to that, to read those signals instead of the notifications on my phone screen. I felt the current under my skin, the pulse of blood rushing from my center to my farthest extremities. The heat. I relished the fact that there was no indication of where I was, no pin on the map that placed me in any given place. Without an ID or a phone, and on foot alone in the city, I became no one. I could be anywhere, everywhere.

———

That night, the girls convened in the living room to discuss the latest developments. It was just a rehashing of everything that had happened, all the sordid details, but with Malcolm's name scribbled in, his body filling out the broad lines they had painted earlier in the day when he was an anonymous victim.

"I bet he was wearing one of those flashy tops in silver or gold or something."

"Do you think it was a fraternity guy who did it?"

"Maybe a kidnapping gone wrong? His family was pretty rich."

"There's a cult out in Laurel Canyon. They call themselves the New Masons."

"Mansons, you moron."

We moved to the dining room to eat the foraged fare Julie had picked up at the farmers market, shit you'd see literal squirrels eating on a bus stop bench. I'd need to leave for a solo grocery run later.

"I hear his younger brother hated him. Probably wanted his share of inheritance."

The girls were in a rapture. Everyone except Emily. She had joined dinner late. She had a clarity to her eyes. She wasn't drunk, I realized. Her eyes probed me, worry written all over her face.

I swallowed my mouthful of spaghetti squash, the limp imitation of noodles. I smiled and winked at her.

Her face crumpled, and she slid her chair from the table so quickly it looked like a magic trick. She was up the stairs before I could say a word.

———

I decided to visit Weston at work the next day. Just as he had never been to my room, I realized I'd never seen his office before. In all our dating, the closest I'd gotten was hearing the groan he let out every time we crossed the Santa Monica–Wilshire junction near his office building.

I missed him. He hadn't called in days. All I'd gotten were a few stray texts. But I didn't let that discourage me, dampen my amazing mood after Malcolm's murder. I decided that I would surprise Weston, bring him lunch. I found his address on one of his old business cards. I was able to scan the card's QR code and load the address directly into Google Maps. The building was large, a standard luxury corporate complex in Century City.

I located Weston's floor—the seventh—and prepared to find him. It was a lot easier than I anticipated. No receptionist station, no tall looming front desk surrounded by potted plants to check into. The floor plan was open, and the color scheme could best be described as transparent. It was all glass. Everyone had a little plot of it, enclosed in tiny square, transparent boxes. I scanned down a line of six pods, spotting Weston in the fifth one. I guess I was expecting a little more mahogany, a splash of emerald the color of money, the higher-ups cloistered away in cigar smoke.

Weston's office was large, if you could consider it an office. There wasn't much other than his desk and a flat screen mounted high against one of the glass walls, errant cable wires showing.

"What are you doing here?" he asked, after I endured a painfully long walk under his gaze.

"I was trying to surprise you." I pulled out my bag. "I got sandwiches."

I was also going to blow you under your desk, I wanted to add. I looked around. A nerd at a copy machine and two cows over by the water tank turned their heads away, as if they hadn't been staring at the two most attractive people in the office.

"Open office model. Supposed to promote synergy and all that bullshit."

What was the point of his supposed power if he couldn't get away with anything?

Weston wouldn't have his sandwich, so I was left staring at mine, unable to eat something that huge under his gaze and the two dozen people with open access all staring in.

"I told you I hated this place," he said.

"Are you off soon?" I asked.

"I'm getting drinks with a couple of the guys after work. But I'll meet you back at my place," Weston said.

I knew what that meant. I wanted to catch him before he was three drinks deep.

"I guess I'll see you later then."

———

I spent the rest of the evening masturbating in bed, punctuating each orgasm with checks on Malcolm's hashtag. The story was still trending, fifteen million now.

I drove over to Weston's a little after ten. I didn't waste time; I climbed onto him on the sofa in a floor-length silk shift.

I had doused myself in J'adore perfume but received no reaction. He wouldn't stay hard.

"Sorry, I don't know what's going on," Weston said, but it didn't feel like an apology to me.

"It's because you drank too much. Again."

"Thanks, Mom."

"Does this feel good?" I reached between his legs.

"No."

I got off him and poured myself a tumbler of whiskey. I looked at myself in the mirror over his bar. I'd have to go out again tonight, swallow up the hungry gazes of strangers until I found a victim who I could eat whole. I'd feel better after. I always did. I'd never cheated on Weston. I shared each victim's last gasp instead, his warm blood instead of come. Thinking about that special moment, I emptied my glass in one swallow and refilled. I was pouring a third glass when Weston grabbed the bottle from my hand.

"Jesus. Slow down."

"What? Are you worried I won't leave enough for you?"

We glared at each other. Then I tried again, climbing back on him, not caring if my knees pressed into his stomach. I shoved his shoulders against the couch. I pushed my lips onto his, barely a kiss. I bit his lower lip. Tasting Weston used to feel as good as a kill. I wanted that back.

"It's fine, let's just go to bed," he said.

This wasn't about sex anymore.

"I'm not ready for bed. I want you to wake up!" I yelled. "Look at me! Feel something!"

The whiskey had flooded my veins, made me loose and powerful. My good mood was ruined. I wanted a release, swift and hard and a little painful.

"I can't," Weston said, squirming away from me.

"Do you feel this?" I asked, and slapped his face with my open palm as hard as I could. There was a crack, and his head whipped back.

I had hit Weston without thinking. It was the first time I had ever been physical with him, had hurt him the way that I'd done so many times before, with so many other boys. It had been as easy as releasing a long, deep breath. It terrified me. I tried to pretend it was nothing.

"It won't bruise," I started to say, but Weston was getting up, shoving me off him. I landed on the hardwood and grabbed for his ankle. "Wait, Weston."

He kicked at my arm. I reached for him again, and this time his foot connected hard into my shoulder. He didn't even stop to check on me.

"Go the fuck home!" he screamed.

He slammed his bedroom door, and I heard the door lock.

I sat on the floor and rubbed my shoulder. Weston had ruined this whole night. My anger returned, steady and strong.

I could get in there if I wanted to, I almost screamed. Weston couldn't keep me out if I really wanted in.

27

ASHLEY WAS ON HER PHONE BLOCKING THE STAIRS WHEN I came back to the house that night. I tried to storm past her. My night had already been ruined. I was all momentum, no brakes.

"Tiffany, Emily is acting super weird."

"Don't care," I said.

"Something's wrong with her."

"Zero fucks."

"She told me to watch for you. Like give an alert or something if you were coming home. You were supposed to stay over at Weston's."

Ashley had my attention now. I thought about the butcher knife I kept under the cashmere sweaters in my bottom dresser drawer. Had Emily been rooting through my things like a little truffle hog?

"I'll deal with her," I said. "I'm sure it's nothing."

Ashley gave me a funny look. "Why is she so freaked?"

I thought fast. "She borrowed my Givenchy top without asking."

"That little bitch."

I opened my bedroom door gently enough that Emily didn't hear, didn't turn around from the closet. Her meager share of clothing was off the hangers, thrown across her bed, and she was frantically stuffing items into her battered roller suitcase.

I waited until I was directly behind her.

"Going somewhere?" I said.

Her head darted my way, and I spotted fear behind watery, wide eyes.

"I didn't mean to scare you," I lied.

I blocked the door and gave it a hard swing, so it clicked shut.

"You still haven't answered my question," I said. "Where are you going?"

"I need some time to think," she said.

"About what?"

"About everything. I'm leaving for a week or so. I'll be back."

That last sentence, it really gave everything away.

"Where?" I asked.

"What?"

"Where are you going? Your grandmother's dead. All your friends are here in this house."

Emily set a sweater down. "I just want to get the fuck out of L.A."

"Why?"

She moved away from me and started pacing like a caged animal, cornered and suddenly dangerous. "Oh, I don't know. Because my closest family is dead. Because there's a new murder report on my phone every day. Because I can't stop drinking. Because I went on my first date and woke up in blood. Because my roommate—"

She stopped.

"What? Finish your sentence. Your roommate what?"

Emily moved for the door. I grabbed her by the arm and pulled her close, so close I could recognize the scent of cheap wine.

I tucked a curly strand of hair behind her ear and leaned in. "Sisters are forever. You and I, we're bonded now."

"I won't tell, if that's what you're worried about."

"Why?" I asked, suddenly curious. There was no use pretending I didn't understand what she was saying, that she didn't know. Emily was never stupid, only naive.

"Telling on Malcolm only made everything worse for me."

I laughed, catching on. "Well, on the off chance unsavory evidence gets traced back to me, just remember: this is your room as much as it's mine. And I'm the one with the lawyer."

Emily winced.

I was suddenly dead serious. "Want to come with me one night?"

Emily pulled away and looked me in the eyes, defiant. "You have to stop."

"Why?" I sneered. "Because I'll get caught?"

"Because you won't," she said, her voice wavering. "I think I've known the entire time."

I grabbed her face in both my hands and brought her forehead to mine, mimicking that closeness I remembered seeing between Weston and Dean that night at the club.

"Look me in the eye and tell me you didn't want Malcolm dead the next morning. Look me in the eye and tell me you didn't imagine it. That your cunt didn't skip a beat when you heard the news, that you didn't feel something powerful and real from the news reports. That tingle you felt, the one that scared you, that was happiness. That was satisfaction." I searched her face. "Come on, I can see you."

Emily shook her head and tried to pull away.

"You wanted to be seen. To be popular. To have a little of what I have. Don't lie."

She whispered, "I didn't want Malcolm to die."

But her voice was edged with doubt, razor sharp. She'd spend the rest of her life trying to figure it out, who she really was and what she was capable of.

"It will be our little secret," I said.

My hands were still in her hair. I trailed my fingers down to her neck and brought her closer to me. Without thinking, I kissed her, on the lips, her mouth still half open in surprise. I tasted the wine she had been drinking and realized there was also some vodka mingled on her tongue.

Then I felt the blade of a knife against my throat and realized that Emily had in fact found her way into my secret stash. She held a paring knife I'd hidden in my sock drawer. I had to begrudge her a bit of respect, almost pride.

"I'm nothing like you," she whispered. "I'm leaving this house. For good. And then I'll never think of you again."

"Try," I said. "You've already proven my point. Are you going to stab me now? Do you think I'm afraid?"

I laughed, and Emily shoved me away, the knife pointed in front of her. She held it firmly, with control. I wouldn't be able to just knock it out of her hand the way you see killers do to dumb blondes in horror movies.

She turned back to her suitcase and zipped it, a sleeve still hanging loose out one end, her sad accumulation of the past year all stuffed in one piece of luggage. She slung a backpack over her shoulder and pulled up the handle to her suitcase, the knife in her right hand still trained ahead of her. What would the other girls think, seeing her leave like that, so suddenly, with a knife and an old suitcase?

I decided not to stop her. Emily had already been silenced after she accused Malcolm. No one would believe her, not without any money or connections to back her claims. Besides, I realized, for the first time, I wanted someone else to know, to also carry my secret, to read the future news stories and think of me, imagine the knife in my hand, the blood on my face.

"Goodbye, Emily."

———

That night I sent Weston at least a dozen texts. I even left a voice mail, short but pleading. No answer. I was alone. During the day, with nothing to do, I stayed at the house, waiting for my phone to vibrate on the bed, for updates from the outside world. I posted back-piled photos from two years ago just to keep up on social media. I pretended it was normal that my boyfriend was ghosting me, that my roommate had gone MIA, carrying all my murderous secrets along with her.

I checked the safe under my bed a few times a day, ran my fingers over the rings, watches, and fraternity pins. I counted them in moments of sudden panic. The final count was up to seventeen. Seventeen kills. Some nights, I locked the door to my room, crawled under the bed, and fell asleep there on the floor. I'd wake up to sun hitting my legs, feel the weight of metal and mattress above me, and panic before I remembered where I was.

When I picked up my phone, I saw headline after headline. Scrolling through socials, I saw a video of a student lighting his desk on fire during a final, a professor getting slapped on the ass and then punching the student right back. It was a viral shit show.

It hadn't just been Emily. People were leaving campus daily. Classes were canceled. First, it was only the humanities classes, the bullshit subjects like philosophy and communications, but then the engineering and chemistry professors started bailing, and I realized it was serious. Girls slowly drifted off, back to strange corners of California, closer to the center of the country. They had never liked L.A. anyway, they all said. Too much traffic and too little water.

I started having nightmares again. Weston passing me on the street, walking right past me on San Vicente Boulevard. He didn't know me, his eyes barely registering me, glancing over to another blonde walking in another direction. Then the dream collapsed, re-formed, and I saw Emily on *TMZ*, telling the entire story to the news raptors, men and women covered in scales, ready to feed on the grisly details.

I think I've known the entire time. Her words echoed in my head.

Emily would be a liability for the coming years. That twinge of relief she felt at Malcolm's death: What if it was followed by guilt? The sudden need to empty out the truth like a good purge? Nobody would believe her, but if she had concrete proof, if she had found a way into the safe, captured a photo on her phone before leaving . . . What had I done? Why had I let Emily go so easily?

———

I left the next day to find her. I packed two knives, industrial tape, all in a small gym bag. I had gotten her grandmother's address from the Panhellenic directory and was surprised when I plugged the address into my phone and saw a thin line stretching ten miles directly south of Westwood. I hadn't left the five-mile radius of campus in weeks.

I had to connect from the 405 to the 105, watch the exit signs grow distant and unfamiliar as I drove my Mercedes farther south and east. A stack of black smoke from a fire in the distance formed ahead, growing nearer.

I had hit 100th Street by the time I pulled off the freeway. I wound my car under an interchange of spiraling off-ramps and connectors, crumbled concrete pillars holding everything up. I parked several blocks away and quickly felt vulnerable, out of place, walking along the sidewalk. The walkway disappeared when I turned onto her street. This wasn't the L.A. I knew, the city I felt comfortable in. I was being watched. There were so many people on foot, at the crosswalks, on sidewalks, across from two liquor stores squeezed next to each other.

I remembered when Pam had visited the sorority house, the only time, a little over a year ago. She had been all smiles and compliments for the girls as I showed her upstairs. She had told Emily she had beautiful skin, that her cheap Forever 21 top was cute, then flashed me a look.

I wasn't like Pam, in so many ways. I almost liked Emily, despite our differences, despite our eventual falling out. But I did need to kill her. There was no other way.

I found the address number in faded blocking across the curb, the tiny plot of concrete surrounded by an angular square of lawn. The front porch faced the freeway, yet there was still a set of chairs, a side table, potted plants.

I looked for a doorbell and settled for a few raps on the metal skeleton of the screen door. A woman emerged from the green-blue glow of a TV-lit room. She opened the door wide, met my gaze, but stayed silent.

I had a speech prepared, but I lost my words. "I'm looking for Emily." She shifted her weight slowly.

"Her grandmother lived here," I explained.

"She's dead."

"Yes, but do you know where I can find her relative? Emily."

"She isn't here." Her face was already turned away from me. I backed away before the woman replied, loud this time, "I told you, she isn't here."

I walked away, already regretting the long trip back to my car. I wouldn't be returning this far south, and I had no other leads on Emily's whereabouts. So this was what it meant to have nothing left to lose. All these nights I thought I was roaming free. Emily was invisible; she could be anywhere right now. She had left no footprints, no tracks. She could hide in any spare space in the city, every rotting corner.

———

I went for a run the next afternoon to let off steam, but it had become harder and harder to find a suitable route. Neighborhoods on the Westside were roped off. Armed guards patrolled the streets, and signs were posted on sidewalks, warning against intruders, even those walking by, even joggers who looked and dressed like me. Bel Air and Beverly Glen wanted none of it, nobody passing through who didn't live there. I resorted to running laps around the deserted campus.

And then one day I saw it, something that stopped me in my tracks, forced my fingers to feel for my AirPods and pause my playlist. A solid human chain, at least three hundred people long, wrapped around the entire campus perimeter, faces all covered, duct-taped, in black sweatshirts. I felt a heavy weight in the center of my stomach. I slowly backed away from the crowd and headed home.

"What's happening?" I asked Mandy when I returned to the house.

"Protesters have plenty of time now that classes have stopped. And people are joining from everywhere, all across the country. You can't have two shootings in a row and expect nothing."

"That's what they're protesting? The shootings?"

"Who knows? I can't keep up. All I know is Sushi Friday is gone. They're serving caloric crap like Del Taco at the food hall since so many workers have left campus. I can't live like this much longer."

———

Two days later, there was a third shooting about a mile from campus, ten dead. Then school permanently shut down; gates we never knew existed were closed and locked. Like magic, rows of street parking suddenly opened along the edges of campus.

How was it fair that some twat could go out there with a semi-automatic and match almost a year of my hard work in just ten minutes? It was the difference between a Pollock and Seurat. Messy splatter versus refined artistic vision.

I visited the warehouse for the last time to clean out all my equipment. It had already been tagged, taken over by new owners. Besides, there was plenty of space in the sorority house now to store my weights.

Only five girls remained in our sorority, and they stayed solely because of the fact that Coachella was still scheduled this April. It was the only thing keeping the last few of the sorority members in L.A. Mandy and Amy were among them.

"After weekend one, I'm out," Amy explained. "First time I ever skipped both weekends, but circumstances are dire. I'm totally done with Southern California. They did not put this shit on the campus brochure."

"What about you, Tiff?" Mandy asked. "You leaving after the festival?"

Where was I supposed to go? I didn't have a middle-American plot of land to pack up to. This was it.

The days were stretching longer, and when they ended, the sunsets were brilliant. The sun went down in a bloodred explosion each evening. I fried bacon every morning and sirloin each night, shoved raw meat in the otherwise empty fridge, and didn't bother putting on all my clothes most days. If this was the end of the world, bring it. I'd greet the apocalypse in lace lingerie.

And still, Weston didn't answer my texts.

At night, I went out, but I didn't stray far. I just watched mostly, stood outside houses whose sidewalks hadn't been blocked off or staffed with guards. Frat row had more holdouts than the sorority, a few brave heroes determined to stick out protests, riots, fires that I could now catch sight of farther south.

I watched in the darkness behind lit windows, watched boys goofing off, ordering takeout, getting dressed. I wasn't looking for them to get naked—that was too easy. If I really wanted sex, I could walk in and get it myself in a second. I was looking instead for those candid moments, when they picked their noses, or the little quirks of their eating habits, the way they might pluck out the cilantro in a taco. When they got that distant, lost look watching porn right before they came, and then that moment after when they were left alone with the mess in their hands and their boxers at their ankles, when they had nobody around to come on. And yeah, sometimes I killed them, sometimes I couldn't resist. But mostly, I watched.

Things were changing. I thought of the Pike house, all the members packing handguns where they used to keep their weed jars. A knife wouldn't cut it anymore, not in this city. I saw the eruption of flame from the barrel of a gun, and I knew I had to make a brief visit back to Orange County.

It was time to go home.

28

PACKED MY CAR, CHECKING THAT THE TRUNK WAS STOCKED with a clean crowbar in case I came upon someone I liked on the drive back. I knew I had crossed the county line from Los Angeles to Orange County when both the traffic and smoke cleared, and the freeway expanded into a ten-lane speedway like magic. The loops of distant roller coasters rose above the palm trees as I entered Anaheim. I exited a half hour later on PCH, flying straight toward the ocean.

Then it was winding roads through Monarch Estates, up the cliff-lined beach, the sea salt texturizing my hair, giving it a little body. It was only a ninety-minute drive from L.A., but the rules were different here. There would be no protesters, no signs, no random gatherings, no distant fires, only stacked mansions and luxurious vistas, closed gates impervious to strangers. Orange County kept its dirty secrets inside the homes.

I pulled up to the gate at the top of the hill and faintly recognized the guard. I flashed him a bit of leg. It was warm again, spring finally, and I had worn a slinky silk sundress cut three-quarters up my thigh.

"Welcome back, sweetie," he said. "How long you staying?"

"This is a quick trip. I have to return to L.A."

"You be careful up there," he said, and looked down at his computer monitor. "You're not listed on the address. I'll have to write you a guest pass."

None of Pam's cars were in front of the house. The place appeared to be empty, just the typical half dozen or so gardeners hacking away at the property. I ignored their surprised, wordless faces. I could tell some of them remembered me, enough to probably know my appearance wouldn't be welcomed by Pam. But she didn't pay them nearly enough to challenge me.

I walked around through the pool gate, passing an old man lugging a giant water hose. I entered the house through the side French doors. The downstairs was empty, not even house cleaners wiping counters. I was in luck.

I moved upstairs to the bedrooms, slipping on a pair of gloves. Celeste's door was closed, the only one in the row, and I could hear synthetic pop music from inside. She wasn't a real problem. I moved on to the master bedroom and closed the door behind me.

I had one specific purpose, small but important. If I was lucky, Todd and Pam might not even notice it was missing. I started by checking the bedside table, not the obvious drawer, but the hidden one underneath. It was still there. I pulled the .22 out and checked the chamber. Loaded, no surprise. Pam had started keeping it there after the night my father had successfully flung her down the stairs. But I knew the gun I really wanted would be in the safe.

It was the same monstrosity from my youth, a three-hundred-pound slab of concrete preset to three numbers. And I still remembered them. My father had given me the combination at the very end, after the cancer had eaten through and he could barely stand. Back then, the safe had been kept in his office, before the room had been cleared and redecorated with a Pilates reformer. The attorneys who had me open it never asked me why I had the combo, why his daughter and not his wife knew the secret numbers.

8-12-21. It opened. I searched through bank statements and foreign currency until I found it. I pulled out the long-barrelled .357 Magnum, the one that had always been my favorite.

I checked the cylinder, and it was loaded. Six bullets would have to do for now. I pulled the hammer back, and the old feeling hit: power and sex all rolled in one.

Celeste's door was open when I emerged from the bedroom. I spotted her strung out on the couch in one of the downstairs dens, taking a series of selfies. I moved fast enough to make sure the gun was concealed in my purse. I wouldn't be able to escape her notice, though.

"What are you doing here?" she asked, but I knew she wasn't really concerned because she kept her phone in one hand, watching her reflection, puckering her lips.

"Nice way to greet your sister," I said. "Why are *you* home? Shouldn't you be in college by now?"

"I'm taking fashion classes at FIDM. Mom wants to get me into Princeton next year."

"She'll need to put down some serious cash to make that happen."

"Tell her yourself." Celeste looked behind me.

Pam emerged from the kitchen, her face tighter, her forehead shinier. Platinum extensions stretched down to her ass. They only made her look older.

"What are you doing here?" she repeated Celeste's question, her keys in her hand.

"I can't stop by for an afternoon, say hello?"

"You know you need to call if you want to come over."

"This is my house, too. Now you're going to ban me from my own home?"

"I always invite you back."

"Bullshit."

"Why are you being this way? After all I've done for you."

"You haven't done shit for me," I said.

"Have you lost your mind? I've given you everything, Tiffany! Anything you wanted, I made sure you got. Clothes, vacations, cars."

It was so easy to set Pam off. I could still do it in less than ten seconds.

"Those were all things *you* wanted," I said.

"You're getting a great education because of me. A little thanks would be nice."

"I could have gotten into college on my own," I said.

Pam circled around closer, her hand clutched around her keys, a useless weapon. "Then why didn't you, Tiffany? How's the school year going? Are you still failing your classes?"

"I don't care."

"Do you care about anything?"

"Not like you."

"Well, excuse me. I just wanted you to have more than I did."

Celeste slipped past us and up the stairs, picking up the scent of coming blood. I thought of slamming Celeste's head against the wall: one swift, easy move, and I could knock her out. Or one pull of the trigger of the gun in my purse, and I could take her head clean off.

I turned my attention back to Pam. I wasn't done yet.

"You cared about having the perfect life so bad you let yourself get the shit beaten out of you for it. And you want to stand here and give me advice?"

"It's a lot easier to fall into than you think," Pam said. "I hope you don't find out one day," she added, but the way she delivered it, the barbed emphasis on each syllable, sounded like a threat.

She met my gaze, and for a moment, I felt a flash of dread. I reached for my necklace. It felt tight against my throat.

"Why do you hate me so much?" Pam said.

Her eyes welled up. I didn't know if she'd be able to get a tear out, her lids were stretched so tight. She was back to her old refrain, back to being the victim. For all the years she'd tried her hand at acting, this was the only part she had ever learned to play.

I relaxed.

"I'll drop in again after the school year ends, Pam, and we can revisit this conversation. Tell Todd I said hello."

But I didn't leave right away. I walked through the French doors to the backyard. I could smell smoke. Somebody had used the fire pit yesterday. I approached the pool. It was covered with a thick blue tarp. It reminded me of the coroner's blanket at the scene of a crime.

The gun had still been in the safe. It was mine now. It hadn't gone missing, like some of the other items I discovered around my father's death. The cash I had expected to disappear. Pam and her attorneys scrounged up every last cent. But there was another thing, something that, when I first discovered it by myself, had been an intriguing puzzle.

I found it the week before my father died. It was a small, compact jewelry chest, and I knew in the instant of discovery, without him ever saying, that my father had left it for me. The items were beautiful, classic, and understated. Nothing like Pam's gaudy jewelry. The pearl-drop necklace immediately stood out, for both its smooth shape and the fact that it still had blood crusted over it. I took the necklace before Pam could learn where it came from. I cleaned it off and wore it that night. I pretended he had given it to me. In a sense, he did. When my father died, the attorneys took over, and I never saw the box again. Maybe it was in Century City right now, with Slade in his office.

At the time, I thought the box revealed my father's illicit affairs. I wasn't able—or maybe willing—to put it together. It didn't hit me until I started slowly filling my own safe, until I had my own secret chest.

I slipped off my sandals and sat cross-legged at the edge of the pool. I spotted motion from the house and could see Celeste jerk away from the upstairs bedroom window, caught. Pam was at the kitchen bay window, not bothering to hide her surveillance. I turned back to the pool.

I had made my last stand against Pam here, a few weeks after my father's death, after Todd had moved in like a jackal that smelled fresh money about to burn.

I was seventeen and a fuming rage. It was the first time I had felt something so deep and relentless I couldn't shop or fuck my way out of it.

I had returned home half drunk from a bonfire party, cutting through the fog blanketing PCH to find the house deserted and dark. There was fresh dog shit across the entryway, but Tiki and Sergeant Sparkles were nowhere in sight.

I had wound my way up the stairs to my father's empty room, hunting for something I couldn't name. The space gave off the scent of sour decay, even though a cleaning crew had come through right after he died. A flutter of panic had surfaced for a moment as I visualized my father's body rotting somewhere under the floorboards.

Then I had sniffed it out. It was from the dogs. They had pissed in every corner of the space.

I remember not even thinking, doing it so quickly I couldn't recall the details, even now. I don't remember where in the house I had found them. I don't remember the dogs biting me. But I did remember the dogs barking, both of them, that shrill, awful screech, and I did remember the way their bodies hung suspended in the air for a moment when I pitched them over the safety fence into the pool.

I hadn't even watched. It must have been a good two hours until the screams started, and I knew Pam and Todd had returned home.

I had found Pam collapsed by the pool, sobbing over their deflated bodies. Todd was drenched, standing uncertainly behind her.

"Why?" she had screamed over and over. "Why?"

Todd had watched on in horror, dripping water, finally realizing what he'd gotten himself into when he joined this family, the price he'd have to pay.

I looked at the pool now, covered over, another secret forgotten and buried.

Why did I kill them? The answer was simple. Because I could.

29

O N MY WAY BACK TO L.A., I GRABBED A GLASS OF WINE AT A rooftop deck in Laguna. I kept the gun right in my purse for the thrill of the risk, like facing a crowd of boys seated in a miniskirt and no panties. I could stay here, check into the Montage for a week. Inside its suites, I wouldn't even need a gun. I could ride out whatever violence was gripping the city. But the truth was I wanted to see everything ignite and explode.

I didn't match the rest of the diners. I didn't belong here anymore, sitting across from women with plunging necklines that fought against the counter-buoyancy of swollen, hard breasts. I didn't have any make-up on, though my skin was clear. I had long ago ditched fake lashes and acrylic nails for the liability they posed if left behind at a kill. I searched through the men at various tables, all too old, and thought about how many of them I could bring down if I wanted to.

I missed Weston.

Driving north, I decided to stop at his house. I couldn't take the silence. I didn't call or text him a warning. I didn't want to give him a chance to say no. I couldn't be alone anymore, spend another night by myself with just my mementos. I pulled off the 405 two exits early and parked my car in front of his house when I saw his lights on. I took the gun out of my purse and held it, feeling the weight of it restore my con-fidence. I wanted it with me, touching my flesh, but I thought better and shoved it in the glove box.

Weston answered only a few seconds after I knocked. He turned and left the door open, wordless, and I followed him into the living room.

"Is it okay that I stopped by?" I asked.

"I guess."

"I'm sorry," I said. "I just wanted to tell you I'm sorry."

I hoped he recognized that I wasn't the type of person to apologize, that it went against every fiber in my genetic makeup.

"Why wouldn't you answer my texts?" I asked. "Do you not want to see me?"

"I don't want to be alone," Weston said. He was drunk, eyes bloodshot. It was only 8:00 P.M.

"I don't, either. That's why I came here. Then you forgive me?"

"Yeah. Just stop being so crazy. Stop messing with me."

He opened his arms, and I leaned into his chest. His shirt smelled worn and unwashed, but Weston could never smell bad.

I let him lead me to the bedroom.

Then the unbelievable happened. He was drunk, but he managed to get hard. He reached between my legs and opened them up like I was in bloom. The taste on his tongue was strong, almost pungent, but soon his lips were off mine and moving down my body, settling between my thighs.

I wanted to tell him that being with him when he was here with me—not floating, but when he was grounded and hard—felt better than any kill, even when the blood was still warm and that luscious red hue. I'd handcuff him to the bed if I needed to, just to keep him like this with me. But I couldn't say any of that, so I just slipped his finger in my mouth and moaned.

Afterward, when I was naked and loose, I wanted to tell Weston something that was true, even if it was only part of the truth, only one tiny piece of the puzzle.

"Emily is gone," I said.

"Where?"

"I have no idea. I tried to find her but couldn't."

I stopped and waited, choosing my next words. He was suddenly alert, interested.

"She was drugged. Two weeks ago. There were other things. I think she wanted to escape."

"I liked her. Not that way," he quickly added, but I understood. He took a drink. "It must be something, to be a woman."

He spoke in such general terms, but it was all true. I reached for his free hand.

"I'm sorry to hear about Emily," Weston said. "I hope she's okay, wherever she is."

We were silent, and I was close to sleep when Weston continued. "I wonder what Dean would be doing right now, where he would be if he was still here."

And there it was, the ever-present ghost in the room.

I didn't answer. Instead, I held Weston closer. The harder I pressed, the more alone I felt.

———

I woke up by myself in the middle of Weston's bed. My head pounded even though I'd had only the one glass of wine yesterday. Wind rattled the windows, and I remembered hearing a warning that the Santa Anas were coming. I slipped on my underwear and reached to find the rest of my clothes.

Weston was gone, a three-word note left behind: *Work. Talk soon.* And like that, all the promise of last night evaporated.

I stepped outside and felt dry air tickle my face. I thought about a shopping trip on Rodeo Drive, but the stores were all boarded up. There were fewer and fewer places left to go. I weaved my car around the palm fronds that covered the streets like little bodies. The Santa Anas meant fire. It was starting.

30

THE POWER WENT OUT TWO DAYS AFTER THE WINDS STARTED. Palm fronds settled precariously over cable wires. Afternoon stretched on, and the lull of the AC as it slowly powered down sounded normal at first. I didn't notice the electricity was out until night set in. I had no candles, just a flashlight in my car and my phone, which sported 20 percent battery. I forgot how complete darkness could be when an entire neighborhood was out, how entire blocks could plunge into black because of one short circuit.

I took the flashlight, held it between my teeth, and climbed up to the roof to see how far the outage stretched. California was transitioning into spring in a spurt of heat and awe. I saw fire, the faint outline in the distance, at least five miles away. Somehow, I knew that it was coming my way.

I woke up later and thought the power had returned, my bedroom was flooded with so much light. But it was the brilliance of midafternoon. I had slept for I wasn't sure how long. My phone's battery had died overnight, and I couldn't find a single clock in the entire sorority house.

I faintly remembered screams woven into my dreams, the cries of young people, and I wondered if I had really heard those sounds last night, if any of it was real. It was silent now, the streets mostly emptied.

I had a slow day. Was this how generations before felt? No social media, no texts, calls, updates; it was as though the entire day was spent in secret, just as my nights had been when I left to kill.

I downed a beer on the roof. I counted the fires burning: they were up to four now, but they were starting to blur into one, inching closer. There appeared to be no attempt to fix the outage, no workers in the distance, but I wasn't worried. I looked north to Malibu, where the sky was clear. Did they know what was coming?

The immediate neighborhood was empty, but the streets that funneled toward the 405 were filled with cars. To make sure, I focused on one, a red Lamborghini, and waited to see when it'd get to the nearest traffic light. It was still sitting there at the end of the day.

I went inside when the sun moved west. I took a cold shower and decided to dress for the evening. I chose a long flowing Anthropologie skirt and sleeveless top I'd found in Mandy's empty room. I put my hair up, spritzed on Gucci. The sun had started its descent, tingeing my room with pink. I was feeling that magnetic pull toward my safe when I heard the front door slam. One of the girls was back.

I moved to the upstairs hall. "Hello?" I called.

He stood at the base of the stairs, a welcome sight.

"Weston. What are you doing here?"

He gave a short, confused laugh. "Coming to rescue you, I guess. I thought for sure you'd be gone to Orange County. But I couldn't reach you, so I stopped by on my way to the airport. Are you okay?"

He joined me upstairs, skipping every other step. He was in jeans and a T-shirt. Was it a weekday? I couldn't remember anymore. There was something else different about Weston that I couldn't place.

"I'm not leaving," I said.

"Anyone in their right mind would be gone by now. I only stayed this long because I was boarding up the house. I should have left yesterday with everyone else."

"Is it that bad?"

"Haven't you seen the news reports? They've announced evacuations across most of the city. The winds are picking up, and arsonists are having a field day. It took me over an hour just to get here from Mar Vista."

"I mean, if I left, I'd have to put a few suitcases together. Maybe hire a mover."

"Tiffany, you're not going to be able to hire someone to move your stuff. I don't think you're understanding the situation."

"Well, I'd at least need a couple hours to properly pack." The safe weighed on me, kept me from straying too far from the house.

"I can help you load everything into your car."

"My car?"

He gave me an awkward look. I suddenly remembered he had mentioned the airport.

"Where are you going?"

"New York."

"Scared off so easily? You're going to feel pretty stupid when everything dies down. Just give it a few days."

"That's not happening."

I thought about New York in the spring, Park Avenue and Barneys. The flowers along the High Line in full bloom, sepia tones of light.

"I mean, I guess I can go to New York. That might not be such a bad idea, in fact. Just for a week or so. How long were you planning on being gone?"

He sat down on my bed and motioned for me to join.

"Sit down," he said, and my stomach dropped.

I joined him and caught a whiff of his breath. Weston was completely sober, completely alert, for the first time in so long.

"Tiffany, I'm not coming back."

"You're staying in New York? Not returning to L.A.?"

"Yes."

"So you're dumping me?"

"The decision has nothing to do with you. I'm going back home. L.A. has run its course. It's not you; this whole place is just not working out."

Not you—the words rang, carved out a hole in my stomach, and I worried I'd keel over and vomit. I realized I hadn't eaten yet today.

"What about your job? Your house?"

He paused, his head down. "I put in my notice at work a month ago. The house, well, I might not have one anyway by the end of this." He gave a weak laugh. "If it's still standing, I'll put it on the market."

Weston was interrupted by the sound of a helicopter circling low over the house. We waited for it to pass. I clenched my fist around my comforter, tears smarting my eyes.

I thought of Weston pulling away, his slow desertion. All the effort I had made to meet him in the middle, to try to make it work, and he'd been sitting on a bombshell for the last month, probably hoping I'd just give up on him and take the fall for our relationship's ruin. I thought of all the nights we had spent together when he already knew it was over.

"So you've known this whole time?" I asked.

"I didn't want to hurt you. But you had to have felt it, too."

"So now it's my fault I didn't pick up on your nonverbal signals? Your passive-aggressive cues? You're dumping me like this, and you have the nerve to hope I don't get hurt?"

I stood up suddenly. My body chemistry was shifting. I pushed back tears and let myself welcome a more familiar rush of anger and pride. I didn't need him. He wasn't going to sit on that bed, trying to soothe me like I was some sort of child, when he was the pathetic one, the one who let himself be worn down by Dean's death, who gave up on the city because of a few fires and some shootings. I went for the throat, the deepest nerve I could rip into.

"I should be dumping you. You're worthless! You're on more medications than a reality TV housewife. You can't even get hard. Why couldn't you have added Viagra to the stack of pills in your cabinet?"

"That's enough."

"I'm not done. Not even close. You're a fucking baby. You think I couldn't hear you in the middle of the night? Wailing like a child? You're not even a man."

"I understand you're angry, but I'm not going to engage in this."

He claimed to be above it all, but I noticed his hand was slightly shaking. I felt the anger in him spreading. I was working into him, kneading under the muscle—I had almost broken under the skin. I leaned closer.

"Oh, now you're above it? You weren't when you were groveling on your knees, begging me not to leave you that night at the airport. You needed me then, when you cried Dean's name all night, when you told him 'I love you' in your sleep like a fucking—"

Weston sprung to his feet and shoved me hard against the bed.

"You think you were there for me?" he spit out. "You didn't console me. You only care about yourself—your nails, your hair, your body. Talk about worthless? Have you ever worked at anything in your life? Have you ever given a shit about anything other than yourself? You're the shallowest person I've ever met!"

"You have no idea who I am or what I can do," I said. "What if I told you I can take down a two-hundred-pound man, that I can carve out a man's stomach like a surgeon? That I roam the streets every night? That after I fuck you—on those rare occasions—and you're asleep, safe in your bed, my work is only beginning?"

I stepped up to his face and said, "You have no fucking idea what I can do. Do you want me to show you?"

Weston shoved me away, and I released my breath, my secrets finally out in the open. It was a wave, a feeling of relief like emptying myself after a heavy meal. I couldn't control it, and I wouldn't regret it. I waited for Weston's reaction. I searched his face, but it was calm. I backed away as I slowly realized what I had done.

There was a part of me waiting, hopeful that knowing the truth about me would change everything, that maybe now that Weston understood me, who I was, he might stay, take back everything he had just said. He might have a newfound respect for all that I did in secret, what I couldn't reveal to just anyone. Maybe it was a secret we could share, now that he knew the real me.

But Weston's face was impassive. He suddenly gave a short laugh.

"You're such a shitty girlfriend. You're such a shitty human being. And you have a real sick sense of humor. Have a nice life, Tiffany."

He turned and walked away.

I let out an animal cry. This was it. I'd revealed everything, and he'd get the last laugh. It took every ounce of self-control to remind myself that I was lucky he didn't believe me, that he didn't truly know who I was after all.

It was still humiliating, though, that he'd think so little of me. I walked over to the bedroom window and looked out, not wanting him to see any tears in his last passing glance, if he even offered one.

I waited to hear his steps on the stairs, his Porsche start up. I'd watch him leave and that would be the last I saw of Weston. I already knew he'd never answer any of my calls, if I could ever get my phone charged. I saw a picture of myself cataloged in his mind, as Blonde Number Whatever, that crazy one from Los Angeles, another headshot in a sea of ex-girlfriend money shots. I'd be put away with all the others, just as Dean had promised.

I waited for what I knew was coming, so complete in my certainty that it must have been a solid three minutes, maybe more, until I felt Weston's presence still in my bedroom. He had moved to leave, had opened the door, but he had never left my room. He was turned away from me. I couldn't see his face, but I could sense his muscles tightening, his hand still frozen in midair near the doorknob. I recognized the calculated, full-bodied thinking he used the few times he was working and not drinking. The times he had to piece together raw data and numbers, fit them into a workable solution.

I faced him slowly, unable to speak. At least another minute went by. When Weston turned around, and I could finally read his face, I knew he had figured it all out.

He took a step forward, and I retreated one step, calculating how long it would take to reach the knife in the drawer of my desk. I realized suddenly the disadvantage I had, barefoot, in a long, clinging skirt. He was clad in loose, comfortable clothing, and I'd be constricted. If I had been more observant, I would have slipped the skirt off while he was calculating, removed the extra confines, so I had room to dodge and dance. Now it was too late.

Weston took another step forward, still silent, and we began a slow circle around the room.

I tried to think of something that might calm or at least slow down the quick synaptic connections I knew were firing at light speed through his head. I came up with nothing.

I killed men, and I liked it. What more was there to say?

I had another knife in my dresser, but the drawer was heavy, and the weapon was nestled under a thick stack of sweaters. There was no way I could reach it before he was on top of me.

Weston was closing in. He reached for my hand. I relied on gut instinct and let my body take over, all those months I had sharpened my reflexes. I backhanded him with my closed fist, instantly regretting the move. Weston seemed stunned at first, a dribble of blood escaping his lip.

Then he lunged, and I sidestepped lightly away from him. I waited for him to lunge a second time, dodged him again. He was off-balance, and I shoved him hard, so hard he went sprawling across the floor. I went for the dresser, opening it and feeling among the clothes. I found the knife after he was already up, and he slammed the drawer closed just as I grabbed the weapon.

I didn't plan on stabbing him; I only wanted to slow him down, get him to turn the predatory instinct off for a second, so I could find the right lie to feed him, take back everything I had just let slip. I gripped the knife tightly, slashing through the stale air in front of me. I simply wanted to subdue him and slow down the momentum that I could feel was building in his favor.

"Get back—" I started, but never finished. He ignored my warning and barreled headfirst into my stomach, knocking the knife from my hand and sending me crashing onto the hardwood. I scrambled to find the knife, reaching it just as he stood up. Weston landed his foot hard on my hand, and I heard a crunch. He picked the knife up as I tried to get back to my feet. My heel caught on fabric, and I ripped the left side of my skirt.

A second instinct took over—flight—and I turned to flee the bedroom. I had to get to the staircase and tumble down the stairs if I had to, so I could escape Weston's avalanching anger. I ran across the threshold of the bedroom just as I felt my weight shift under me. Weston had tripped me a second time, sending me on my elbows. He pulled me by the leg back into the bedroom.

I kicked him hard in the face and got to my feet, in disbelief at the direction this was going. Yes, I had attacked, but he didn't seem to care how badly he was hurting me.

He swung me off my feet and into the mirrored closet, and the room exploded in glass. I crunched along on my hands and knees away from him, feeling bits and pieces burrow into my skin.

He flipped me onto my back, and then he was on top of me, pulling me closer to him until my skirt was bunched to my stomach and the backs of my legs were shredded raw.

I started to feel a tingle between my legs to see him unleashed like this, nascent power and awakened muscle. It all seemed to be leading toward a giant, passionate climax. Maybe we could fuck it out on top of all the broken glass. The pounding in my head from where he knocked me on the floor matched the rhythm of my pulse. I knew he must have felt it too, that energy that came from the coppery taste of blood, from the pain of two bodies colliding. We hadn't yet done anything to each other that couldn't heal.

Weston grabbed me by the throat and pulled my head close to his. He finally spoke, but I couldn't understand the words. I wondered if he wanted to know how I had done it. I'd gladly tell him.

Weston repeated the question, and this time I heard it.

"Was it you?"

I didn't understand what he meant.

"Did you kill him?" His hands tightened against my neck.

"Who?" I choked out. All that mattered to me in that moment was the two of us, the violence that we now shared.

He slapped me. "Did you kill Dean?"

This was going in the wrong direction. I wanted this to be about the two of us, about him and me. I squirmed away. I couldn't fight him properly. I didn't have that same bloodlust, and I was already hurt.

Weston pulled me closer and then slammed my head against the floor, so hard I saw stars. He let go of me and watched me stumble around. He was toying with me. I knew, because I had done it myself so many times, with so many men.

"Did you kill Dean?" His words were calm and tempered this time. The heat inside me quickly cooled. "You did, didn't you? You beautiful, little cunt," he said, stroking my hair, and I realized I had underestimated Weston this whole time, what he was capable of. I had mistaken grief for weakness.

He held the knife to my throat. "Did you do it?"

My right arm was free, and I wrapped my fingers around a sizable shard of glass on the floor, feeling it cut into my hand. I knew it would never work. Weston had already won.

"Did you kill him?" he asked again.

I smiled, feeling blood bubbling warm between the sliver of my front teeth.

I cleared my throat. I wanted him to hear and understand.

"Yes."

Weston took the knife, turned it hilt side down, and connected it with my face. Again. And again. I felt the glass slip out of my hand.

A second later, I wasn't holding anything, my hands were numb, and I was on the other side of the room, near Emily's dresser. It was dark, and I noticed it was snowing. I tried to focus, to make sense of the bloody scene around me.

The snow was pieces of my hair, blond tufts fluttering across the room. I slowly began to recognize items as mine, parts of me coming off: my hair, a piece of skirt in the corner, my blood in a jagged trail across the room.

Then I was pulled by the back of the head. I heard screams, sirens; saw a flash of red and blue from just outside my window. The city was converging on the both of us, and I realized this was what it felt like, to finally be caught, to have nowhere to go and nothing to hide behind. Emily's face flashed before me.

Weston hauled me to my knees and gripped his fist around my hair, pulling at every last strand that wasn't already floating around the room.

He brought my head back, so I saw straight into his eyes. He looked like he was about to kiss me. Then he slammed my head into the dresser so hard the front of my face crunched straight through wood, through the entire dresser it seemed. I thought my mouth had sawed through the entire block of furniture when I realized the pieces of wood filling my mouth were my teeth. I couldn't see anymore. I was on my back again, and I struggled not to choke on all the blood and strange fragments sliding down my throat. My mind tried to piece together the situation, but my body was giving out.

Weston had my knife. I couldn't see, but I could feel its smooth, cold edge against the inside of my thigh. I'd recognize the feel of it anywhere. If I was a victim, this was where the kill would finally come, when the toying grew tiresome and it was time to shift to a new diversion, the spilling of blood in earnest, the wait for the heart to beat out.

I felt the point of the knife press down along my outer thigh. Weston was feeling along for the best spot, a soft square of flesh where he could be sure the knife could fully slide into. It didn't take long for a thigh wound to bleed out. I remembered how fast the blood had come out of Tristan that first time, that first kill. I closed my eyes and imagined I was back there, back at the beginning of the school year, dressed in that black-and-white dress. I could have ended it all, and none of this would have happened.

The knife stopped its searching, and I knew Weston had decided on a spot.

"Don't," I said, but I'm not sure if the word ever came out.

Pain exploded through me, and my leg burst in flames. I knew in the distant way of a bad dream that the knife had gone into my thigh all the way to the hilt.

Then it was completely dark, and Weston was gone. I knew what I had to do, what my only option was if I didn't want to bleed out.

I reached down and felt the handle of the knife in my thigh, coated in blood already starting to congeal. I left it in. I rolled myself over, the pain starting to break. I sensed Weston nearby. He was rooting through the room; I could hear him looking for something.

I army crawled for the bed, only a couple of feet away, but I knew I was making noise, grunting. I had to pull myself across on my stomach, the knife digging farther into me like an electric rod that had replaced my right leg. I bit my lip to keep from screaming and felt a bottom tooth detach from my gum. I swallowed it and kept crawling, pulling myself under the tight safety of the bed. The longer strands of my hair caught along the bed springs, but I kept inching forward.

I had to reposition my leg to fit it through with the knife, and I gave out my first scream. I felt footsteps, the hardwood vibrating against my cheek.

"Get out," Weston said.

I'd have to be quick. I felt Weston tug at my ankle, and I scooted to the dead center of the bed. I tried to twist the knob on my safe, but there was no way I could see the tiny tick marks separating each number. I closed my eyes and relied on gut instinct, muscle memory. I had opened the safe so many times in darkness.

My hands were bloody and stiff, and I could barely wrap my thumb and index finger around the knob. They slipped along the tiny ridge marks.

I was still struggling when Weston tried to get at me again, snatching at my feet. "You think you're going someplace?"

I knew he couldn't fit under the bed, but I didn't have much time until he figured a way to pull me out.

I was on my third attempt at the lock combination when I heard a jerk of wood and metal. I thought at first something had struck the house, when I realized it was Weston, trying to move the bed, unaware it was bolted to the wall. The groan of metal grew louder, harsher, and I could see bits of plaster raining down on the floor beside me as he worked the bed right off its hinges.

My trainer, Sergio, always told me the body could do miraculous things in a moment of panic. It just needed a shock to the system. I didn't know if I ever bought into that; I'd seen too many heaving bodies give up in front of me to believe in that sort of bodily magic. But I opened that safe somehow, just as Weston tore the bed from its wall. Then I had the gun positioned in my right hand. I didn't have the eyesight to aim, but I pulled the safety and slipped a finger over the trigger.

Weston had me by both ankles and wrenched me out into the open. I focused only on keeping the gun tight in my hand, my aim steady.

Weston slid me toward him, and I used the momentum to propel myself forward into him. I noticed one of my knives in his hand, aimed at my throat, but even through all the blood, I saw how much farther away Weston's hand was than mine. My right hand was able to reach his head. I felt the gun's barrel connect against his temple before I pulled the trigger, and Weston's head exploded off in a jet of fire.

The room was plunged into red. Blood, fire, sirens, and then a deafening silence.

I dropped the gun, the shot still reverberating against my skull, the room closing in. White noise roared in my ears, but I thought I heard a man whisper:

"It's over."

Was it my father or Weston?

My sight came back, and I realized the room was black. The only light came not from streetlights but from ambulances, from police cars. I couldn't hear the sirens, but I could see the streaks of red and blue across the walls.

This was it. They were coming for me, finally, after so long. I pulled myself to sitting, and I took the gun in my mouth, feeling a sizzle from the heat of the barrel against my cheek. I was breathing hard, but I wasn't scared. I'd wait until the police and the firefighters got to the room and blow my brains out in front of them.

It was over. Romeo and Juliet. This was how it ended for them, right? I never read the play, but I had seen the movie plenty of times. The woman was always the last to die in a tragedy. She had to lose everything, see it burn before her until she could end the story.

I waited, watching the lights circle across my ceiling, unsure of the exact moment the cops would burst in since I could no longer hear. It was fine. I had all night.

31

I WOKE UP ON THE FLOOR OF MY BEDROOM, THE GUN HANGING out of my mouth. My jaw was sore, my skin raw. I threw the weapon away from me in a panic. It was almost light outside. No one had come: the lights, the sirens, they all had been after someone else.

I began to smell it as soon as the sun came up and the room started to warm. I was on fire with fever. I was wet with sweat and blood, most of it mine, but I noticed that a puddle from Weston's head had worked its way toward my legs. I needed water, but I couldn't move.

I closed my eyes and tried to ignore the stench.

When I woke again, it was scorching. I was shaking, unable to feel my legs, unable to stop the shivering. Then I saw her. Emily was reaching over my desk, wearing my black-and-white Dior dress. I looked closer and saw bloodstains, streaks of dark copper across the fabric over her stomach, down her abdomen.

"That's my dress," I tried to whisper, but my lips were chapped, glazed shut in blood and spit. She was at my safe, picking through my mementos.

"Those are mine," I whispered.

"You've lost everything, Tiffany. What does it matter?"

She stopped for a second, turned my way, and smiled. In her hand, she held my pearl-drop necklace. I thought I had been wearing it. I was too weak to reach for my throat, to confirm if this was all a dream.

Emily's eyes settled over Weston's body.

"Leave him alone." I couldn't tell if the words came out of my mouth.

"Don't worry. I think you've done enough."

"Don't leave," I pleaded. "Help me."

She was at the door.

"Too late."

———

When I woke up again, I wondered in a distant way if I had dreamed up Emily, if my safe was empty. It didn't matter anymore. I was still feverish, still burning up, and I could feel pain now.

I sat up and looked down at my leg. The knife was still in my thigh. I took a deep breath and clenched my teeth. In one motion, I wrenched it out. It took a few seconds for the blood to start, but then it flowed in a steady flood, a heavy wash over my legs. I wrapped a blanket around my thigh as a tourniquet. I needed to get to a shower, to wash off all the pieces of glass still in my legs. I couldn't stand, and I was shaking even harder.

I dragged myself across the room to Emily's side and searched her bottom dresser. I found a bottle of Popov, half full and doused myself in it, taking out the bigger chunks of glass, and pouring vodka over the tiny cuts.

I tried to reach beyond the fever and pinpoint the exact points of pain across my body. I felt stinging from the glass, but the knife wound was the most severe, a sharp, persistent throbbing reaching from my legs to my fingertips and into my very jaw. I reached and felt my face, then my forehead past my hairline. I couldn't find any hair at first, only flakes rough as nail files. I pulled what seemed like dandruff and realized it was a piece of my bloody scalp. I tried not to hyperventilate. I poured vodka over my head and screamed through it.

I scoured every low space on Emily's side of the room, looking for pills, but came up empty. I took several swigs of vodka and dragged myself across the hall to Ashley's room. I went right for her stash, finding a bottle of unlabeled pills behind her TV, washing them down with more vodka. I dragged myself to her dresser and sniffed through prescription bottles until I recognized the mildewy scent of antibiotics. I took three.

I couldn't make it back to my room and collapsed on the floor in the hall. I was exhausted and thirsty. I might die here, I realized. Dying slowly, alone with no witnesses, was so much more pathetic than going out in a burst of glory in front of the police.

I closed my eyes and imagined being set on fire, bursting into flame before turning to dry ash and floating away in small pieces.

In my dreams, I was whole again. I was flying over the bluffs of Monarch Beach toward the estate. Then my feet settled on grass, and I could walk. I was fine, I was strong, the gun in my back pocket. I stood outside the house, and I could see Todd, Pam, and Celeste through the dining room window. I moved with speed, with purpose, past the side gate, around the pool.

I walked in on all of them sharing a family meal, frozen in terror over the breakfast table, Pam with a smoothie, Todd with pancakes, and Celeste with phone in hand, taking a photo of her steel cut oats. Pam dropped her smoothie, and it shattered bright green on the tile.

I shot Todd first, took him out square in the chest. Celeste was next. I hit her in the shoulder, and she flew off the chair. I missed Pam on the first attempt and shot out a window. I aimed again and hit her in the stomach, right in the gut. I went back for Todd and shot him in the head. I was standing over Pam, watching her stare at the gaping hole in her belly, when my cell rang. I pulled the phone out of my front pocket.

It said *Unavailable*, but I knew exactly who was calling me. I raised the phone to my ear and whispered, "Daddy?"

I woke up in the hallway, confused and sore. I was no longer burning up, but the pain was still breaking through in thunderous rolls. I could feel how far into my brain a back molar's roots went. I looked down. My leg had stopped bleeding, but I could see it swelling against the bandages.

I poured more vodka on everything. It was the only solution I had. I dragged myself back to my room and noticed the spackling of blood across the hardwood, a piece of Weston's skull. I had just touched the bony shard when I heard a sound, a beating, coming from my bedroom, from down on the floor, from Weston himself. *His beating heart,* I thought briefly with horror, until I saw a fluorescent glow near his pocket and realized it was the buzz of his iPhone.

I inched closer and pulled the phone out, trying to touch as little as possible of him. I caught a brief glance at the caller—*Mom*—before the vibrations stopped and the phone went black.

"Why did you have to ruin everything?" I shouted at Weston, finally forcing myself to look at him. He was a dead body in fitted jeans and relaxed cotton, nothing more. His head was gone, just blood, pulp, and stray pieces of dark hair. I swatted away at the flies that were gathering in small clouds around him.

I thought about Weston's mother somewhere in uptown Manhattan, having a glass of sauv blanc over a view of skyscrapers, wondering why he hadn't taken the town car back yet to meet her. She didn't have a face, either; Weston had never shown me pictures.

I looked at him again. Everyone said first love was a bitch, but this was brutal. At least I had closure—staring at the pieces left of him, there was no denying that it never would have worked between the two of us, that we had never fit together. It had been doomed from the beginning.

32

THE NEXT DAY I HAD TO FACE SOME DIFFICULT TRUTHS: MY back molar wasn't getting any better, and my leg needed to be cleaned out. I still couldn't stand. I dragged myself up and down the stairs on a pained scavenger hunt for materials: more alcohol, gauze, fresh antibiotics, tweezers. And pliers.

But something darker nagged at me. I still hadn't seen myself in a mirror. The glass closet had shattered in my room, and the rest of my mirrors were at standing level.

I dragged myself into the bathroom and felt along the counter for a hand mirror. I grasped a metal handle and brought the mirror onto my lap. I took a breath and turned it over.

I should have expected it, but it was still a shock to see what Weston had done to my face, how lopsided it was, how little my left matched my right. My left eye was almost swollen closed; no wonder I had so much trouble seeing. My bottom lip was cut open and stretched over my entire chin. Everything was either blackened or bright red. My nose was clearly broken. And my teeth—I was missing three, I already knew, but the ones still left were jagged and mangled. I checked my scalp and saw that much of what I thought had been blood was now pus.

I stared, memorizing the new lines, curves, bruises, and gashes, committing my new face to memory. I put the mirror down, then looked again over and over. I stared until I started to recognize myself.

It was still me. My new face started to seem familiar, like those mangled features had always been there, hiding right under the surface.

Every time I pulled something out—my loose back molar, a clump of congealed blood the size of a softball on my leg, the blistered pus that had popped on my head—each time a new piece rotted and fell off me, I prepared for the worst, the fact that I might not pull through, that I'd lost too many vital parts of me to live on.

But even as it all fell away, I knew I was getting stronger day by day. I was able to walk soon, with the help of furniture, putting tentative weight on my stabbed leg. My gums started healing over the craterous holes where my teeth had been, craters that stopped tasting of iron every time I ran my tongue over them. I stopped waking up surprised to not be able to slide my tongue over a row of teeth, to feel a full head of hair settled on the pillow. The bruises transformed from black through a rainbow of colors, settling into a dull yellow. When my scalp stopped oozing, I took an electric razor from the bathroom and shaved off the hair still left on my head. I started to resemble a human again; granted, I looked like a mutilated, used-up Barbie after a girl had taken scissors to her. But I was human. And alive.

I could drink water; in fact, I could never get enough of it. I was always thirsty. I started eating again, only soft foods: mostly tuna straight from the can.

I knew I'd live, not by the healing of my body, not by the slow effect of the antibiotics, not when the gash in my leg finally started to close up, but by the dull hunger that slowly returned, the familiar voice that told me to get stronger, return to the city, and find another. Kill again.

I'd survive. There was no doubt about that.

33

IT WAS ANOTHER HOT AFTERNOON. THE POWER STILL HADN'T come back. Had it been two weeks since I killed Weston? A month? I was slowly picking up sounds from the outside world. I heard cars, more sirens, as the area was becoming repopulated, people slowly, tentatively returning.

I still was surprised when I heard the front door of the house open and slam shut. I thought immediately of Emily. But it was Mandy, in a sundress with a suitcase and a butcher knife. I peered through the upstairs banisters.

"Is someone here?" she called.

Anyone could rip the knife right out of her hand. She held it all wrong.

I stayed hidden, unsure of her motive. Then she caught sight of me near the staircase.

"Tiffany? Is that you?"

"Hello," I said, unsure what to do.

"Tiffany! Pack up! We have to leave! I came from the Palisades: PCH is blocked, the 405 is gone. We have to head east. It's the only way out! Dan is waiting in the Rover. I can't believe I let him talk me into staying around here."

Mandy went on, never bothering to look my way, rustling downstairs through the kitchen cabinets. I stood up.

"He said the frat would be safe. It went up in flames! We barely escaped. There are tanks across Hilgard—tanks! It's like we're living in a foreign country or something. We have to leave. What is that smell?"

I heard her finally reach the foot of the staircase.

"Tiffany, did you hear me?"

I rose and walked to the edge of the stairs. I heard a choking sound as I rounded the corner and faced her.

"Tiffany, what happened to all your hair?"

I felt the blistered skin of my shaved scalp. I smiled.

Mandy's hand flew to her mouth, and she dropped the knife.

"Where are your teeth? What did they do to you?"

She had stopped her climb up the stairs. Her voice was trembling.

"What is that smell?"

Then she was stepping backward, away from me.

"Why does it smell like that?" she said, the terror in her voice unquenchable. I let it grow.

"Things didn't work out with Weston," I said.

"I have to go," Mandy said, reversing her course down the stairs. She missed a step and twisted her ankle, grabbed the banister with one arm and held her other arm out at me, as though to guard against me, what I had become.

"Didn't you want to come upstairs and pack some of your things?" I asked.

Mandy didn't answer. She took in my new look one last time, turned, and ran screaming.

She left the front door open, and I saw a Range Rover reverse and peel out of the driveway.

I went down the stairs and looked outside. The sun was bright. It was a gorgeous day despite the haze from the fires, the ash coating everything, raining down like Los Angeles snow. Summer was around the corner. In L.A., summer was the most dangerous season, the most unpredictable. The city had binged and purged itself, and only the strong, the true stans who loved the city and all its fire and destruction, would stay. The chaos wouldn't last. Things would calm, order would be restored, but until then . . .

I opened my mouth and let a few pieces of ash dot my tongue. I tasted burned earth and violence. It was delicious.

I thought about my dreams of fire, about how everything had come true. I was ready to leave Weston and the sorority behind, to see what had become of the city.

Was my Mercedes still there? It didn't matter. I picked up the knife Mandy had dropped and walked into a brilliant spring afternoon.

ACKNOWLEDGEMENTS

Immense gratitude to my agent Nat Kimber for being an endless advocate for this book and for Tiffany in all her bloody glory. Thanks to the team at The Rights Factory, including Milly Ruggiero, Karmen Wells, Sam Hiyate and Tamanna Bhasin.

Thanks to Chris Heiser, Allison Miriam Smith and Unnamed Press for providing the perfect home for my debut. Thanks to Jaya Nicely for creating the delicious cover.

Kill for Love wouldn't have entered the world without the recognition and support from the team at Book Pipeline. Special thanks to Peter Malone Elliot and Matt Misetich.

I wrote the first draft of the novel during my MFA program at Cal State Long Beach. Thank you to my creative writing professors and workshop members for the razor-sharp feedback, which challenged me to deepen the story. Thanks to my many other early readers and mentors at the UCLA Extension Writers' Program and Writing Workshops Los Angeles.

Thank you to Steven Lowy for your wisdom and keen eye. Thanks to my friends and family, who have supported and rallied behind my writing over the past years. I offer my utmost gratitude for your encouragement, love and patience. To my parents, thank you for instilling in me my love for reading – though I sincerely hope you haven't gotten this far into the book.

And, Maceo, thank you for always being my first reader, my partner and my North Star. I'm so grateful that I stole your drink at DTD fifteen years ago. Finally, to all dear readers, thank you for joining Tiffany on her wild journey.